She was pregnant

"Unplanned" was putting it mildly. Until Johnny came along, there had been only her work, her career—she hadn't considered the possibility of a relationship, let alone a family. And as well as she knew Johnny, as much as she loved him, she had no idea what *his* reaction would be.

And yet, as she neared Johnny's boat, she felt a glimmer of excitement. *A family.* First Johnny's proposal, and now the pregnancy. Maybe life wasn't always careful planning and long-range goals. Maybe sometimes it just happened. In a heartbeat...

She saw Johnny on the deck and waved, hoping to catch his attention.

There was absolutely no warning. One moment there was Johnny, the boat, the clear blue water in the sunlight....

And then—in a heartbeat—everything erupted in one shattering blast.

Dear Reader,

I've always been a die-hard romantic and would like to believe that
everyone has at least one true love in his or her life. The adventure
begins with finding that love...and it continues throughout a
lifetime shared together. I've found *my* love, and hope that each
book I write reflects that, and reminds my readers of the first flush
of romance, the deepening passion and the enduring devotion. And
of the miracle of cherishing and being cherished.

Sincerely,

Morgan Hayes

P.S. I love to hear from readers. Please write me c/o Harlequin
Superromance, Harlequin Enterprises, 225 Duncan Mill Road,
Don Mills, Ontario M3B 3K9, Canada

Books by Morgan Hayes

HARLEQUIN SUPERROMANCE
591—TWILIGHT WHISPERS
623—PREMONITIONS
722—SEE NO EVIL

DECEPTION
Morgan Hayes

Harlequin Books

TORONTO • NEW YORK • LONDON
AMSTERDAM • PARIS • SYDNEY • HAMBURG
STOCKHOLM • ATHENS • TOKYO • MILAN
MADRID • WARSAW • BUDAPEST • AUCKLAND

For Bonita, sister and best friend.
And to Lise Walsh and Dave Cooper—
whose love shines brightly.

ISBN 0-373-70773-8

DECEPTION

Copyright © 1998 by Illona Haus.

DECEPTION

CHAPTER ONE

THE PHONE PEALED shrilly. Shelby Beaumont moaned, loath to abandon her pleasant dream, and waited for Johnny to answer it.

With her eyes still closed she felt his broad chest press against her back. Then he braced one hand on her shoulder and reaching over her with the other, grappled for the receiver.

"Spencer here.... Yeah, Nick, I *was* sleeping. It's barely six—what did you expect? Mm-hmm... At the waterfront? Damn. And for sure it's Feeney? What the hell was he doing down there? Mm-hmm... No, no, don't let the medical examiner move him. I'll be there. Give me fifteen minutes. Yeah, I know... Okay."

Shelby heard Johnny's weary groan as he replaced the receiver. He brushed aside her hair and grazed her cheek with a kiss.

"You awake, love?" he whispered.

He must have seen her drowsy smile, because he kissed her again and nudged himself into the curves of her body.

"That was Nick. I have to go," he said, releasing a frustrated sigh. But he held her tighter, as if by doing so he could ignore the early-morning call and stay with her in their bed.

Shelby wished it could be that simple. But ever since the murder of the wealthy industrialist Anthony Morelli three weeks ago, the phone had been ringing day and night. With such a high-profile case and with the entire police department's reputation on the line, Johnny and his new partner, Nick DaCosta, had been scrambling for anything that resembled a lead. When the phone rang these days, it almost always meant that Johnny had to rush off. It was what his life had become. And by association, her life, too.

"They found Frank Feeney's body down at the docks," Johnny said, leaving their bed at last. "It appears he was shot. Nick's already there."

Shelby opened her eyes. Between the slats of the window blinds, the sky was still a deep black-blue.

"Who's Frank Feeney?" She rolled over and pulled the duvet around her. Johnny searched the floor for his jeans, his lean muscled physique highlighted by a shaft of light from the street lamp outside the window. Shelby smiled as she remembered how powerful and consuming that body had been last night when they'd made love.

Johnny found his jeans and pulled them on. "Feeney worked for Morelli," he explained, buckling his belt.

Shelby propped herself up on one elbow and watched him tug a wrinkled Fairfield Police sweatshirt over his head.

"So you think there's a connection?" she asked.

"More than likely." He was searching the floor again. "My guess is Feeney knew something he shouldn't have. Are my sneakers over there by your side?''

Shelby smiled. *Her side*. Johnny hadn't been living with her in the loft apartment above her storefront boutique all that long, yet already they sounded like an old married couple. If Johnny had said, ''It's your turn to cook tonight, love, and don't forget the dry cleaning,'' it wouldn't have sounded at all strange.

She found the leather sneakers on the floor and handed them to him. When he sat at the end of the bed to tie his laces, Shelby couldn't resist snuggling up behind him.

''I wish you didn't have to go,'' she murmured, wrapping her arms around his chest and kissing his shoulder.

''Me, too.''

Johnny met her kiss. When he did, Shelby caught his chin in the palm of her hand and kissed him more deeply, as though she could persuade him to stay a few moments longer.

It seemed to work.

With a soft moan, Johnny turned more fully into her embrace, matching Shelby's hunger with his own. As she drew him down on top of her amid the tangle of sheets, the stiff denim of his jeans brushed her naked thighs. The stubble on his unshaved chin prickled her cheek, then her throat as his kisses trailed greedily downward. With one hand she smoothed his thick black hair, still mussed from sleep, and with the other caressed the ripple of his stomach under the soft fleece of his sweatshirt.

''Shel, I can't do this,'' he said with a gusty breath

that fanned her breasts. "You know I want to stay, but…"

Johnny held her gaze, the regret in his dark eyes unmistakable.

"I know you do." She pushed herself upright to give him one more kiss before he left the bed.

"So you won't forget about tonight?" she asked, swinging her legs to the floor and reaching for his robe at the foot of the bed.

"What's tonight?"

"Dinner. Remember? Aidan's coming over. Kate's still out of town, and we promised her we'd have him over."

"Right." She knew he *had* forgotten their arrangements with his ex-partner. "I'll be home before six. Do you need me to pick anything up?"

Shelby shook her head, drawing the flannel robe around herself. "All I need is you," she said, crossing the bedroom and putting her arms around him again. With her head nestled against his chest, she could hear the strong rhythm of his heart. "Promise me you'll be home on time."

"I'll be home on time."

Shelby watched him reach for his shoulder holster and buckle the straps. His expression was hard and focused as he checked the clip of the police issue .38. Only when he looked back at her did his stern mouth lift at the corners. It was an all-too-familiar smile, the one Johnny gave her whenever her apprehension showed.

Johnny liked to joke about how being a *senior* detective largely working homicides meant his life wasn't at any great risk because he dealt mostly with dead people. But Shelby knew that in reality Johnny ran just as many risks as any other person on the squad.

"Be careful, Johnny." Her voice sounded thin.

"Always," he said, giving her another kiss, which she eagerly devoured. She could feel his arousal, too, hard under the restriction of denim. "Why don't we continue this tonight?" he whispered, his mouth barely leaving hers. "After dinner. After Aidan's gone."

"Will you remember where you left off?"

"Oh, I think so." She felt the curve of his smile as he took one final taste of her lips. And then he was gone.

She listened to his footsteps as he moved down the stairs to the boutique on the main floor. Tightening the sash of her robe, she surveyed the bedroom. Even in the half-light it was obvious the place needed a good cleaning. Both she and Johnny had been too busy over the past couple of weeks to stem the gradual rise of disorder around them. But then, most of the mess was hers, she thought as she started to gather clothes from the floor.

Before Johnny had moved in, she'd had this space to herself. There'd been no need to define her work area. Her drawings and designs, along with swatches of material, migrated freely throughout the apartment. Sketches accumulated on the coffee table, the kitchen counter, the dresser, even in the bathroom. Post-it notes were stuck to every available surface—reminders of meetings with clients, presentations, deadlines, fashion shows.

Living with Johnny had changed that. But Shelby never regretted the loss of her personal space, as long as the loss was to Johnny.

Not that she hadn't had her doubts at the beginning. Before Johnny had moved in, she'd cherished her privacy. She'd put a lot of money and effort into the old storefront unit, remodeling it into a boutique, studio and loft apartment in one. Practically living with her work had allowed her to keep her own hours, often working late into the night and sleeping in when she wanted to, answering to no one's schedule but her own.

But then she'd met Johnny. In a matter of months it had become obvious he was spending more time at her place than his own bachelor apartment, and moving in together had been a natural transition. Besides, most of his things had already found their way to the loft by then.

They'd been "a couple" for a year now, living together for the past six months. But neither was willing to move on to the next logical step. Marriage.

Marriage meant permanence. It meant compromise. But most of all it meant staying in Fairfield. And for Shelby, that meant giving up a lot of her dreams.

When she'd left Manhattan and returned to her hometown of Fairfield in northern New York state two and a half years ago, she'd come back with only one suitcase. She'd left most of her belongings in the small two-bedroom SoHo apartment she'd shared with her younger sister, Cora, who'd been attending NYU.

Shelby's return to Fairfield was to have been no more than a few months, which was what the doctors had estimated for her mother's recovery after the initial diagnosis of cancer and the first round of chemotherapy.

Those few months, however, became a year. Her mother's condition had only worsened. During the illness Shelby had turned to her work for comfort, handling her career as best she could from outside the fashion hub of New York City. She'd always intended to go back, knowing that her career could never reach its full potential unless she did. But by the time her mother had passed away, her life had become almost totally enmeshed in the Fairfield community. She had the boutique—and she had Johnny. She hadn't planned on either.

"Hey, Shel, do you know where my keys are?" Johnny called up from the bottom of the stairs.

"They're on the desk."

"Got 'em," he said. "See you tonight."

Shelby heard him unchain the front door, and then the click of the dead bolt locking into place. Dropping an armful of clothes on the foot of the bed, she moved to the window and peered through the blinds.

In another week they'd be setting back the clocks. The crisp late-October mornings would be marginally lighter, but for now, it was still dark. In the yellow glow of the sodium lamps that lined the near-deserted street below, she watched Johnny sprint to the Cavalier parked behind her Lexus. The vapor from his breath lingered for a moment in the cold air like a halo as he unlocked his door. She heard the roar of the engine, and in moments the car pulled away from the curb and headed south down Jefferson Street.

When she could no longer see the taillights, she turned from the window and gathered the robe more snugly around her. She could smell traces of Johnny's scent, combined with his aftershave, and closed her eyes for a moment, recalling last night's lovemaking.

When she opened them again, she saw the bright red digits of the electric clock on the nightstand—6:00 a.m.

There was no point in going back to bed, as inviting as it looked. In three hours Doreen Nash, her assistant, would be rushing into the boutique with her usual breathless flurry of apologies for being late. If she started work now, Shelby decided, she'd be able to put in a couple of uninterrupted hours of sketching.

She padded barefoot out of the bedroom and into the kitchen, where she turned on the coffee machine. Then she moved through the sprawling apartment to the studio in front, gazing over the balcony railing into the boutique on the main floor. Motionless figures, draped in shadow, ringed her cluttered drafting table like a small immobile army. She smiled, remembering Johnny's initial reaction to the half-clothed manne-quins; they'd given him the creeps. And little wonder. In the grayness of early morning, there was something eerily lifelike about the figures.

Shelby turned on the desk lamp. The mannequins' frozen gazes stared back at her. Wheeling her chair up to the drafting table, she searched for a pencil among the jumble of sketches.

A couple of hours of drawing, several more reviewing schedules with Doreen, then a lunch meeting with a client, and finally a long-overdue doctor's appointment at three—it was going to be a full day.

THE CHURCH BELL at the corner of Young and Charles was tolling four o'clock when Johnny parked outside O'Neill Investigations and jogged up the steps to the glass doors. He passed the receptionist's desk with little more than a nod and strode into Aidan's office.

Aidan O'Neill was leaning back in his chair, his feet propped on the corner of the paper-strewn desk. He spiraled a ballpoint pen through the phone cord as he spoke into the receiver tucked under his square chin. Nodding to Johnny, he shoved a hand through his red-blond hair.

"Mmm-hmm...yeah. And your flight gets in when? Mmm-hmm... But, Kate, only one day? Can't you stay home longer this time? Okay, talk to your boss. See what you can arrange. I'll call you tonight... Yup, me, too. Bye."

Aidan lowered his feet, let out a frustrated groan and reached across the desk to replace the receiver.

"Trouble in paradise?" Johnny asked.

Aidan shook his head. "Only that she's never here. Some paradise."

"So what is it this time?" Johnny asked.

"Kate's got this trial down in Newburgh. And when she isn't stuck in the courtroom, she's running all over the place digging up dirt on the prosecution's string of character witnesses. It's ridiculous. Between her job and mine, we can count on seeing each other maybe one weekend a month these days. But I know you didn't come all the way over here to listen to my relationship woes. What's up, John? Can't be a social visit. Word on the street has it you and that new partner of yours are busting your butts these days over the Morelli case. Let me guess. You're here to get a professional's take on the case, is that it? Or maybe you want to hire me yourself?''

Johnny gave his best friend and former partner a weary smile. Ever since quitting the force a year ago, Aidan had done well with his private detective agency. He'd been busting his butt, too, but that didn't stop him from ribbing Johnny about the fact that at least he kept his *own* hours, instead of the police department's.

"Any progress?" Aidan asked.

"Not on the Morelli case."

"And what about Feeney? I heard you guys found him belly-up at the waterfront this morning."

"It was a professional hit. No doubt connected to Morelli, but we don't have the evidence to prove it. Feeney worked for him, though. He knew who was on Morelli's payroll, and whoever killed Morelli probably figured Feeney would talk sooner or later. It's just too bad it wasn't sooner."

"And what about your own contacts? You're not going to tell me you don't have someone on the inside."

"Feeney *was* my contact," Johnny confided. "He was supposed to meet me this afternoon."

Johnny paced the length of Aidan's office. At the window he stopped and watched a whirlwind of dead leaves scurry along the sidewalk.

"You don't have any other contacts?"

It wasn't a lack of trust that kept Johnny from sharing the details of his investigation with Aidan. In fact, he would have preferred to tell his ex-partner everything. It always helped when he and Aidan put their heads together; they'd made a good team.

"There may be someone else I can talk to." Johnny continued staring out the window. "But I won't know until tomorrow."

"You're playing this one awfully close to the chest, John." A note of warning entered Aidan's voice.

Johnny heard Aidan swing his chair around, but he didn't turn. He only shook his head. "I have to."

"What about Nick? Was he in on this meeting with Feeney?"

"No."

"He didn't know anything about it?"

Johnny shook his head again and at last met Aidan's gaze.

"Come on, John, you can't do this alone. I know you'd prefer it that way, but you've got a new partner now. You need him."

"There's something about this case, Aidan."

"What?"

"I don't know yet. Just...something."

But he couldn't tell Aidan. As much as he wanted to, as much as he needed a second opinion, he didn't dare voice his suspicions to his best friend. It would only put Aidan's life in jeopardy, as well.

Frank Feeney had known too much. And that knowledge had proved fatal.

"It's probably nothing," Johnny said eventually.

"Besides, with a little luck, I may have this whole mess wrapped up by tomorrow afternoon, anyway."

They'd known each other for five years. Long enough for Aidan to recognize when it was time to leave well enough alone, Johnny thought gratefully.

Still, his ex-partner was right. He *was* playing this case dangerously close to the chest. But he had to. From what little he'd gotten out of Frank Feeney the other day, Johnny could smell a bad cop all over the three-week-old Morelli murder investigation. But now he would never know what information Feeney had been ready to offer him—or on whom.

And until he had more to go on, Johnny could trust no one. Experience had taught him that. Before he'd come to Fairfield from New York City five years before, he'd honestly believed he had a secure future with the NYPD. He'd put in his years as a beat cop, walking the same streets he'd grown up on, and then three more years working Narcotics until he'd finally secured a position in Homicide. It was there that the trouble started.

Before he'd even completed a full two years with the squad, Johnny had detected the vein of corruption that pulsed through the ranks of detectives. Foolishly he'd taken his knowledge to the Internal Affairs Bureau, and within days he'd been roped into assisting in a major cleanup operation. In the end, however, *he'd* been the one to come out looking dirtier than the detectives he'd been sent in to expose.

Things had gotten out of control. When Johnny had tried to warn two of his fellow detectives unconnected to the corruption that they were about to be framed,

IAB pulled its backing. And Johnny had been left hanging. No one on the force would ever trust him again, and IAB had blacklisted him, calling him unreliable. From whatever angle he was viewed, Johnny Spencer was bad news. There'd been no other choice but to leave—the force and New York City. And there was no going back.

He was not about to have the same thing happen a second time. It had taken five years to develop the sterling reputation he had in Fairfield, and he was not about to lose it the way he had in New York City. No, he wouldn't be as hasty as last time. He'd be sure to have concrete proof before he made any allegations of police corruption. It wasn't just his reputation on the line, it was his career. And his life.

Johnny crossed the office and planted himself on a corner of his ex-partner's desk. It wasn't the Morelli case or Feeney or even the suspected corruption he'd come to see Aidan about. It was something far more personal.

In the pocket of his leather bomber he felt for the small jeweler's box he'd tucked there only an hour before. His fingers trembled slightly as they brushed the velvet surface. For four months he'd had the jewelry store down on Brubacher put the ring on layaway for him. For four months he'd wrestled with his doubts. Even now, he wasn't certain what had led him to finally put down the rest of the money and pick up the ring.

And that was what he'd come to see Aidan about this afternoon. He felt compelled to show the ring to his friend first. After all, it had been Aidan who'd introduced him to Shelby a year ago. It had been Aidan who'd given him Shelby's unlisted phone number after he'd hounded him for it. And it was Aidan who'd been their closest friend all along.

"What do you have there?" Aidan asked when Johnny finally drew the box from his pocket.

Johnny said nothing, only snapped open the lid and turned it so Aidan could see the glittering diamond ring inside.

"Well, as long as I live and breathe—John Spencer buying a diamond ring. I don't believe it. You're actually going to ask her?"

"Tonight." Johnny nodded, unable to resist a small smile as he imagined Shelby's reaction. But looking at the diamond now, his smile faltered slightly.

"You don't seem so sure, pal."

Johnny shrugged, then met Aidan's cool blue-eyed gaze. "I guess I'm not. No."

"So what's the problem?"

"I don't know. I still worry about Shel, you know?"

"About her being a cop's wife, you mean?"

"Yeah, that's part of it." Johnny nodded. "You know, you go through training at the academy and then years on the force, and you figure you'll never allow yourself to get into that dilemma of marriage versus the force. There's something very comforting about being single, in not having anyone count on you. You see the other guys rushing off to their wives at the end of their shift and—"

"And you haven't been doing just that ever since you met Shelby?"

Johnny looked at the ring. "Yeah." He'd rushed to Shelby's loft at the end of every shift for the past year, and he'd lost count of the number of times he'd even snuck off in the middle of the day to see her.

"But marriage, Aidan, it's so...so big, you know? I mean, with marriage you've *really* got someone counting on you."

"You mean someone who gets left behind if you're killed. Why don't you just say it, John?"

"I saw what it did to my mother, Aidan. The morning she answered our front door and found my father's partner standing there on the porch... She was never the same after that."

Johnny could still see his mother's face when she'd been told the news of the shooting, of his father's death. He'd watched her turn pale and collapse into the officer's arms. He'd been fourteen at the time and had already known he wanted to be a cop like his father; the devastation of that day hadn't changed his mind. Instead, it had strengthened his resolve; he wanted to continue the career that had been his father's before he'd been so prematurely snatched away. But it was also the time that Johnny had vowed never to marry. Never to put someone through what he'd seen his mother go through.

"I know how hard it's going to be for Shelby," Johnny said. "She worries a lot. All the time. She doesn't talk about it, but I know she expects the worst. Whenever I'm late or she hears something on the news...I know it upsets her."

"You could always quit."

Johnny was shaking his head, but Aidan went on,

"Private-investigation work isn't that bad. And God knows, I could use someone with your expertise. We could make it a partnership if you wanted, John. All you have to do is give me the word and that sign outside will have your name on it, too."

Johnny shook his head. "Sorry, my friend—" he smiled "—it'll never happen."

It wasn't just his father, he thought. Even his grandfather had been a cop. And a good one, too. It was a Spencer thing. And no matter which way Aidan sliced it, no matter how rosy he tried to make it look, PI work just wasn't the same as being a cop.

God forbid there should ever come a day that he'd have to choose between the force and Shelby.

"So what's the other part?" Aidan asked.

"The other part?"

"You said that asking Shelby to be a cop's wife was only part of it. What else?"

Johnny touched a finger to the sparkling diamond, unable to take his eyes off the object that could mark the beginning of so much happiness and yet represented so many doubts.

"It's Shelby's career," he answered at last.

"What about it?"

"She could make it big, Aidan."

"She *is* big, John."

"I mean *really* big—a household name. God knows she's got the talent. And the reviews and acclaim to prove it."

"So what does that have to do with your marrying her?"

"New York."

"I don't understand."

"She told me herself when we first met that if she wants to get anywhere in the fashion industry, she has to move back to Manhattan. 'To be in the thick of things,' she said. In fact, she was about to do just that before we met. She even had boxes packed."

"And you can never move back to New York because of that whole IAB thing, is that it?"

Johnny nodded. "You *know* what went on down there, Aidan. You know I can't go back. Not if I want to be a cop. There's nothing for me in New York. Hell, even if I took to PI work there, with my reputation I wouldn't survive."

"So what are you saying? That Shelby will have to choose between you and her career?"

"Basically yes. I'm holding her back even now. And if we get married, I'm as good as signing the death warrant to her career."

"I think you're exaggerating, John."

"No. I don't think I am."

"Well, as far as I can tell, John, you've got only one choice."

"What's that?"

"It's Shelby's future. You have to let *her* decide."

Johnny snapped the ring box shut and jammed it back into his pocket along with his clenched fist. He shouldn't have bought the ring today—or ever. He should have listened to his head, not his heart. Shelby probably wasn't going to say no, and then he'd have to live with the fact that she'd given up the full potential of her career for him.

He switched topics. "So what about you and Kate, then?"

"What about us? You mean, are *we* ever getting married?"

"Yeah, *are* you?"

Aidan gave a cynical laugh and shook his head. "Who knows? If we could actually spend more than one weekend a month together, maybe I could answer that. But frankly, John, I have no idea. We don't have what you and Shelby have, I can tell you that much. Then again, I doubt *anyone* does."

"SHELBY, YOU'RE MAKING me dizzy pacing like that. He'll *be* here." Aidan was sitting on her couch sipping a glass of wine. "Are you sure you wouldn't like something to drink? It'd help you relax."

"I *am* relaxed, Aidan. Really." But Aidan recognized the veil of calm she skillfully wrapped around her unease. As she continued to pace the hardwood floor, the brown pantsuit she wore, obviously one of her own designs, showed to advantage her tall lithe figure. When at last she sat down on the other end of the couch, she offered him another of her easy smiles, and Aidan was struck, as always, by her natural beauty.

Her lustrous black hair was swept casually over one shoulder, revealing the fine definition of her jaw and cheekbones, and when she tilted her head back to take a swallow of her soda water, Aidan eyed the curve of her neck—the kind of curve a man yearned to press his lips to, he'd often thought.

Shelby caught his admiring gaze and smiled again,

bringing an unparalleled radiance to her face and lighting up her wide brown eyes. It didn't matter how many times Shelby directed that smile at him, Aidan knew he would never tire of it.

He wondered if Shelby ever noticed just how admiring his gaze was. But then, how could she *not* have noticed—all those years of growing up together, his kid sister's best friend. From the first time he'd laid eyes on Shelby Beaumont—the rough-and-tumble tomboy from down the street—Aidan had had a crush on her. He'd always figured it would pass, that it was a childhood fancy. But all that passed were the years—and the opportunity.

Now here they were, all grown-up. And Shelby about to be proposed to by his ex-partner, of all people. John had known her barely a year. And Aidan, he'd known Shelby practically all his life, and he'd never even been able to muster the nerve to ask her for a date.

Still, if there *was* regret, it was softened by the happiness he felt for John and Shelby. After all, they were two of his favorite people in the world, so why shouldn't he be happy?

"John will be here," he told Shelby again, seeing her fidget. He drained his wineglass and immediately regretted having done so. Shelby was up like a shot, heading to the bar for the bottle.

"Any word on that break-in?" he asked, trying to distract Shelby from her worry.

She shook her head. "Johnny talked to the responding officers. They figure it was just a couple of kids. It's been quiet around here ever since."

Aidan nodded, letting her refill his glass as he fingered a tassel on one of the cushions. A week ago a storefront window three doors down had been smashed. When he'd first heard about it from John, he'd wondered if it was the beginning of another rash of break-ins in the Jefferson Street district.

At least this time he wouldn't have to be quite so concerned about Shelby. Now she had John. The last rash of burglaries in the area had been a year ago. Shelby had been living alone in the loft when the boutique had been broken in to. Her sudden appearance from upstairs had frightened off the intruders before they could wreak any significant damage, but still, when Aidan had received the call and crossed the north end of the city to the boutique, he'd found Shelby badly shaken.

That was the first time she and John had met—late at night with squad cars flashing their lights out in the street and cops scouring the area while Aidan had tried to comfort her. It was later, in the car outside Shelby's place, that John had asked about her. And at first Aidan had tried to discourage John's interest—not so much out of jealousy but out of concern for Shelby.

For in the years that he'd shared an unmarked car with John Spencer, Aidan had learned that John had had quite a succession of women in his life and appeared to have left the proverbial trail of broken hearts. So at John's spark of interest in Shelby, Aidan had been determined to prevent Shelby from becoming just another brokenhearted victim.

But who'd have figured? Certainly not Aidan. He would have been the last one to believe that John

Spencer could settle down. Yet he'd seen the diamond ring himself this afternoon.

It shouldn't have surprised him, Aidan thought now as he watched Shelby ease back against the cushions of the couch, trying her best to appear relaxed. If any woman could compel a man like John to take stock of his life and commit, it was her.

SHELBY NOTICED Aidan's casual glance at the clock on the wall. She followed his gaze. It was already seven.

"He usually phones," she said. "I'm sorry about this, Aidan."

"You don't have to apologize, Shelby. Not to me. I know what it's like. Listen, he's probably gotten tied up somewhere, that's all. If he isn't here soon, he'll call. Don't worry."

"I'm not worried," she lied, wondering if her smile betrayed the true extent of her anxiety. She took another sip of soda water, wishing it was wine. But she couldn't drink. Not after her annual physical this afternoon.

Her period was late this month, she'd admitted to her doctor. Only by a few days, though, and she'd shrugged it off as stress due to her upcoming presentation to Maison de Couture. But when Dr. Williams had handed her the blood-work card she was to take with her to the lab, Shelby had noticed the box that was checked at the bottom of the scrawled form—PREGNANCY.

The thought of hearing back from her doctor's office caused another swell of apprehension. She and

Johnny hadn't even discussed marriage, let alone a family. It was one of those things, she decided, that neither of them dared to mention for fear that the other might have entirely different expectations and desires, that this difference could be the one thing to darken their perfect and happy life together.

Besides, even if they did both want children sometime in the future, it would have been just that—in the future. Not now. Not when they were both absorbed in their careers. Not when she was beginning to make real headway with her designs in New York. And not while Johnny was still on the force.

Shelby got up from the couch again. She couldn't sit still. Not until she heard Johnny come through the door and call her name. She again paced the floor in front of the windows. Through the open blinds she could see the dark street glistening in the light drizzle. Any moment now Johnny's Cavalier would pull up to the curb and she'd see him jog across the wet street, hear his footsteps on the stairs and see that infectious smile on his lips as he apologized for being late yet again.

When the phone's piercing ring shattered the silence, Shelby jumped. She spun from the window and snatched up the receiver.

"Shel, it's me."

Her grip relaxed around the receiver at the sound of Johnny's voice. In the background she heard cars, other voices, and then the squawk of a police radio.

"I'm sorry, Shel. I wanted to call you earlier, but we've had our hands full."

"Where are you?"

"Down at First and Carnegie," he said over the clamor around him. "We had an armed robbery. It's a real mess."

Aidan was at her side now. A gentle smile eased across his lightly freckled face, and his bright blue eyes seemed to question her.

"He's at First and Carnegie," she whispered to him over the mouthpiece.

"Listen, Shel," Johnny was saying, "I'm only a few blocks away, and we're just wrapping things up. I'll come straight home from here. Is Aidan still with you?"

"Yes, he's here. We'll wait."

"All right. Look, I won't be long, I promise." Behind him, someone shouted and there was the sound of tires skidding across wet pavement. Then Johnny's voice again. "I love you, Shel," he said, his words sounding like a confession over the phone line.

"I love you, too, Johnny," she whispered. Her lips brushed the mouthpiece as though she could feel his mouth on hers. "I'll be—"

But her words were cut off by an earth-shattering explosion of gunfire. There was yelling, frantic voices and a loud clatter, which Shelby imagined was Johnny's cellular phone smashing to the asphalt.

And then there was another shot.

CHAPTER TWO

"JOHNNY!?"

When she heard the second shot, Shelby's heart stopped. She clutched the back of the sofa for support, her senses reeling.

She closed her eyes for only a second, but it was long enough to envision the scene at the other end of the line: Johnny's Cavalier parked askew on the street, along with several patrol cars, the blue strobes lighting up the night as officers rushed to the scene; the cellular phone lying on the wet asphalt; and finally Johnny, in a pool of blood, his gun not even drawn.

"Johnny! Are you there? Johnny!"

There was only frenzied shouting, more cars and slamming doors.

Aidan's voice, gentle and calm, slipped into the periphery of her awareness. "Shelby, what's happening?"

"Johnny!" she cried desperately into the receiver again, her hand aching from the pressure with which she clutched it. "Dammit, Johnny, answer me!"

"Shelby..." Aidan's hand wrapped around hers holding the receiver. "Shelby, let me have the phone."

"Johnny!" she screamed once more, panic clawing at her.

Aidan grasped her shoulder firmly and turned her so she was forced to look at him.

"Shelby, give me the phone."

And it was then that one voice could be heard over all the others, over the squawk of the police radio in the background and the footfalls of running officers. "We need some help here," the voice yelled above the confusion. "Call the paramedics. Officer down. Officer down!"

Shelby's stomach pitched sickeningly and the apartment whirled. Aidan didn't have to fight for the phone now. It almost fell from her loosened fingers as he took hold of it, one steadying hand remaining on her shoulder.

"Hello? Is anyone there? Hello! This is Aidan O'Neill. Is anyone there?" Shelby thought she heard fear in his voice. She saw his knuckles whiten around the receiver.

Trembling, Shelby hugged herself, as though to literally hold herself together.

"Shelby, what did you hear?" Aidan looked at her, the phone still to his ear. "Tell me what you heard."

"There's..." She swallowed hard, tasting the sourness of her own fear. "There's an officer down."

"John?"

"I...I don't know."

When he replaced the receiver in the cradle, Shelby lunged forward, trying to stop him. They couldn't just hang up. They couldn't break their only link with

Johnny. She stared blankly at Aidan's hand on the phone.

"The connection was broken, Shelby. I'm sorry."

Her gaze lifted to Aidan's face. But all she could see was Johnny lying on that dark wet street.

"Listen, Shelby, let's keep calm. We don't know anything for certain."

"Aidan, he was on the phone." She struggled to bring her voice under control. "I heard the gunshot—two of them. I'm sure he dropped the phone. Then—" she shook her head "—I heard someone say...there's an officer down!"

"But we don't know it's Johnny. Not for certain. Shelby, listen to me." He gripped both her shoulders now and gave her a little shake, as if to break her away from the hot fear flooding through her. "Pull yourself together. I'll call downtown. Maybe they can tell us what's going on."

Shelby watched Aidan punch out the precinct number. It wasn't her imagination that his fingers shook.

She'd known this would happen. She'd known all along. From the moment she'd met Johnny, she'd understood the dangers. She should have heeded that warning voice deep inside, should have paid attention to all the fears that had churned in her stomach every time Johnny had been late, every time the phone or the doorbell had rung.

But no, she'd believed she could live with the fears. Ignore them and they wouldn't be real. And foolishly a part of her had genuinely believed that it would never come to this, that Johnny would never be taken from her.

"Who is this?" Aidan was asking into the phone. "Joey, yeah, this is Aidan O'Neill. You've got an officer down at Carnegie and First? What the hell's going on there? Do you know who…mm-hmm…mm-hmm… Well, who?… Yeah…no, I understand that, but…"

It *was* Johnny. Shelby pushed away from the couch. Johnny had been shot. She couldn't just wait here.

Carnegie and First. It was only minutes away. Ten at the most.

There were sirens now in the distance. The ambulance.

She crossed the living room and grabbed her trench coat from the tree by the door, still hearing Aidan on the phone: "Yes, Joey, I understand. It's just that John's down there…. Yeah, he was talking to Shelby when the shots were fired, and we…yes, that's right. Mm-hmm… Well, listen, you'll call us the second you know something, right? Yeah, I'm at John's."

From the side table Shelby snatched up the keys to the Lexus and bolted for the stairs. Her heart raced. She visualized the ten-minute drive, how she'd do it in five. How she'd turn up at Carnegie and First and see the patrol cars and the ambulance….

The siren was louder, shattering the night, as she flew down the stairs to the boutique and the front door.

She hadn't heard Aidan hang up the phone, nor had she heard him charge down the stairs after her. But when she reached for the dead bolt, he was right behind her.

"Shelby, wait." He pulled her around forcefully,

restrained her with his arms. "Shelby! The station will call as soon as they know something."

"I have to go to him, Aidan!" She clenched her fists and felt the car keys dig into her palm.

"Shelby, we don't know it was John. Listen to me..."

But she was already twisting away, struggling with the dead bolt. He grabbed her a second time.

"Listen to me! Shelby, you're being irrational."

"Irrational?" She spun around to face him. "Irrational? Aidan, you didn't hear what I did. Johnny's been shot! I am *not* going to just sit here and—"

"No!" When Aidan reached for her this time, his hands clamped her arms like steel vices.

He was every bit as frightened as she was, she realized. His eyes seemed darker somehow and his freckles stood out against his pallor.

"You can't just run out there, Shelby." His voice wavered and his jaw clenched. "We don't know if it was John. *We don't know!*"

Aidan's grip relaxed to a small degree, as though he was still uncertain whether he could actually trust Shelby to stay put. But when he finally released her, Shelby's only move was to let out a shuddering breath. If he'd held her a moment longer, she was sure the tears burning behind her eyes would have flowed.

"We have to wait, Shelby. The precinct will call the second they know."

THERE WAS A LOT of blood. Then again, as the medical examiner would confirm later, the caliber of the bullet was a .357 magnum. The damage was irreparable, the wound fatal.

The shot had come out of nowhere. They'd been wrapping up the scene. Everything was secured. Everyone had holstered their weapons and was packing it in. It was supposed to have been safe.

No one had known that the armed felon who'd attempted the liquor-store heist had an accomplice. That the accomplice had scrambled to the roof at the arrival of the first patrol car. And in a last-ditch effort to rescue his friend had drawn his gun and started shooting.

Johnny had been the closest to Officer Seth Cushing when the rookie cop had taken the bullet in the chest. The shooter needn't have fired the second round; the first had killed Seth, in spite of Johnny's efforts.

As the men charged to the rooftop and fanned through the dark alleyways to apprehend the sniper, Johnny had dropped the phone and rushed to Cushing's side. He'd applied pressure to the gaping wound, feeling the man's life pulse out beneath his fingers.

"Come on, Seth. You can make it," he'd pleaded with the young officer. "You gotta stay with me now, you hear?"

The rookie had nodded weakly, his face twisted in agony.

"You gotta hang on. For Susan. For the kids. You hear me? They need you, Seth. Just hang on!"

But Johnny had known that Seth wasn't going to make it. "Don't worry, Seth," he'd said when he felt him weaken, when he knew that the next breath might be Seth's last. "We're going to get the son of a bitch who did this. *I'm* going to get him, you hear? And we'll look out for Susan.''

Officer Seth Cushing was dead before the paramedics had even reached him. Nevertheless they'd done everything possible to revive him before lifting his body onto a stretcher and into the ambulance.

"Damn." Nick DaCosta came up beside Johnny and followed his somber gaze to the ambulance. "I don't believe this."

A paramedic had handed Johnny a towel, which he used to wipe the blood from his hands. He watched the attendants close the doors. "Anything yet on the shooter?"

Nick shook his head. His dark rain-matted hair gleamed in the light from the red strobe atop the ambulance. His eyes narrowed under his heavy brows as he looked up to the roof from where the shot had been fired. "Nothin'. We got more men coming down to search the area, find out if anyone saw anything."

To Johnny, Nick's expression seemed more haggard than usual, his thin face paler. No wonder, given what had just happened. But in truth Johnny had noticed his partner's tension and fatigue earlier. Particularly this morning, when he'd arrived at the waterfront and found an exhausted Nick nursing a steaming cup of coffee as he examined the Feeney crime scene. Maybe it was all the overtime the two of them had put in lately.

"I know what you're thinking, John," Nick said, breaking the bleak silence.

Johnny dropped his gaze to the stained towel in his hands and said nothing.

"I want this guy, too," Nick continued. "But with the Morelli and Feeney homicides, I wouldn't count on the captain letting either of us work on this one. It's too much, John."

Johnny only nodded. Nick was right. Their load was heavy. It wasn't likely that Captain Barnes would let them investigate this shooting. Still, he'd try. It wasn't that he'd had close personal ties to Seth Cushing. Sure, he'd spoken to him at the precinct often enough, seen him at a couple of police barbecues with his wife, Susan, and their two little girls. And three weeks ago Cushing had been one of the responding officers on the Morelli homicide. But it didn't matter how well Johnny did or didn't know him—Cushing was a good cop. And losing one of their own dealt the entire force a blow.

Danny Ogden, Cushing's partner, walked slowly over from the ambulance as it pulled away. His uniform was soaked with rain, and his blond hair was plastered to his head. His cap hung limply from one hand.

"Thanks, Detective Spencer," he mumbled. "I... uh...I know you did everything you could."

"You okay? Are you going to be able to handle talking to Seth's wife?"

Cushing's partner didn't answer. His eyes had locked onto the bloodstained towel in Johnny's hands.

"Danny?" Johnny waited until the officer met his gaze. "Do you want me to talk to Seth's wife?"

"No. No, Detective Spencer. Thanks." He cleared his throat. "He was *my* partner. I'll...um...I should go now. Be with Susan."

They looked after their own, cops did. Seth Cushing's family was going to be struck hard by this, and it was Danny Ogden's responsibility to look out for Susan and the girls. Johnny could see by the way the young officer's jaw set and his stance straightened that he was accepting that duty, no matter how difficult.

"I'm sorry, Danny," he said again, reaching out to grasp the man's shoulder. And when he met Danny's pain-filled eyes, Johnny recognized the look that told him Danny Ogden would never forget this day. He would never forget his first partner or Susan Cushing's face when he told her that her husband was dead.

"Yeah, I'm sorry, too," Danny replied at last, and turned to leave.

That was how it usually happened. In an instant. One bullet from some two-bit thief and a life was over. A family was shattered.

Even more unsettling was the thought that it could quite easily have been Johnny shot tonight. He'd been standing close enough to Cushing. He could have been the one who'd taken the bullet, the one lying with his life drained out of him in the back of that ambulance right now. And then it would have been Nick, not Danny Ogden, trudging off as the bearer of bad news. It would have been Shelby hearing how he hadn't suffered, how he'd died almost instantly....

"Omigod! Shelby!" Johnny spun around to the Cavalier, scanning the glistening pavement for the cell phone.

"What?" Nick was right behind him. "John, what's wrong?"

"I've gotta call Shelby."

He scooped up the phone and jabbed frantically at the number keys.

Aidan answered on the first ring.

"Aidan—"

"Dammit, John, what the hell's going on down there? You've scared Shelby half to death, for God's sake!"

"I'm fine. Put her on, Aidan. Please." Johnny leaned against the fender of the Cavalier and watched several patrol cars pull away. He waited, listening to the static over the line, and knew Aidan was having to convince Shelby to take the phone.

Johnny could almost see her face: the usually smooth forehead furrowed with worry, her sparkling dark eyes even darker with fear. He'd scared her half to death. It would be a wonder if she came to the phone at all. When she finally did, her hello was audibly unsteady.

"Shel? Shelby?"

"I'm here."

"Shel, I'm sorry. I didn't mean to frighten you."

Silence.

"Shel? Listen, I'm okay. We, um, lost an officer tonight." He would never tell her that he'd been standing right beside the man when it had happened. "Are you all right?"

No answer.

"Shelby, I'm fine, you hear? I'm sorry I didn't call you right back, but I kinda had my hands full here. They're still looking for the shooter. We didn't know there was a second guy and—"

"I thought you'd been shot, John." Her voice trembled, sounding as if she'd been crying. Or, more likely, knowing the invincible front Shelby endeavored to maintain, he guessed she'd been holding back the tears too long.

And she'd called him John. He didn't think she ever had before.

"I'm sorry, Shel. I'm coming straight home. I'll be there in ten minutes."

More silence.

"I'm sorry," he said.

She didn't hang up the phone immediately. Instead, there was a long spell during which Johnny imagined her listening to his breathing, perhaps still uncertain whether to believe he was truly safe. Eventually, though, he heard the click as she replaced the receiver, then he flipped the switch on the cellular before tossing it onto the passenger seat of his car.

He raked a hand through his wet hair and swore.

"She thought it was you?" Nick asked.

"Yeah. I was talking to her when Cushing was shot."

"Oh, shit. That's rough."

But Johnny didn't expect Nick to truly understand what effect it had had on Shelby. Nick was single. There was no one in his life, only the occasional fling that he'd mention when they were driving. No different from himself not too long ago—before he'd first laid eyes on Shelby Beaumont.

"She'll get over it, John. Shelby's tough."

"Yeah, right." Not as tough as everyone pegged her, though, Johnny thought as he slipped his hand into the pocket of his jacket and felt the jeweler's box.

He'd seen her fear and her doubts too many times. Usually it was just under the surface, just beneath that strong facade, but it was there. And tonight he'd heard it loud and clear in her voice.

It wasn't too late. He hadn't asked her to marry him. He could still return the diamond ring and swear Aidan to secrecy. Shelby would never have to know.

Sure, it'd be hard at first, being apart from her. It would be hard on both of them. But in the long run... And in time Shelby would meet someone else—it was inevitable, given her grace, her beauty, her boundless passion—someone who could offer her stability, a secure life, children.

And then maybe, one day she'd understand that his leaving her had been for the best, that she was better off without him, without the worry and the risk that went hand in hand with being a cop's wife.

AIDAN SAW Shelby's hands shaking when she hung up the phone. Immediately she moved away from him, no doubt reluctant to further reveal the fright she'd suffered.

She sat on the couch but had little success in appearing calm and in control. In moments she was up again, resuming her anxious pacing until she stopped at the island that separated the kitchen from the living room.

"I'm sorry about dinner, Aidan," she said finally, offering him an apologetic smile.

It was clear that her chicken Kiev would go untouched tonight. "Don't worry about it, Shelby. We'll do it another night."

She only nodded, crossed her arms over her chest and leaned against the counter. She let out an unsteady breath.

"Are you going to be all right?" Aidan asked, wanting to go to her. It hurt him to see her like this, her usually strong exterior crushed, leaving her looking fragile, vulnerable. She didn't deserve this, he kept thinking. And more than anything, he wanted to take her into his arms and comfort her.

"I'm fine, Aidan. Really." She smiled again, brushing her hair over one shoulder. "And I'm sorry...for my reaction. You were right. I shouldn't have jumped to conclusions."

"It's understandable, Shelby."

There was another long silence. Shelby looked down at her hands and turned a wide silver ring around one trembling finger. John was planning to ask her tonight, Aidan thought, imagining the diamond ring on Shelby's finger. He couldn't help wondering if John's proposal, like the dinner congealing in the oven, would also be postponed.

"Do you think he'll ever quit, Aidan?"

He wasn't sure what surprised him more—the bluntness of the question or the flat, almost lifeless tone of her voice. When she looked across the room at him then, her eyes seemed to plead with him, as though he was the only one who could possibly convince John to leave the force.

Aidan sighed and shook his head. "I don't know, Shelby." It wouldn't help matters if he told her he doubted John would ever quit the force, if he reminded her that being a cop was a Spencer tradition, not to mention John's life and passion. "I really don't know."

He wished there was more he could tell her, more he could offer to ease her fears. But even if he'd known what to say, he didn't get the chance.

For at that moment they heard the door open downstairs.

SHELBY DIDN'T MOVE.

When she heard Johnny's footfall on the steel stairs and then the squelch of his wet sneakers against the hardwood of the second floor, she didn't budge. Even when he stepped into the living room, his black hair soaked, his face still glistening from the rain, she couldn't bring herself to go to him.

In fact, the second Johnny turned his dark gaze on her, she looked away. Just the sight of him sent another nauseating wave churning up from the pit of her stomach and into her throat.

In *her* mind Johnny had been shot. The instant she'd heard that first discharge of the gun, she'd felt his loss. Aidan had tried to convince her she was jumping to conclusions, had even called her irrational, and maybe she had been, but she still felt the keen and terrifying emptiness in her life.

She swallowed hard, fighting back tears of relief and anger.

"Shel, I got here as soon as I could."

She dared another glance at him. His jeans were wet, as was the front of his sweatshirt; beads of rain glittered on his leather bomber. One corner of the jacket was flipped back, caught by one of the straps of his holster. Shelby looked from the gun to Johnny's expectant expression. She only nodded, knowing that if she attempted to say anything, her voice would betray her shattered emotions.

"Shel."

He took a step toward her, obviously hoping to close the seemingly insurmountable gap between them, but Shelby shook her head and raised one hand. She started to back away, retreating behind the island and into the safety of the kitchen.

She couldn't allow him to touch her. If he did, she knew she'd fall apart.

Johnny seemed to understand. His lips pursed, and he gave her a barely perceptible nod before turning to Aidan.

"I'm sorry about all this."

"It's okay, John."

Silence fell between the two men, and Shelby understood that Aidan wanted to ask Johnny about the shooting. But he wouldn't. Not in front of her. Not when he saw how upset she was.

The tension in the room was electric. Aidan glanced from Johnny to Shelby, then back again. "I'll, uh, head out now. It's getting late."

Johnny nodded, turning to walk his friend down to the main door. As Aidan left, Shelby caught his reassuring nod and smile, and tried to return it.

She listened to them take the stairs and cross the darkened boutique to the front door. She heard their hushed voices rise to the loft apartment, but she couldn't make out the words. No doubt Aidan was asking about the dead officer.

Shelby gripped the edge of the counter. The room threatened to spin again. She needed to get a hold of herself, put this behind her. But...it had been so close!

She should have been happy, grateful Johnny was alive. She should have been flooded with relief the second she'd found out, run into his arms the moment he'd come into the room. Yet all she felt was the terrible emptiness that had gripped her when she'd heard the shots over the phone. Even with Johnny home, his voice coming up from the front door, the emptiness was still there, and the deep and sickening knowledge of what could have been—and almost was.

CHAPTER THREE

"WHO WAS IT?" Aidan asked when he stopped in the open doorway of the boutique and fished his keys out of his pocket.

Johnny looked past his friend and watched the rain shimmer down to the quiet street in the long shafts of lamplight. "Seth Cushing."

"I don't think I knew him."

"He was a good cop."

"Married?"

Johnny nodded. "With two daughters."

"Damn." Aidan shook his head, closing his eyes briefly.

"I was standing right beside him, Aidan. Not a foot away. It could've been me."

"Don't think about it."

Johnny let out a tense breath. "Yeah, you're right. Listen, thanks for being here tonight. For staying with Shelby."

"She was scared."

Johnny nodded.

"I don't think I've ever seen her that scared," Aidan said.

"I know." Johnny recognized the genuine concern

in his friend's voice. He knew he could count on Aidan to be there for Shelby if he couldn't be himself.

Like tonight.

"Thanks again," he said, but he needn't have voiced his gratitude. Aidan understood.

"Talk to her, John. She'll be all right, but you gotta talk to her."

"Yeah." Johnny shoved his hands into his jacket pockets, but removed them again when he felt the jeweler's box. "Listen, are you going to be at your office tomorrow afternoon?"

"Should be."

"I mean late afternoon. Maybe five-thirty or six? I have to talk to you about something. I might...I think I need your help."

"What is it, John?"

"Tomorrow, Aidan. I can't get into it right now. Shelby... I should get upstairs."

"Sure." Aidan nodded. "I'll see you tomorrow, then."

"Thanks." Johnny closed the door behind his friend and looked around the dark boutique. Shelby's mannequins hovered in the shadows like ghosts, seeming to watch him. More like judge him, he thought, as he felt for the ring box again.

Aidan was right. Shelby had never been so frightened. At least not as long as Johnny had known her. Before he'd walked into her life, her world had been stable, secure. Furthermore she'd known exactly what she wanted from life and had set herself on a direct path toward it.

But now, although her dedication to her work hadn't

waned, some of the dreams seemed to have been discarded along the way. Earlier on, when they'd just been getting to know each other, she'd spoken of returning to New York City. Since they'd started living together, however, she never mentioned the move. It was as if she'd become satisfied with Fairfield and her life with him, as though she was happy to sacrifice her dream.

Johnny fingered the velvet-covered box again. After what had happened tonight, her sacrifice didn't seem worth the life he could offer her.

He took a deep breath and headed for the stairs.

He found Shelby at the far end of the living room, her back to him, gazing out the window. Her arms were crossed over her chest and her body was rigid.

Johnny shrugged off his wet jacket and went to her. When he put his hands on her shoulders, he felt them stiffen.

"Shelby."

She didn't reply.

He pushed aside her hair and lowered his mouth to the nape of her neck, pressing a kiss to the delicate skin. She gave a quiver, then her shoulders relaxed slightly and he kissed her again, inhaling her intoxicating scent. He encircled her with his arms and drew her back against his chest. "I'm sorry, love."

She didn't reply. After a moment she lifted her hands to his. Her fingers trembled.

"The last thing I'd ever want to do is frighten you."

"I know," she said, and gave his hands a gentle squeeze.

"I just...when the shots were fired, I just reacted."

He pressed his cheek against her head, and felt her nod. "A cop was killed tonight."

"I know," she said again.

There was comfort in the silence that fell between them, in the intimate embrace they shared. It felt so right to hold her in his arms—as if nothing else mattered. He could stand here forever with her, forget that the rest of the world even existed. For him, there was only Shelby.

How could he *not* ask her to marry him? How could he even consider leaving the only person he'd ever loved so much it almost hurt when he wasn't with her? And how could he possibly turn his back on Shelby now, walk out of her life forever? He couldn't bear the thought of never again hearing her laugh or seeing her smile, of smelling her sweet scent and feeling the electrifying tingle that quivered through his body when she touched him. He'd be lost without her.

No, he couldn't leave her.

It was selfish of him. He knew that. He should have the strength to walk away, knowing she could have a better life without him. But it wasn't that easy. Without Shelby, his own life would have no meaning.

No, this was not a decision he could make for the both of them. He wasn't strong enough for that. Aidan was right—it would have to be up to Shelby to decide whether or not she could live with the risks and the dangers of his job.

"I thought it was you, Johnny. I thought you'd been killed." The flatness and detachment in her voice took him aback.

"I know you did."

"It *could* have been you tonight."

"But it wasn't." He brought his hands up to her shoulders again and turned her to face him. Her eyes appeared darker than usual, glistening with unshed tears. Johnny realized this was the closest he'd ever come to seeing her cry.

"It wasn't me, Shel," he repeated, lifting her chin. "I'm here. With you."

"Promise me you'll be careful. That you won't let anything…"

"I promise, Shelby." He traced the line of her jaw, then fanned his fingers into her hair and drew her to him. "No matter what, I will always be here. With you. Forever."

He needed to be with her tonight.

When he lowered his lips to hers, Shelby lifted a hand to his chest, bracing herself. The other trembled against his cheek. He kissed her gently at first, giving her the time she seemed to need to deal with the emotional overload. But when his kiss became more intense, when he cradled her face in his hands, he heard her soft whimper.

And still she held back her tears.

Her lips almost shivered against his and her body trembled. It was a kiss, he thought, that possessed all the hesitancy and all the quivering anticipation of their first one.

As long as he lived, he would never forget that first kiss. The soft glow of the street lamp on her skin, her gentle smile and the softness of her hand when she'd slipped it into his. They'd had dinner at Tony's Trattoria. They'd talked about his career and then hers, about her moving back to New York City one day and making a bigger name for herself in the fashion industry.

Shelby didn't need to tell him that she hadn't planned on having a relationship, that she hadn't thought herself capable of making the room for someone in her life; it had been obvious to Johnny. She was committed to her work. Still, when he'd kissed her that first time, her initial hesitation had been crushed by eagerness and desire.

They'd slept together for the first time that night, as well. It had been obvious they were meant to be together, almost pointless to prolong the inevitable, their passion for each other so absolute, so consuming.

Now, as Shelby's fingers trailed to the back of Johnny's neck and slipped into his hair, her response became undeniably urgent. She devoured his mouth with an almost desperate hunger. Her hands dropped to his waist, pulling him closer, and she pressed herself against him as though needing to touch every part of him, to be consumed by his love in order to believe he was alive and here with her now.

She was still shaking. And as they continued their fevered kisses, Johnny heard a small cry escape her throat. He felt her breath shudder and for a moment wondered if she was crying.

He drew back far enough to see her face, brushing aside a long strand of hair. Then he tilted her chin so that she was forced to look at him.

"Shel?"

"I'm all right, Johnny." Her voice trembled.

On his lips he could taste her familiar sweetness.

He held her gaze, his hand never leaving her waist, as he reached for his jacket and pulled out the jeweler's box.

"I know this probably isn't a good time to be asking," he began, searching her face. "But I've been planning this all day...well, all year actually."

Why was this so difficult? He'd rehearsed in his head a thousand times what he wanted to say to her. Was it because of what had happened tonight? Because he'd finally seen the kind of life he was asking Shelby to commit herself to?

"Johnny, I—"

"I love you, Shel. More than anything. More than I'll ever be able to find the words for. After tonight...after what happened, I shouldn't be asking you this." He snapped open the small box and watched Shelby's overwhelmed gaze as the diamond caught the light. "I only wish I'd had the nerve to ask you long before now. It's just that...it's a big step, you know?"

Her gaze lifted to meet his. Her eyes glistened and her mouth curved in a gentle smile. But in that gentle smile, Johnny glimpsed the tiniest fear.

"Johnny, I don't know what to say. I—"

He placed a finger over her mouth, and her smile faltered. "Don't say anything, Shel. Please. Not yet."

"Johnny—"

"Shh." He pressed a kiss to her lips. "Don't answer right now. I want you to think about this. Being a cop's wife, Shel, I know it's not what you planned. And I know it's not easy. I see it every day on the force, see what it's like worrying, not knowing—like tonight. I just...I want you to really consider what you'd be getting into, that's all. By marrying me, you'd be marrying the force. I...I don't want you to rush into something like that."

He fingered a long strand of dark hair as he waited for her nod. When it came, he said again, "I love you, Shel. I'll love you forever, but I want you to be sure."

She nodded, then stepped into his embrace and met his kiss with a passion that made him wonder who needed the other more just then.

"Make love to me, Johnny." Her voice was so quiet he wasn't sure if she'd actually spoken the words or if he'd felt them in her driving desire. "I need you."

Later, Johnny didn't know who led the way to their bedroom or who pulled the blinds. All he knew was Shelby—Shelby and her desperate need to be with him.

In seconds he'd unbuttoned her pantsuit and slipped the silky material from her shoulders, discarding it on the floor and falling with her onto their bed. Then he straddled her, wanting her to feel his arousal.

She tugged at his shirt and pulled it over his head. Her hands were still trembling as they glided down his bare back and moved around to the buckle of his belt. When at last she'd twisted it free and unzipped his jeans, Johnny couldn't remember if he'd ever wanted her more than he did right then, if he'd ever *needed* her more.

He stopped. Beneath him, Shelby, too, caught her breath. In the shafts of streetlight that knifed through the partially closed blinds, Johnny looked down at her, watching the excited rise and fall of her chest.

A part of him wanted to take the time to unclasp

the white lace bra that contrasted so with her olive-toned skin, to cover her breasts with his kisses, to suck each perfect nipple in turn, and to taste every last delicious inch of this woman he loved like nothing else in this world. But another part of him yearned fiercely to bury himself inside her, lose himself in her longing, crush both their fears with his love and his desire for her.

When he kissed her again, Shelby matched his intensity. She tugged down his jeans and he moved over her. In one final frenzied moment, when he knew neither of them were capable of further restraint, he plunged into her.

With a gasp of rapture, Shelby lifted her hips and Johnny grasped them, plunging more deeply with every thrust. It was as if their very lives depended on their union tonight, as if it was the last time they would ever be together.

Somewhere in their gasps were words—declarations of love and cries of devotion—but these were lost in the pounding urgency of their lovemaking. He was vaguely aware of the shudder that ripped through Shelby's body as he moved with her. And when he looked down into her eyes, seconds before they came together in that one shattering and desperate instant, he saw the tears on her cheeks.

"OMIGOD, THAT WAS Lauren Dametto!" Doreen hung up the phone and spun around to face Shelby. "She wants to bump up the date of your presentation."

Squatting in front of a scantily clad mannequin, Shelby muttered a curse between the row of dressing pins pinched firmly between her lips. Even so, she continued to calmly pin the hem of the black velvet cocktail dress. "How soon?"

"Three weeks."

Shelby stopped. She shot a glance at her assistant, and they shared a brief look of exasperation. Lauren Dametto represented the biggest names in the fashion industry. It wouldn't have mattered if her personal assistant had called to say Ms. Dametto wanted to see Shelby's designs tomorrow morning; Shelby would have had to be ready. There were no second chances when it came to Lauren Dametto.

Shelby got to her feet and calmly removed the remaining pins from her lips. She took a deep breath. "Well, it looks like we've got ourselves a new deadline, doesn't it?"

"You think we can actually make it? I mean, we've still got so much work to do on those designs for Maison de Couture coming up, and...well, you know, then there's everything else, and..." Framed by a mop of tight red curls she struggled to keep at bay with a huge barrette, Doreen's round face screwed up in worry.

"I've never missed a deadline before."

"I know, Shelby, but—"

"We'll manage, Doreen." She gave her assistant a fleeting smile—one that concealed her own uncertainty—and draped her measuring tape around her neck. "Don't worry."

"Okay." Doreen still sounded doubtful. "You're the boss. I'll let you worry for both of us."

"In the meantime, I've got some new sketches I need you to run over to Peter," she said, referring to her couturier. "If we're bumping up production by three weeks, I want him to start these right away. I'll go get them."

She went upstairs and crossed to her drafting table, immediately noticing Johnny's T-shirt amidst the clutter. A smile touched her lips as she picked it up.

Johnny had been asleep when she'd slipped from their bed that morning. She hadn't had the heart to wake him; he'd looked so peaceful. Instead, she'd tiptoed to her studio and immersed herself in her work. She'd been startled from her concentration when Johnny padded into the studio an hour later and wrapped his arms around her.

Spinning her stool around, he'd brushed aside the edges of her robe and stepped between her bare legs. He'd taken her face in his hands and gazed into it for the longest time, caressing her cheeks with his thumbs, and then he'd kissed her. Soon he'd drawn her up from the stool, and it wasn't long before his T-shirt had been discarded among the drawings on her table.

They'd stumbled back through the apartment to the bedroom and made love slowly, tenderly. This time without the frantic desire, fueled by the fear of losing each other, that had driven them the night before. She'd cried again this morning, but unlike the previous night they were not tears of relief, but her realization of the overwhelming extent of her love for him. And for the unknown. For the uncertainty of their future, despite Johnny's proposal of marriage.

The phone rang, breaking Shelby's reverie, and she dropped Johnny's T-shirt onto the desk.

"I've got it up here, Doreen," she called, grappling with the receiver. "Shelby Beaumont."

"Hello, Shelby. This is Dr. Williams."

"Doc." She was pretty sure she knew why he was calling. Even though she'd been Evan Williams's patient since she was a child and she'd celebrated more than a couple of New Years at the Williamses' annual bash, he'd never *personally* called her. So this had to be important.

"I hope you're sitting down, Shelby," he said, his voice far too cheerful.

Shelby swallowed hard.

"I just received the results of yesterday's blood tests, and—"

"I'm pregnant." Her words came out in a trembling gasp.

"Congratulations."

Shelby groped for the stool and sat. Everything in the studio seemed to blur except the photograph of Johnny on the corner of her desk. His easy smile beamed back at her. She wondered if he would give her that same smile when she told him the news.

"Shelby? Are you there?" Dr. Williams sounded concerned.

"Yes, Doc, I'm here."

"I...I take it you and John weren't planning this?"

"No. Not exactly."

"Oh." He hesitated. "I understand. Do you want to arrange an appointment, Shelby? There are...well, options we can discuss."

"No. No, it's nothing like that," she assured him. "It's...it *is* good news. Just...unplanned."

"Well, you should come in nevertheless so we can go over the details of your pregnancy."

"Sure, Doc."

"How is Thursday afternoon next week for you?"

Shelby took a deep breath, wondering if Evan Williams could hear the shiver in it, and tried to calm her racing heart.

"I don't have my calendar with me right now. Could I call back later?"

"Sure. You can arrange it with Marsha."

"I'll do that."

"And congratulations again, Shelby."

"Thanks, Doc."

As she replaced the receiver in its cradle, Shelby's mind was churning. Pregnant? Now? Yes, she hadn't used her diaphragm a couple of times in the past few weeks, but she'd checked her calendar and thought she was safe. So "unplanned" was putting it mildly. And what made the news more unnerving was the fact that, as well as she knew Johnny, as much as she loved him, she had no idea what his reaction would be. They'd never discussed having a family, at least not seriously. And before she'd met Johnny she'd never even considered the possibility of a relationship, let alone a family. There'd been only her work, her career.

Yet, in the midst of her apprehension, there was a glimmer of excitement. A family. First Johnny's proposal and now their pregnancy. Maybe life wasn't always about careful planning. Maybe sometimes it just happened. In a heartbeat. Fate.

"Was that Peter?" Doreen called from below the balcony, her round smiling face turned upward.

"No," Shelby managed to answer, her hand still resting on the receiver.

"Who was it?"

"Oh, no one." She slid the measuring tape from around her neck and dropped it on top of her drawings. And when she reached for the black ring box which she'd placed on a corner of her desk, her fingers trembled. "Nothing important," she told Doreen.

JOHNNY WEDGED his foot against the corner of his desk and leaned back in the battered oak chair. The wing that housed the detectives' division was unusually deserted. In fact, if Johnny hadn't been so anxious to speak to the captain, he would have been out, too, canvassing the city with the rest of the men for any leads on Seth Cushing's killer.

From the window by his desk, the late-afternoon sun filtered through the dingy pane. It washed over the files and mounting paperwork, and made the brass picture frame on his desk gleam.

Mindlessly he picked up a small, black rubber ball and worked it between his fingers as he studied the five-by-seven photo of Shelby. Her lovely mouth was curved in an alluring, almost mysterious, smile that was undeniably Shelby. He liked to believe she'd been thinking of him when the picture was taken. It was the same smile that greeted him every morning when he rolled over in bed, the same smile that never failed to make his heart skip when he pulled her into his arms.

The smile he knew he could never, in a thousand life-times, tire of.

If a year ago anyone had told him he'd be proposing marriage, he would have scoffed. And if they'd said the woman he'd be proposing to was Shelby Beau-mont, he probably would have had them committed. Even now, Johnny still had to pinch himself on occasion. A high-class refined woman like Shelby and a working stiff like himself—who'd have thought? Every day, every time he lost himself in her smile, Johnny wondered how he'd gotten so lucky.

Maybe that was what nagged in the back of his mind now; even though he knew Shelby loved him, it still didn't really make sense to him sometimes. It was that nagging voice he'd listened to last night when he'd given Shelby the ring but refused to allow her to give him an answer.

And then this morning, after finding her at her desk, after they'd made love once more, he'd wanted to ask her again. He'd wanted to suggest they spend their honeymoon on his boat, take a few weeks and sail down the coast with no set destination. Just be to-gether.

But he hadn't brought it up. As much as he wanted to hear Shelby say yes, he'd remained silent. Even when he'd kissed her goodbye and headed to the front door, he'd looked up to catch her watching him from the studio railing. Her face was pensive, her smile flickering, almost melancholy. Again, he'd wanted to ask, but said nothing.

He'd wait for her answer—no matter how long. He wanted Shelby to be sure. And if the worst happened, if she said no, he would understand. He'd respect her decision, no matter how devastating. Maybe they'd stay together, or, more likely, he'd leave and let Shelby get on with her life.

"Hey, John."

Johnny glanced up as Nick crossed the near-empty room and dropped into the chair behind his desk.

"What are you still doing here?" Nick asked. "I thought you were going to work on your boat this afternoon."

"I am." Johnny lowered his feet and checked his watch. He was running late. "I have to talk to the captain first. You seen him?"

"I think he's on his way up. He was just downstairs—" Nick barked a laugh and shook his head "—helping Dabrowski and Reynolds wrestle with some punk they brought in on an assault charge. I tell you, John, those boys wouldn't know how to cuff a guy if he held out his hands and begged them to. By the way, they're starting up a fund for Cushing's family, if you're interested."

As Nick began fingering through a stack of files, Johnny watched him for a moment. Nick was younger than he was; not by much, but he still had that hotshot attitude of a rookie out to prove himself, an attitude that only invited trouble and resentment from the squad. He'd transferred from New York City ten months ago, obviously believing he could wrap the Fairfield department around his little finger with all his big-city smarts. Instead, he'd been greeted with a collective cold shoulder.

It didn't seem to matter that he'd been partnered

with Johnny, either. No matter how much respect the other men on the squad had for Johnny, they certainly hadn't gone to any great effort to demonstrate the same for Nick. But then, Nick hadn't put in any great effort himself to become a member of the team; he rarely showed up at police barbecues or other social functions, and only once or twice had he joined them down at Al's Saloon for a pint after their shift. In fact, Nick's interest in the collection for Seth Cushing's family was the first sign Johnny had seen that the rookie was attempting to become a part of the Fairfield force.

Maybe he'd hoped for too much in his new partner, expected the same bond he'd shared with Aidan. Or maybe it just took time. Still, in spite of the months together, he couldn't claim to really know Nick DaCosta. At first he'd thought the junior detective was simply reserved, possibly shy around the senior detectives.

But since the Morelli and Feeney shootings, Johnny had begun to wonder if there were other reasons behind Nick's apparent reluctance to enter into friendships with the other men on the squad....

Johnny glanced at his watch. "I thought you said Barnes was on his way up."

Nick nodded, and as if on cue, Captain Barnes pushed through the swinging door that separated the detectives' wing from the rest of the precinct.

Dan Barnes crossed the room, his jacket slung over one shoulder, his shirt rumpled and his tie hanging crookedly from his collar. Exhaustion racked his weathered face. Still, he didn't look bad for a guy well into his sixties who'd put in forty solid years with the Fairfield Police Department, and who, year after year, refused to address the issue of retirement.

When he *did* retire, though, Johnny would miss Dan Barnes. He'd run the precinct like a tight ship for more than fifteen years now and had always been there for any officer who needed him, Johnny included. Johnny only hoped that today Dan Barnes would support him yet again.

CHAPTER FOUR

"CAPTAIN." JOHNNY GOT UP from his desk.

"What are you still doing here, John? I thought you were kicking off early today."

"I'm just on my way out. But I wanted to see you first. Got a minute?"

Barnes checked his watch with an impatient flip of his wrist. "That's about all I've got. What's on your mind? You have something for me on the Morelli case?"

Johnny exchanged a glance with Nick. "No, nothing yet."

"What about ballistics? You get that report from Corky?"

"No. As far as I know he still hasn't examined the slugs from the Feeney scene. He figures he might have something by tomorrow. But that's not what I wanted to talk to you about."

Barnes shook his head, a muscle twitching in his jaw. There was more behind the captain's impatience than fatigue, Johnny sensed, and he knew enough not to take it personally. "John—"

"Dan, look, all we know right now is that the slugs from the two scenes are the same caliber. So that means we're probably looking at the same shooter in both the Morelli and Feeney hits. Other than that, we've got nothing to go on.''

"Nothing?"

Johnny shrugged. "I'm working on some angles, looking into a couple of leads." He held the captain's hard gaze, wondering if the man recognized his bluff. "But since Nick and I can't move anywhere with these cases until Corky comes through with the ballistics report—"

"Get to the point, John."

Johnny shoved his hands into the pockets of his jeans and leaned against his desk. He'd not asked many favors of Dan Barnes over the years. Perhaps that was one of the reasons Barnes had always been so supportive of him.

Barnes waited, his arms crossed over his broad chest.

"I want Cushing's case," Johnny said.

"What?" Barnes let out a gruff laugh that sounded more like a smoker's cough. "You're kidding, right?"

"No, Dan, I'm not. I want to handle the investigation."

"Oh, for crying out loud." The captain shook his head and began to weave his way through the desks to his glass-enclosed office.

"Dan—"

"Forget it, John." He held up one beefy hand to put an end to the protest, but Johnny was right behind him.

"Dan, I was there. I was standing beside the man when he was shot. It could have been me. I think—"

"No!" Barnes had reached his office and swung to

face Johnny with a suddenness that stopped him in his tracks. "Look, I've got every available officer out on the streets right now looking for that cop killer. We can't do any more than that."

"Dan—"

"John, you're the best this department's got and—"

"All the more reason for you to let me lead this."

"What? The Morelli and Feeney cases aren't enough work for you?"

"It's not like that." Johnny tried to temper his voice.

"No? So what're you planning to do, then, John, hmm? You going to work triple shift or something? A one-man crime squad?"

"If that's what it takes."

"No."

"Dan, come on. You know I wouldn't be asking unless—"

"No. And that's the end of it. I'm sorry."

Barnes crossed to his chair and dropped into it, then wheeled up to his file-strewn desk. When he picked up his pen, Johnny saw the captain's knuckles whiten with the pressure of his grip.

Propped at one corner of Barnes's desk were two framed photos. Johnny couldn't see them from where he stood, but he knew what they were—one was of the captain's wife and the other was his daughter's college-graduation picture.

And it was thoughts of his wife, Johnny suspected, that might be the real cause of the captain's gruff manner this afternoon. A year ago she'd been diagnosed with cancer. Perhaps she'd had a relapse or other complications, problems that Barnes's professionalism would never allow him to bring to the precinct, but that Johnny knew wore away at the man's spirit.

He studied the captain. There were dark circles under his pale eyes, his forehead seemed permanently creased with worry, and his shoulders were slumped in defeat. Realizing he couldn't push the man further, Johnny turned to leave the office.

"I'm sorry, John," Barnes said, lifting his weary gaze from his work. He set down his pen and rubbed one eye with the heel of his palm. "I know what you're asking. And why. Of course you're welcome to help out. You know that. But I've assigned Michaels as the primary investigator. You've already got too much on your plate."

"I understand, Dan." Johnny offered him a brief smile.

"Now get out of here and go work on that boat of yours."

"Sure." Johnny closed the captain's door and crossed to his desk.

Nick was waiting for him. "So, what angles?" he asked, leaning back in his chair and lacing his fingers behind his head.

"What?"

"Angles, John. You told Barnes you were working on some angles. That you had a couple of leads. How come I don't know anything about these?"

"Because there aren't any."

"But you told him—"

"You've got a lot to learn, kid." Johnny shook his head and reached for his jacket.

"So there's nothing?"

"Nothing you don't already know about." Johnny pretended to check his holster; he couldn't look Nick in the eye when he lied to him. He hadn't told his partner about his too-brief conversation with Frank Feeney the day before the man's body was found at the waterfront. Feeney had tried to keep his cool over the phone, but Johnny hadn't been fooled. Feeney had been scared. And Johnny had a pretty good idea what he'd been scared of—the entire setup smelled of a bad cop.

So Johnny had kept his mouth shut, which was as bad as lying. He hadn't told Nick about Feeney or about his other possible contact. And he wouldn't. Not until he was more certain of Nick.

"So are you off to the boat now?" Nick asked.

"Yeah."

Nick's phone rang just then and Johnny checked his watch—it was already after four. He had to get moving if he was going to be at the docks by four-thirty.

"I'll see you tomorrow," he called, then swung open the door and turned down the main hall of the precinct. He shrugged into his leather jacket and was halfway down the stairs when he spotted Corky McNair. He hurried down the remaining stairs to the lobby and caught up with Fairfield's ballistics expert just as he was heading down another corridor.

"Corky. Hang on a sec."

The stocky figure spun around abruptly, startled by Johnny's approach. The man was out of breath, as he generally was, and his eyes, huge behind the thick lenses of his glasses, flitted nervously from Johnny to the files in his hands and back again.

"I've been trying to reach you."

"Sorry, Detective. Been busy. Very busy."

"Obviously. Listen, do you have anything yet on the slugs we brought you from the Feeney scene? I know you said tomorrow—"

"Actually I had a quick look at them late this morning. Nothing extensive, mind you. Just preliminary." He lifted a thick-fingered hand to smooth a wisp of hair over his bald pate.

"And?"

"One of the slugs was particularly good. As you suspected, the riflings match the one pulled from the wall at the Morelli scene. It's a .357 magnum for sure."

"Can you tell the make of the gun used?"

"Like I said, I only had a preliminary look."

"Well, what's your guess?"

Corky McNair hesitated. In spite of his nervous temperament, he was respected as a man of precision, not someone who jumped to premature conclusions.

"A guess, Corky," Johnny prompted. "That's all I'm asking."

The man leaned closer to Johnny and spoke softly, as though to impart the secret of life, instead of a ballistics analysis. "If I *had* to guess, judging by the lands and the grooves and by the twist on the slug, I'd say you're looking for a Distinguished Combat Magnum."

"But that's—"

"Exactly. A Smith & Wesson 586—police issue.

Thing is, Detective, they're not used on the force any-more. Haven't been for a few years now. Quality-control problems. Repeated reports of cylinder jams, so they were replaced. Not that this means it was a police weapon that killed those men. Just, if it was, well, it'd be pretty rare, you know?''

Corky shifted his weight and started to turn away. "I gotta run, Detective."

"Yeah, I have to be someplace myself. Listen, can we talk tomorrow?"

"You know where to find me. I'll probably have something more concrete for you by then." About to head down the hall again, Corky stopped suddenly and turned to Johnny. "One more thing, Detective."

"Yeah?"

"Well, I was just thinking, maybe you're not in any particular rush for the paperwork on this?" Corky raised one eyebrow. "I mean, given the possi-ble...implications of this information..."

Johnny shared a knowing look with the ballistics expert. Corky was right. Until Johnny had a better idea of what he was looking for, until he figured out if there was any connection between Morelli and the Fairfield Police Department, it wouldn't hurt to delay the re-ports.

"No, Corky. No rush. I understand you're very... busy."

"Right, Detective. I'll see you tomorrow."

Johnny nodded as Corky McNair moved quickly down the corridor, his files gripped tightly under one arm.

He could only hope that Corky would be able to

give him something more definite tomorrow, that the man could substantiate his guess. And that no one, including Nick, would go to the ballistics lab to nose around for himself in the meantime.

IT USUALLY TOOK Shelby about fifteen minutes to drive from the north end of the city to the downtown precinct. This afternoon, however, the drive seemed agonizingly longer. After the call from Dr. Williams, Shelby had handed Doreen the sketches for Peter, grabbed her car keys and headed out. And during the drive, she'd rehearsed the words she'd use to tell Johnny the news of the pregnancy.

But at every traffic light the script in her head changed—each version becoming more excited and more certain than the last as she neared the precinct and Johnny.

The initial shock of the news had worn off somewhere between Glade Street and Twenty-second. And by the time she'd turned onto Main, Shelby found herself reflecting on some of the more imminent changes a child would bring to their lives. She knew Johnny liked kids. She'd seen him often enough horsing around with other officers' children at police functions. And last Christmas, when they'd spent four days at his sister's house up in Maine, his two nieces had instantly taken to Shelby. But it was Johnny they'd been most enamored with.

For the two girls, ages three and five, Uncle Johnny was their god. They followed him everywhere, mimicked his every gesture, hung on every word. They'd even ended up crawling into bed with him and Shelby on their third night there.

Yet somehow, like the topic of marriage, she and Johnny had always managed to avoid discussing having children of their own. Well, it was definitely shaping up to be a week for confronting those previously avoided issues, Shelby mused as she steered the Lexus into a parking spot at the back of the precinct. She pulled the keys from the ignition and drew a deep reassuring breath before she unclipped the seat belt. Then she placed a hand on her flat belly and smiled thoughtfully. Somehow, just like the first time she'd set eyes on Johnny Spencer and knew it wouldn't be the last, she knew he'd be elated at the news.

As she jogged up the steps of the precinct, she could imagine that smile of Johnny's lighting up his face. She pulled open the heavy doors and stepped into the lobby. It was nearing five, and still the place was a madhouse.

Shelby twisted her way through the confusion of uniformed officers and civilians, dodging two plain-clothes detectives and a handcuffed offender who was shouting obscenities. From his perch overlooking the lobby, the desk sergeant gave Shelby a smile of recognition and a wave as she stepped through the gate and headed up the stairs.

The detectives' wing was tranquil in comparison to the main floor. Several detectives worked at their desks under the harsh light of fluorescent bulbs, while others lounged around the water cooler. Whether on the phone or in discussion, none of them missed the opportunity to wave to Shelby—it truly was like one big family, she thought. And once she said yes to Johnny, she would become a permanent member of that family.

Heading to the back of the room, Shelby's smile faltered when she saw Johnny's empty chair. Nick was sitting at the adjacent desk, poring over a case file, his thick brown hair fastidiously combed and his shirt appearing freshly pressed. Shelby had always thought him extremely attractive. She'd even told Johnny that if her sister, Cora, hadn't lived so far away, she'd have set her up with Nick.

He looked up then and saw her. "Shelby. Hey—" a smile softened his angular face as he stood to greet her "—how are you doing?"

"Fine, thanks. Yourself?"

"Busy." He sat back down and gestured at the stack of files on his desk. "But you probably know that. So, you looking for John?"

"Is he around?"

"Afraid you just missed him," he said, tapping a tattoo on his desk with the end of his ballpoint. "He left about fifteen minutes ago."

As usual Nick seemed uncomfortable. He stopped the nervous tapping of his pen and crossed his arms over his chest as though not quite sure what else to do with himself.

Once, Shelby had mentioned to Johnny the effect she seemed to have on his new partner, but Johnny had only teased her, joking that she had the same effect on most of the guys at the precinct.

She smiled at Nick. "Is he out in the field or—"

"No. He said something about going to the docks to work on his boat."

"Great. I'll head down there."

"Okay. I'll, uh, see you around, Shelby."

She was about to turn when Dan Barnes stopped her.

"Shelby." The captain stepped out of his office and closed the distance between them. "How're you doing these days? I haven't seen you around in a while."

"I'm fine, thanks, Dan." Shelby buried her hands in the deep pockets of her leather trench coat—in one, she worried her set of car keys, and in the other her fingers stroked the velvet surface of the jeweler's box. "It's been a bit crazy lately."

"Yeah, my wife just got back from a shopping trip in New York City with her sister. They went to some big fashion show down there and saw your designs. She was really impressed."

Shelby smiled. "I'm pleased."

"Yeah, she says you were a real hit down there."

"Well, I'll have to thank Barbara personally the next time I see her." Her fingers continued to rub the ring box. As much as she liked Dan Barnes, she had to go. All she could think of was getting to Johnny, rushing into his arms, telling him her news and losing herself in his embrace.

Dan Barnes was nodding, seeming to have all the time in the world. "Actually I'm glad I saw you, Shelby. I was going to ask John to talk to you, but I'd rather ask in person now that you're here."

"What is it, Dan?"

"Seth Cushing."

"The officer who…"

The captain nodded. "Do you know Susan very well?"

"His wife? Not really. I mean, I've met her a couple times."

"I was hoping you might consider attending the memorial service for her husband. I think it's important that some of the wives and significant others attend. You know, kind of like a support group for her."

"Of course I'll go."

"Thanks, Shelby."

"Listen, Dan, I'm sorry, but I really have to run," she apologized, waiting for his nod of understanding before she turned to leave. "I'll see you soon," she called.

"Take care, Shelby."

Dan Barnes and Nick watched her leave in a swish of silk, her long skirt fluttering as she moved. Only when she was out the door and beyond earshot did Nick shake his head and let out a low whistle.

"Man, that is one stunning woman."

"Yup, she sure is," Dan Barnes concurred, his gaze sliding from the swinging door to the detective. "One fine lady."

"She sure is something to look at."

"Well, you better get a good look, DaCosta, 'cause that's about all you're ever gonna get. Just remember, she's your partner's girlfriend." He gave Nick a friendly nudge and headed back into his office.

DAN BARNES'S MENTION of the memorial service darkened Shelby's mood as she pulled her car out of the precinct lot and into the southbound traffic. It brought forth a flood of memories from last night— the fear and panic she'd felt, followed by the sickening relief when she'd found out it wasn't Johnny who'd been shot.

Not until this morning had she given thought to the dead officer, Seth Cushing, and the family he'd left behind. Then it had weighed heavily on her mind. So she hadn't brought up Johnny's proposal this morning, saying nothing even when he'd left for the precinct. She'd been that uncertain of her eventual answer.

But now, as she neared the docks and Johnny, things had become clearer. Perhaps it was the brilliance of the late-afternoon sun on the autumn-hued leaves, or maybe it was the news from Dr. Williams and the look of elation Shelby expected to see in Johnny's face when she told him, but somehow last night seemed almost a lifetime ago. So long ago, in fact, that she could almost pretend it had never happened.

And by the time she pulled the Lexus into the graveled lot designated for Fairfield Yacht Club members, her excitement began to peak once again. She found an empty spot amidst an array of heavy equipment and construction vehicles. It had been five months since the yacht club had begun their expansion of the piers, and still the work continued.

Through the windshield she watched a truck careen by, churning up thick clouds of dust in its wake. Past the truck, across the lot, she saw Johnny's Cavalier. A smile curved her lips and she took the ring box out of her pocket. She snapped it open and was struck again by the beauty of the diamond Johnny had chosen. But then, it wouldn't have mattered what the ring looked like, Shelby thought as she slid the delicate band over her finger; the love and the future it represented were far more beautiful than anything perceptible to the human eye.

She wanted Johnny to see the ring on her finger. Wanted him to see it and instantly know there was no question in her mind as to where her future lay.

Leaving the car, she wove her way through the tangle of cranes and backhoes, and followed the makeshift walkway to Pier Eight, where Johnny kept his boat, the *Orion.* A breeze tugged at her hair and beyond the dust and chaos of the construction, the sun glimmered off the rippled surface of the water.

It had been weeks since she'd been down here, weeks since she and Johnny had been able to find the time to go sailing. They'd have to make more time now, she thought as she sighted the mast of the *Orion.* In fact, right after she said yes to Johnny, she was going to suggest they spend their honeymoon on the sailboat. That was, if Johnny ever managed to finish fixing up the thirty-six-footer.

He'd been working on the boat as long as she'd known him and years before that. He'd brought her here on their first date, and she'd recognized his pride in the *Orion* even before he'd helped her onto the deck and given her a full tour. The *Orion* was his special place, he'd told her, and Shelby had felt honored that he'd wanted to share it with her.

That first evening together they'd sat on deck sipping Coronas, listening to the lapping of the waves against the hull and the slap of the riggings against the masts.

No doubt Johnny would be hard at work again this afternoon. Shelby smiled as she imagined him on deck—wearing his threadbare Police Academy T-shirt that should have been demoted to a rag years ago, a pair of grease-stained jeans and his black New York Mets cap, faded and frayed, turned backward as it always was when he worked on the boat.

There seemed no more fitting place than the boat to tell Johnny the news.

And then she saw Johnny on the port-side companionway. She wanted to shout yes right then, but knew her voice wouldn't carry the fifty yards—not over all this construction noise. She waved, hoping to catch his attention.

The loud blare of a truck horn stopped her in her tracks. She waited as the rig lumbered between her and the pier, followed by a dense bank of swirling dust. She waved ineffectually at the dense cloud and started for the pier once more.

And suddenly her world ended.

There was absolutely no warning. One moment there was the pier, the boat, the clear blue water in the sunlight, gulls reeling overhead. And then, in a single heartbeat, everything erupted in one earth-shattering blast.

The explosion splintered the hull of the *Orion.* Shelby screamed Johnny's name and rushed forward, ignoring the flaming debris raining down around her.

The air became thick and swollen with the heat from the first wall of flames.

"Johnny!" she screamed again above the crackle of the flames that engulfed the vessel.

She continued to run headlong toward the inferno that was once the *Orion*. Behind her, men were shouting and taking cover as the flames leaped at the sky. She heard a desperate voice she recognized as her own chanting, "No...no...no..."

When she reached the pier, the heat of the fire blistered her skin. Acrid smoke burned her throat. She cried out for Johnny again and again. She staggered forward, toward the wall of deadly flames, her mind on one thing only—saving Johnny.

It was the second explosion that stopped her. Almost as powerful as the first, it ripped through the shattered hull of the *Orion* as though the boat were nothing more than a toy, spewing out a last violent burst of fiery splinters and burning planks. The force of the explosion hurled her back like a rag doll against the pier. And her world pitched into utter blackness.

CHAPTER FIVE

AIDAN SHIFTED uncomfortably in the hard vinyl chair. Propping his elbows on the side of the hospital bed, he covered his face with his hands and closed his eyes. If only he could open them to find that none of this had happened, that it had been a horrible nightmare.

But it wasn't.

He opened his eyes, blinked against the harshness of the lamp over Shelby's bed and reached up to angle it away from her. Even in shadow, he could see the lingering redness in her face—a slight burning from the heat of the explosion, the doctor had told him when Aidan had first laid eyes on her several hours ago. A purple bruise bracketed the one-inch gash along her forehead. Other than that, the doctor had reported no other detectable injuries, but he would offer no assurances until Shelby regained consciousness. Aidan knew the doctor was worried about the physical blow she'd suffered, but Aidan was worried more about the emotional one.

He reached out and with one finger brushed at a stray strand of hair.

"Come on, Shelby. You can't block out the world forever."

No response. Only the steady rise and fall of her chest.

He studied her face, as he had for the past few hours. To someone who didn't know Shelby Beaumont, she might have appeared at peace, resting calmly. But to Aidan, who knew the radiance that normally shone from Shelby's face, her expression held deep sorrow. It was as though even in her unconsciousness she realized what had happened to John, as though she knew what kind of cruel reality she would be waking up to when she finally opened her eyes.

Behind him the sounds of the hospital were muted by the closed door, but Aidan knew that the corridor was empty at last. News had traveled fast, and there had been a steady stream of visitors—concerned officers and detectives, friends and Shelby's assistant. Captain Barnes had paced the corridor for a good hour and a half as well.

And through it all, Aidan had remained by Shelby's side, not daring to be anywhere else when she finally came to. He'd left the room only twice: once to speak with Barnes about the preliminary investigation into the explosion, and the other to make the necessary phone calls.

He'd called John's sister, Rachel, in Maine, his ex-partner's only family. When he'd told her, he'd heard the receiver clatter to the floor followed by a tormented cry. Eventually John's brother-in-law took the phone, and Aidan had had to relay the news yet again as Rachel sobbed in the background. After promising to call when he knew more, Aidan had hung up and tried to collect himself.

Still in his own daze of disbelief, he'd dropped another coin into the pay phone and called directory assistance for Cora's number in Manhattan. In the same numb stupor he gave Shelby's sister the news. Cora was already on her way.

Aidan let out a long ragged breath and checked his watch. Almost midnight.

"Come on, Shelby," he whispered again, hearing the wrenching grief in his own voice. He took her hand in his and stroked it. Then he stopped short. He hadn't noticed the glittering diamond before, and now, seeing it on her finger, knowing that she'd accepted John's proposal, he felt his heart twist painfully.

"Shelby, I know you don't want to wake up. But if you can hear me, you have got to pull through this. You've *got* to. I can't...I can't lose both of you. Do you hear me?"

He lifted her hand, rubbing it against his cheek as he watched her. She stirred slightly, releasing what sounded like a small cry of distress. But still her eyes remained shut. Her forehead tightened, and she shook her head. No doubt, she was reliving the nightmare of the explosion. Of John's death.

Aidan sat that way for some time, holding Shelby's hand, listening to her low breathing and the occasional whimper, letting the minutes slip by in the hushed confines of the hospital room. It wasn't until the door behind him swung open that Aidan finally moved; he lowered Shelby's hand and turned to see Nick Da-Costa come into the room.

"How is she?" Nick asked, edging up to the bed. "She come around yet?"

"No." Aidan studied the young detective's profile. He'd met Nick only a couple of times: once when Nick had first transferred to Fairfield and again at Aidan's self-thrown retirement party at his cabin outside the city.

"What do the doctors say?" Nick asked.

"They won't say much until she regains consciousness."

"So she doesn't know?"

Aidan gazed at Shelby again. "She knows."

"Man. I can't believe this." Nick dragged a hand through his wet hair and Aidan wondered when it had started raining. For the past several hours, nothing had existed for him beyond these four walls.

"It's a mess down there," Nick went on, his gaze never leaving Shelby. "They've got the dock lit up like the Fourth of goddamn July, and they still come up with squat. We've got the crime-scene unit and salvage teams working overtime, and now they're telling us there could be debris spread for almost a quarter mile, for God's sake. I've never seen such a—"

"Nick." Aidan stopped him. He stood and gestured to the door. "I think we should take this outside, don't you?"

Nick caught his nod toward Shelby and complied. Once in the corridor, Aidan took up a position by the door to allow him a clear view of Shelby.

"So what *have* they come up with?" he asked Nick, lowering his voice.

"Not a hell of a lot."

"Do they know if it was a bomb?"

"They gotta sift through everything first. According

to some of the construction workers who were close to the scene, there were two explosions. And from what the bomb squad's been able to piece together so far, if it *was* a bomb, then the second explosion was most likely the fuel tank. But right now we got nothing concrete.''

''What about... Have they found his body?''

Nick jammed his fists into his jacket pockets and cast his gaze to the floor. Nick had been John's partner too, Aidan tried to remind himself. Even if it had been for only a few months, this still couldn't be easy on him.

''Have they found John's body, Nick?'' he asked again.

''Not much of it.'' When he looked up, Nick's face was ashen.

''What about identification?''

''Dammit, Aidan, what few remains they *are* finding...there's next to nothing to identify.''

''Are they checking dental records?''

Nick rubbed his face as though trying to erase the horrible images. ''They'll be lucky if they find enough to match to any dental records. The lab boys, they...they figure John was pretty close to the initial explosion. He...'' Nick shook his head and looked down the stretch of empty corridor. ''They say his death must've been instantaneous.''

Aidan directed his gaze to Shelby's still form. What on earth was he going to tell her? What could he possibly say? When he turned to Nick again, seeing the strain of exhaustion and the trauma in the detective's face, he was grateful it hadn't been him down at the docks tonight, sifting through the pieces.

"And you're sure it was John on the boat?" he asked at last.

"Who else, Aidan? He left the precinct after four, said he was going straight to the docks. He'd been planning it for a couple of days. Wanted to work on the boat. Then Shelby came by. I told her where he'd gone and she went to find him."

Aidan looked at her again. She'd seen it happen. He'd guessed that from the second he'd received Barnes's phone call and learned that Shelby was at Fairfield General. But when he'd seen her, actually seen the burns she'd sustained from the heat of the blast, Aidan could only guess how close Shelby had been and how much she'd seen.

"I suppose the only thing left is to question Shelby when she wakes up," Nick said. "Find out what she saw. See if she knows of anyone who would—"

"No. No one is questioning her, Nick, you hear me?" Aidan hadn't expected the sudden protectiveness that surged through him. "I am not going to have you or anyone in there hounding her. She's been through enough. She'll answer questions when she's ready and not before."

"Well, someone's gotta talk to her." Nick's tone sharpened.

"I think I can handle it."

"I meant someone who's still with the department, Aidan."

It was an obvious dig and Aidan didn't appreciate it. But there was no opportunity for a rebuttal, because

Nick was already heading down the corridor past the nurses' station.

As he watched him leave, Aidan tried to convince himself that the detective's underlying hostility was only a reaction to the day's events, to John's death, to the loss of his partner. But for Aidan, John had been far more than a partner, and if it was the last thing he did, he'd look out for Shelby.

That was what John would have wanted.

JOHNNY WAS NEAR. She could feel him next to her, holding her hand in his. Strong and comforting. Drawing her from the blackness.

Her head throbbed with a ruthless pain that only sharpened as she clawed her way to consciousness. She felt his fingers brush soothingly across her temple and she nuzzled into his caress.

"Johnny."

She squeezed his hand, holding on to him—her only lifeline out of this shadowy abyss. But as the blackness slipped away and reality ebbed in, so did the confusion.

She didn't understand.

His ring. Johnny's Police Academy ring—he never took it off. But there was no ring on the hand that held hers now. Why would he have taken it off?

Like a jumble of puzzle pieces without a master picture, Shelby struggled to assemble the slivers of scattered memory. Fragments of images rose and pitched in her mind's eye.

She gripped Johnny's hand more tightly, as though it could help her piece the puzzle together.

Johnny's smile. The docks. Sunlight shimmering on the water. Gulls circling overhead. The *Orion* bobbing against its moorings. Johnny on the deck. She was going to tell him...

But there was more.

Yes. An explosion. Flames. Screaming. Her screams.

And heat. The scorching heat of the blaze that engulfed the boat. The blaze that devoured Johnny.

Reality meshed with memory, and this time when Shelby heard Johnny's name tear from her throat, her scream seemed to ricochet off the walls.

"Shelby. It's okay. I'm here, Shelby. I'm right here."

But they weren't Johnny's fingers that tightened around her wrist. They weren't Johnny's hands holding her down in the hospital bed when she struggled to sit up. How could they be? Johnny was dead. She knew it.

Aidan stood over her. Etched in the deep lines of his face she saw the truth. In his eyes she saw his pain. And she knew.

She didn't need to ask, but she did.

"He's dead, isn't he, Aidan? Johnny's dead." She bit her lip.

"Shelby." His voice cracked. He shook his head, and she was only vaguely aware of his hands grasping hers.

She closed her eyes. *This isn't happening. This isn't happening,* she chanted silently over and over. *It isn't true. It can't be.*

But she'd seen it. And she would see it a million

times again in her mind. A million times and for the rest of her life.

When she opened her eyes again and looked at Aidan, she wondered if he'd been crying. She tried to whisper his name, but nothing came out.

There was a soft thump of a door closing, and Dan Barnes took up a position at the foot of her bed.

"I'm so sorry, Shelby," he offered awkwardly, evidently realizing that his words were of no consolation.

"I want to see him." She looked to Aidan then, withdrawing her hands from his grasp.

"What?"

"I want to see him. I want to see Johnny."

"Shelby, you...you can't."

"What do you mean I can't?" In one movement she'd pulled away from Aidan and sat up in the bed. She threw back the starched sheets and swung her legs over the side. "I have to, Aidan. I have to go to him."

"You can't see him."

"I have to!"

"Shelby!" He gripped her shoulders, steadying her. "You *can't* see him, Shelby, because there's nothing... The explosion... It..." Aidan shook his head. "I'm sorry."

She was going to be sick.

The explosion. The flames. She'd seen the destruction, seen what it had done to the *Orion*. And Johnny...

The room spun. She gripped the side of the bed. Her insides coiled, and bile lurched to the top of her throat. She really *was* going to be sick.

Clutching her stomach, she staggered to the open

door of the bathroom, grateful that Aidan didn't try to stop her. She slammed the door closed, barely making it to the toilet in time. And when she finished, she had scarcely the energy to stand. Using the narrow counter for leverage, she dragged herself from the floor and swayed over the sink.

The reflection in the mirror shocked her. In the harsh light of the cramped bathroom, her skin looked bloodless. A small gash on her forehead had been neatly dressed with two thin strips of gauze, but the swelling and bruising around it made it appear grotesque. Her hair hung limply around her face, a disheveled mass of black framing her ashen complexion. And her eyes—they looked more bruised than her forehead—two dark lifeless caverns. It was like gazing into the face of death, she thought. And part of her truly wished that she was.

Johnny was dead. So why not her?

Her grip tightened on the edge of the counter.

Why *not* her?

Tears swam in her eyes, hot and thick. Her reflection blurred and her knees went weak. She wondered if she was going to throw up again.

"Shelby? Are you all right? Do you need any help?" Aidan asked through the closed door.

"No. No...it's okay." She heard the stammer in her voice, barely under control. She had to maintain control. If she allowed herself to cry, she knew she'd never stop. "I'll be right out," she told him at last, and turned on the faucets.

The cold water stung her face; the starched towel scratched rawly against her burned skin. She rubbed even harder, hoping the pain would wake her from this nightmare.

"Shelby?"

When at last she reached for the handle and eased the door open, she prayed that her legs wouldn't give out on her. But even if they had, Aidan would have caught her. For instantly he was at her side, one arm around her waist while the other took her hand, guiding her back to the bed.

"Did you want me to get a nurse?"

"I'll be fine, Aidan," she answered, the words sounding absurd. How on earth could she possibly be fine? Johnny was—

"Shelby, maybe we should get you a doctor or a nurse," Captain Barnes offered.

"No. It's okay, Dan. Thanks."

Aidan fussed over her, straightening the sheets and blankets and plumping her pillow.

"Listen, Shelby." Captain Barnes cleared his throat and shifted his weight from one foot to the other. "I really hate to do this, but do you think you're up to answering some questions?"

"Dan, is this necessary?" Aidan cut in. "Don't you think you could give Shelby a little bit of time here?"

"Aidan, no," she said. "It's all right. Go on, Dan."

"I'm sorry, Shelby, but it's better to ask you this while it's still fresh."

She nodded.

"I...we need to know if it was John on the boat, if you actually saw him."

Shelby looked at her hands, unable to meet Dan's sympathetic expression. Absently she twisted the engagement ring on her finger, turning it around and around. When she looked up again, she realized Aidan had been watching her. His gaze lifted from the ring, and he reached over to still her hands.

He knew. He knew that Johnny had proposed. In fact, given his close friendship with Johnny, she didn't doubt that Aidan had known before she had.

"Shelby?" Dan prompted.

"Yes, it was Johnny," she answered at last.

"And what did you see exactly?"

"Dan—" Again Aidan tried to stop him.

"I saw the explosion."

"Before that, Shelby."

"I pulled into the yacht club and parked. I was heading down the pier towards the *Orion*. I was going to meet him on the boat."

"Did John know you were coming?"

"No. I wanted to surprise him. I was going there to tell him that..." No. Dan Barnes didn't need to know this. No one on the force did. It was between her and Johnny.

"Tell him what, Shelby?"

"Nothing. I was just going to surprise him." Aidan's grip on her hand tightened, as though he understood why she'd gone down there.

"So you saw John on the boat?"

"Yes. I saw him come up on deck. He was wearing his black academy T-shirt, jeans and his Mets cap. I waved to him, but he didn't see me. And then...then there was the explosion."

"Do you remember if it was from the front of the boat or the back?"

"The first one...was from the bow. I think."

"And the second?"

"I don't know." She released the breath she'd been holding. The few times Johnny had talked about his job, about questioning witnesses and loved ones of the deceased, Shelby had wondered about the difficulty in describing to police in such a factual manner an event that had literally shattered your life. But now, even with Dan Barnes hovering over her in this sterile hospital room, the process was horrifyingly simple. All she had to do was close her eyes and she could envision the entire scene as distinctly as if the image of the explosion was burned into her retinas, burned into her memory for eternity.

"Shelby, did you see anyone running away from the boat, maybe when you first got there?"

She shook her head.

"Did you see anyone suspicious in the area at all?"

"No."

"Do you...did John ever talk to you about anyone who might have wanted him—"

"Dan, come on." Aidan moved to the foot of the bed, placing himself between the captain and Shelby. "I *know* this can wait. I really don't think this is the time."

Shelby wasn't certain if Dan Barnes would have protested; he didn't have the chance. The door swung open and the night nurse bustled in.

She stopped short when she saw the two men. "Well, I hope you two are on your way out. Visiting hours are long over," she said, emitting an air of authority even before she elbowed her way between the two.

Dan cleared his throat again. "I was just asking Ms. Beaumont a few questions."

"All the more reason for you to go. This woman needs some rest. Now if you two don't mind..." She nodded at the door.

"Shelby, I'll be in touch." Dan's voice softened, his detective's edge slipping away as he reached past Aidan to pat her arm. "We'll be...there'll be a service for John. I can talk to you later. When you're home. I'm...I'm sorry, Shelby. I truly am. John—he was my best. A good man."

"I know."

She watched Dan retreat, and when the door closed behind him and Aidan came to her side once again, it was Shelby who reached for him this time, clasping his hand in hers.

"Aidan, don't go. Please. I don't want to be alone." But wasn't that exactly what she was—alone? Utterly alone? Johnny was gone. He wasn't on his way over here. He wasn't about to breeze through that door to take her home.

"Please, Aidan. Stay."

She saw him share a quick glance with the night nurse. She'd never needed Aidan more than she did just now; clinging to his hand and his gaze, she didn't doubt that she'd be lost without him.

"Under the circumstances I suppose I can't argue," the nurse said. Then she busied herself with a blood-pressure cuff, and it wasn't until she spoke again that

Shelby dropped her gaze from Aidan's. "How's your head?"

Shelby shrugged. "It hurts."

"Well, your doctor was in earlier. Said we could offer you some Tylenol if you really needed it. But with your pregnancy..."

"I'll be fine without it. Thanks." Shelby closed her eyes, searching for Johnny's smile through the darkness.

Johnny.

Johnny's child.

It was all she had left of him—his child.

And for the remainder of that black night, as she drifted from one nightmare to the next, Shelby's hand never left her belly.

CHAPTER SIX

"SO HOW'S SHELBY?" Dan Barnes fixed Aidan with a hard stare. The ex-cop had pulled up a chair in front of the captain's desk.

It had felt strange walking through the detectives' wing again, Aidan thought. Stranger still to be sitting across from the captain in his office.

"Is she holding up?" Barnes asked.

"She's managing, I guess," Aidan said, and again thought of her pregnancy—news, he was certain, Shelby hadn't shared with anyone except perhaps her sister. In fact, if the nurse hadn't mentioned it that night at the hospital, Aidan wondered if he would have known for some time. Shelby had remained silent on the topic, and over the past week he'd been careful not to press her on it. If Shelby needed to talk about the pregnancy, or her plans regarding it, he knew she'd come to him...eventually.

Aidan glanced over to see Barnes rub at the furrows of tension in his forehead. The strain of the past week since the explosion showed clearly in the man's almost lackluster eyes and careworn expression.

"It's hard to tell with Shelby," Aidan added. But the truth was, it was *impossible* to tell with Shelby. Even though he'd spent as much time with her as she would allow him, he had not once seen her break down.

Even at the combined police memorial service for John and Seth Cushing yesterday, Shelby had maintained her calm, accepting condolences with the same quiet grace with which she'd handled everything over the past few days. After the service she'd permitted Aidan to guide her away from the crush of well-wishers to his car. She'd been silent during the drive back to her place, staring out the windshield and only once or twice letting her gaze drop to her lap where she held the box containing the medal presented to her in John's honor.

Aidan had wanted to stay with her, if only for a couple of hours, but there'd been no convincing her. She'd wanted to be alone, and he hadn't had the heart to force the issue. Giving her a quick hug, he'd left her at the front door, waiting until he heard the turn of the dead bolt before going back to his Skylark.

He'd tried calling her later that night several times, and because she hadn't answered, he'd returned to her place. When he'd pulled his car up to the curb, the boutique had been dark, but there were lights on upstairs. He knew they were the studio lights, and it hadn't surprised him. Shelby had been working practically nonstop since he'd brought her home from the hospital six days ago. It worried him. As it had worried Cora.

"Her sister's staying with her now, isn't she?" Barnes asked.

"Cora? No, she had to return to Manhattan yesterday, just after the memorial."

"You think it's a good idea for Shelby to be alone?"

"No. But you can't argue with Shelby." That was why he'd parked outside of her place last night, sitting for hours in his car. He'd seen her walk past the windows a couple of times: once with swatches of fabric, once with a mug in one hand and sketches in the other, moving between the apartment and the studio. She'd worked long into the night, and Aidan tried to take comfort in the fact that Shelby was burying herself in her work, instead of her grief for John. "She'll be all right," he said.

However, it wasn't just Shelby's emotional state that concerned Aidan when he thought of her being on her own. Someone had killed John. The possibility of that same someone coming after Shelby was remote, but until Aidan figured out the who and the why behind John's murder, he couldn't count on Shelby's being safe.

"So what's the word from the lab, Dan? They know for sure it was a bomb?"

"Yeah."

"Anything the bomb squad recognizes?"

Dan Barnes shook his head. "They're still working on it. It was definitely a homemade job, but there's nothing to link it with any profiles on the database."

"So you're saying you don't have any immediate suspects."

"That's what I'm saying." Frustration dragged at the captain's voice, and Aidan couldn't remember Barnes ever looking as old as he did just now, his bristly chin resting in the palm of one thick hand, his eyes heavy-lidded with fatigue and his face ravaged by tension.

"We've done three canvasses," he continued. "Talked to everyone who was anywhere near the yacht club that day—hell, for the entire week *before* the explosion. Workers, staff, club members, construction crew. Nothing. No one saw a damned thing. But then, how could they have with all the construction going on down there."

"What about past cases? Any recent releases or paroles on John's past convictions? Maybe someone with a grudge?"

"Nick's already gone through the records. There's no one. At least no one who had the means and know-how to make the kind of bomb we're looking at."

"And what about current cases?"

Barnes shrugged. "Aidan, you know I can't—"

"Look, Dan, it's no secret. I know John was heading the Morelli and Feeney investigations. At least tell me if you suspect a connection."

"We're looking into it. We're doing all we can, Aidan. Really. I've got my best people on this one."

In the momentary silence that hung between the two men, Aidan sensed their mutual grief. The late-afternoon sun filtered through the dusty window of the captain's office and raked across the file-strewn desk. How many times had he and John sat in this very office with Barnes over the years? Laughed together, worked together, respected one another as cops and as friends? It didn't feel right, being here without John. He thought it must be the same for Dan.

"I wish you were still working for me, Aidan,"

Barnes said at last, letting out a heavy sigh. "You and John—you two were my best. I sure as hell could use you on this one."

"Dan, you've got me on this one." Aidan pushed back his chair and stood. He was definitely on this case. There was no way he'd rest until he'd found the person responsible for John's death. At the moment, though, he had next to nothing to go on. All he knew was that John had planned to see him late in the afternoon on the day of his death. About what though, Aidan wasn't certain. But he had his suspicions.

John had been too quiet about his leads on the Morelli and Feeney cases. He'd been loath to share information even with Aidan, and that could mean only one thing—John had suspected someone on the police force. But he must have also suspected the danger in involving others or else he would have asked for Aidan's help sooner.

When John had walked him to the door the night Seth was shot, he'd told Aidan, "I think I need your help." If Shelby hadn't been so upset by the night's events, maybe John would have taken the time then to voice his suspicions. Maybe Aidan *could* have helped. And maybe John would still be alive. Maybe, maybe, maybe...

God, he needed more than maybes. He needed something concrete. He had to talk to Shelby. It wouldn't be easy for her, even after a week, but he needed to know if John had told her anything that night, anything that might help him find John's murderer.

"Thanks, Aidan," the captain said. "You'll let me know if you get anything?"

"Of course."

"I just want to get the son of a bitch who did this."

"So do I, Dan. So do we all."

Aidan shook the captain's hand, and headed out the door into the squad room. He stopped at John's chair. He almost expected to see his own files scattered across the top of the adjacent desk. But it was Nick's desk now.

From the corner of John's desk, Aidan picked up the small black rubber ball. He tried to roll it through and over his fingers the way he'd seen John do, but he fumbled it. He never did seem to have the same dexterity John had had.

Aidan replaced the ball and put his hand on the back of John's chair. It was as though his friend was still working, as though he would walk through the squad-room door any second and slap Aidan on the back, maybe rib him about leaving the force. The desk was undoubtedly as John had left it. No one would have straightened it or cleaned it out. Not yet. Not for at least a few more days, if not weeks, as the squad members tried to come to terms with their loss.

Aidan's gaze traveled over the jumble of files as though he expected some answer to miraculously jump out at him. Then he noticed the framed photograph.

Shelby. Even in a photograph, her smile sent a jolt of warmth through him. The radiance and light in her expression was still there. He wondered if he would ever see that same light in her eyes again.

"Hello, Aidan."

He hadn't heard Nick come into the squad room, and he could only guess how long the man had been standing there watching him all this time.

"Anything I can do for you?"

"No." Aidan gestured at Barnes's office. "I was just in to see the captain."

Nick merely nodded, but the tension between him and Aidan was almost palpable. The young detective folded his arms and leaned possessively against the corner of what had once been Aidan's desk.

"Did you want me to take any of John's things over to Shelby?" he asked Nick.

"I think I can manage, Aidan." There was a certain defiance in his voice, and Aidan watched his eyes narrow. "John was *my* partner. I'll look out for Shelby."

"Sure, Nick. Whatever. I was only trying to help."

It couldn't be easy, Aidan thought as he watched a muscle twitch along Nick's jaw. The kid had transferred from New York City, probably figuring that with his big-city experience he'd show the Fairfield force a few tricks, but instead, he'd been partnered with John, filling the vacancy Aidan had left. A year ago he and John had been the squad's sterling team, with not a single open case on the books and an almost unheard-of eighty-percent conviction rate. They'd been the captain's favorites, and anyone who stepped into either of their shoes had a hard act to follow. So Nick's hostility was understandable.

But even after Aidan had said goodbye and left the precinct, as he steered his Skylark through the downtown core, he hadn't been able to let go of one nagging thought—John had suspected someone on the force.

So why not Nick? Hell, why not anyone on the force? Even Barnes, for God's sake. There was no way to tell.

He had to talk to Shelby. He had to find out if John had told her anything. Until then, Aidan realized he could trust no one. Including Nick. Maybe especially Nick.

SIX DAYS. Shelby had had to look at a calendar this morning to know how long it had been since she'd returned from the hospital—six days.

A week since the explosion. A week without Johnny.

In that time nothing had seemed quite real. People had come and gone. Others had phoned or sent flowers. Johnny's sister, Rachel, had come down from Maine with her husband, Steven, and their daughters. And Cora... Cora had been there throughout.

Shelby was glad, though, that her sister had returned to New York. It was easier to be on her own, to submit to the cold and vacant numbness. And it was easier just to work; as long as she worked, she could forget there was life beyond these walls.

She glanced again at the calendar on her desk. Yes, time had ceased to have any meaning for her—not when she couldn't sleep and when she never wanted to wake up. She studied the sketch on the drafting table before her. *Not when she wanted nothing else from life except death.*

She dropped the charcoal pencil and rubbed her face. How many times in the past week had she allowed herself that very thought? Death. The idea of leaving these shattered dreams behind. To be with Johnny...

Shelby tore the sketch from the pad, crumpled it into a wad and tossed it at the overflowing wastebasket. She rolled back her chair and stood. Raking her fingers through her hair, she tied it into a crude ponytail and started to pace.

At the balcony railing overlooking the store, she watched Doreen working on the books at the front counter. As her assistant busily punched out numbers on a calculator with one hand, she penciled in figures with the other. Shelby appreciated the low profile Doreen had been keeping today. After yesterday's memorial service, she'd considered telephoning Doreen to ask her not to come in today. But in all honesty, there was simply too much work to do.

Doreen must have sensed Shelby's presence; she glanced up from the books.

"Can I get you anything, Shelby? A cup of tea?"

"No, thanks, Doreen. I'm all right." Tea wouldn't cut it, anyway. What she really wanted was a drink.

Shelby dropped a hand to her belly and turned from the balcony. She'd told Cora about her pregnancy. Aidan also knew; he'd found out at the hospital and had been graciously silent on the subject.

When Shelby sat down at her table again, her gaze drifted involuntarily to the photo of Johnny. Would their baby have Johnny's smile and those same dark mischievous eyes? And how painful would it be to look into eyes like those again?

At the police memorial yesterday there'd been an enlarged photograph of Johnny. Throughout the ceremony, Shelby hadn't once been able to bring herself to look at it. She'd kept her gaze on her lap, letting the captain's words wash over her. At one point Aidan had placed his hand on hers.

Shelby picked up her pencil again and started a fresh sketch, determined this time to repress the memories of yesterday's service.

She worked for no more than ten or fifteen minutes before the phone rang. The lead of her pencil snapped and she cursed. Then she pushed away from the table and returned once again to the balcony in time to see Doreen pick up the downstairs extension.

"Oh, hi, Aidan." She spoke softly into the receiver. "Yeah, I guess she's all right. No, she won't come to the phone... Yeah, working as usual."

Doreen's face turned up again and Shelby shook her head.

"Aidan, hang on a second, will you?" Doreen covered the mouthpiece with one hand.

"Shelby, why don't you just pick up the phone and talk to him? Tell him you're all right. That's all he wants—to hear it from you himself."

"No, Doreen. Please. I told you, I'm not taking any calls. Tell him I'll call him later."

Doreen gave an exasperated frown. She uncovered the mouthpiece. "Aidan, she'll call you later. I'm sorry. Mm-hmm. Yeah... Okay. Goodbye."

Doreen climbed off her stool and crossed the floor to where she had a better view of Shelby. She planted her hands on her hips.

"Shelby, I'm not going to keep doing this. You're my boss and my friend, but I won't sit here and deflect calls for you all day. Aidan's phoned five times. And he's not the only one you're shutting out."

"Doreen, we have work to do."

"To hell with the work, Shelby. Lauren Dametto's already rescheduled. You know as well as I do that we'll be finished with the designs ahead of time. It's insane what you're doing—working day and night. You can't keep up this pace. You're going to work yourself into an early grave."

Instantly a flush as red as her hair swept over Doreen's upturned face. "I'm sorry, Shelby. I didn't mean—"

"It's all right," Shelby said, and wondered if her assistant knew how much truth she wished was in that last remark.

Through the store's front window, Shelby saw a white van pull up at the curb. She nodded to the door, trying her best to give Doreen a smile. "The courier's here. Should be the samples from Peter. Could you sign for them?"

Doreen reached the door before the bell even rang. Once she'd signed for the delivery, however, Shelby could see that the small box was not the awaited samples.

"What is it, Doreen?"

"I don't know." Doreen unfolded the shipping order and crossed the store to the stairs. "It's not from Peter. It's..."

"What?" But her assistant was already on her way up the spiral staircase. Shelby met her at the head of the stairs. "Doreen?"

"It's...it's from the funeral home, Shelby. It's Johnny's ashes."

Doreen started to hand her the box, but Shelby was already shaking her head. She took a step back, reaching for the railing to steady herself as the room began to tilt.

Johnny. His ashes. She hadn't expected them. Not this soon.

She stared at the package. How could he be...? The box was so small, so unassuming....

"Shelby, are you all right?"

"I'm fine."

"Can I get you anything?"

"No. Please, just...just put it somewhere," she said, her gaze never leaving the box in Doreen's hands.

"Where?"

"Anywhere. It doesn't matter."

"Shelby, these are Johnny's ashes."

"Please, Doreen, just put it someplace, okay?"

"Listen to me, Shelby, you can't do this. You can't just lock everything inside you and not talk about it. You can't shove this box away in a corner and ignore it like you've ignored your own emotions. These are Johnny's remains. The man you loved. Sooner or later you have to deal with it."

"Dammit, Doreen, I'm dealing with this the only way I can!" The sound of her own voice—so harsh, almost cruel, as it echoed through the stillness of the boutique—shocked Shelby. In all her life she couldn't remember *ever* shouting at someone that way.

And judging from the expression on Doreen's face

just then, Shelby guessed that her friend's shock couldn't have been greater had she reached out and slapped her.

She softened her tone. "I'm sorry, Doreen. I didn't mean to shout like that."

Doreen nodded, but didn't seem convinced.

"I *will* deal with the box," Shelby went on. "But please, just put it someplace for now. And...maybe you should call it a day. It's late."

"Sure, Shelby. Whatever you say."

Doreen held her gaze for one last moment, as though assuring herself there really was no way she could convince Shelby to actually take the box. Finally she set it on the chair next to the stairs and turned to touch Shelby's forearm.

"Call if you need me," she said, then headed down to the main floor.

"Thanks, Doreen. Good night."

There was the bang of the door in its frame, followed by the slide of the dead bolt as Doreen locked up behind her, and then silence. Shelby leaned against the waist-high railing, her back to the boutique, and stared at the box on the chair.

Johnny's remains. So neat, so contained. How could a whole life be reduced to a little cardboard box?

Shelby clutched her stomach. How could the man she loved, the man who'd been so full of life and vigor be reduced to such a small nondescript parcel?

She bit her lip hard, wishing the physical pain could overwhelm the sorrow. There was an emptiness about the apartment-studio, an emptiness perhaps worsened by the fact that Johnny's things were still everywhere, but Johnny was not, and never would be again.

She remembered talking to Cora about moving back to New York City, thinking that if she left Fairfield, the pain might dull faster. But she suspected that no matter where she was or what she was doing, she would always feel it. There would forever be a void where Johnny had once been.

Shelby crossed to the chair and stood looking down at the box. So neat. So tidy. She lowered a hand toward it, uncertain whether or not she could even bring herself to touch it. When she finally did, her fingers trembled. And when she picked it up, her hand shook so fiercely she thought she might drop it. She swallowed hard, determined not to cry even though no one was there to see.

"Damn you, Johnny." She clutched the box to her chest, fighting the tears that blurred her vision. "Damn you. You *promised*."

She wanted to throw the box, hurl it down from the balcony and scream. He promised he'd be careful. He'd said he'd always be there for her. *Forever,* he'd told her. *Forever.*

When the front buzzer sounded, she almost dropped the box. Unsteadily she set it back down on the chair. Swiping angrily at a lone tear, she headed down the stairs, and by the time she unlatched the dead bolt, she'd regained her composure.

It would be the courier, at last, with the samples from Peter, she thought as she opened the door. But she was wrong.

"Aidan."

"Well, you can't say I didn't try calling first." He shrugged. The late-afternoon sun shimmered off his hair, highlighting the gold.

She managed a smile and wondered if he could see how close to tears she'd been only seconds ago. "I'm sorry."

"I just thought I'd check in on you. See how you were doing."

"I'm fine, thanks. Working, you know?"

"So Doreen keeps telling me." He dug his hands deep into the pockets of his bomber jacket and shifted uneasily on the step. "Are you going to invite me in, Shelby?"

"Aidan, no." She shook her head, hoping he didn't see how her hand trembled when she swept a stray wisp of hair from her forehead.

"Shelby—"

"Please, Aidan. I need to be alone. I have work—"

"Then I won't stay long," he said, and brushed past her and into the boutique.

CHAPTER SEVEN

THE SECOND Shelby opened the door, Aidan took one look at the dark circles under her eyes and the hollows under her cheekbones and knew he wasn't going anywhere until she talked to him.

But it was obvious the last thing she wanted was visitors. He'd had to practically push his way in.

"Shelby, what's going on?" he asked as she closed the door.

"Nothing's going on. I'm trying to work."

"You won't take my phone calls."

"I'm busy."

There was a pencil tucked behind her ear and a cloth tape measure draped around her neck. She removed both as though to convince him of her productivity and set them on the front desk.

"Too busy to pick up the phone and tell me you're all right?"

She let out a sigh, and when she ran her fingers through her hair, her sloppy ponytail fell loose. Her hair was limp, he noticed, and the dark tresses that framed her face made her complexion appear even paler. Things were worse than he'd feared.

"Aidan, please. I appreciate your concern. I really do. But I'm all right. Just very busy."

She skirted around him and headed to the stairs.

"I don't believe you, Shelby," he said, following her. "And I'm not leaving here until I know for sure you're okay."

"Fine." She whirled around on the top landing, bracing both hands on the railings, and faced him. "I'm okay. Are you satisfied?"

"Shelby..." Aidan reached out and placed a hand over hers. Instantly he felt her tense, as though she found physical human contact unbearable.

"Shelby, talk to me."

"There's nothing to talk about." She offered a smile, one she no doubt hoped would ease his concern. She gently withdrew her hand from under his and brought her palm to his cheek. "You don't have to do this, Aidan."

"Do what?"

"I know you promised Johnny you'd look out for me if...if anything happened. But you don't need to. I can take care of myself."

Dear God, if only she knew that his promise to Johnny wasn't the main reason he was here tonight. If only he could tell Shelby what she really meant to him, tell her how it hurt him to see her like this, to know there was nothing he could do to make her see the good in life again.

And so he nodded. There was no getting through to her. No reaching the despair she'd locked deep inside.

She turned from him, about to walk into her living room, when he noticed her slight hesitation. It was brief, and if he hadn't been watching her, he would never have seen her gaze fix for a moment on the small cardboard box on the chair. As she moved on, he stepped closer to read the courier label.

"Shelby." He waited for her to stop. "Is this...?"

She turned, and instantly he saw her dam come up, the one she'd so skillfully constructed to hold back even the slightest emotion. "Yes," she answered, her voice eerily detached.

He dropped a hand to the box. "Well, shouldn't you...?"

"What?"

"I mean, it's Johnny's ashes, Shelby. Aren't you going to...? Are you just going to leave them here?"

"What would you like me to do with them, Aidan?"

"I...I don't know." He watched her turn stiffly on one heel and stalk around the corner into the living room.

Her sister hadn't had much success breaking through Shelby's dam, either. He'd talked to Cora after the memorial service yesterday, knowing it would be his last opportunity before she headed back to New York City, and Cora had voiced frustration about her thwarted attempts at getting Shelby to open up.

Aidan looked again at the plain shipping box and fingered a corner of the packing tape.

You shouldn't have let this happen, John, his mind whispered. *You should have quit. For Shelby, you should have quit before you got in too deep.* Aidan cursed his friend—not just his ex-partner, not just the man with whom he'd shared the beat-up unmarked Cavalier for five of the best years of his life, but his dearest closest friend. *Shelby deserves more than this.*

More than all this pain and some cardboard box from a funeral home!

When Aidan picked up the package at last, he was surprised—he'd expected it to be heavier. He carried it to the living room and set it on the coffee table. He wasn't sure why he felt compelled to. Maybe because he couldn't stand the thought of the box—his friend's remains—just sitting out there by the stairs like garbage to be taken to the curb. Or maybe because he hoped that by leaving it on the coffee table, Shelby would have to deal with it, with John's death. And face her dark emotions.

She was at the kitchen bar uncapping a bottle of water, and when he looked across the room at her, she pretended not to notice where he'd put the package. Maybe it was the way she was standing, he thought—her hip wedged against the corner of the tiled bar, the bottle in one hand as her arms crossed tightly over her middle—but she looked alarmingly thin. The shirt that hung from her slender shoulders past the small waist of her faded jeans was easily several sizes too large, even for Shelby's tall frame, giving her an almost gaunt appearance. It was one of John's shirts, Aidan was certain.

The counter behind her was bare of the usual clutter of dishes. Given the long hours he knew she'd been working, either Doreen had been keeping up with the cleaning or, more likely, Shelby simply hadn't been eating.

"So where's Doreen?" he asked.

"I sent her home."

"I don't like you being alone here, Shelby."

"Why? Because of the break-in? Aidan, that was weeks ago. It was nothing. Just kids."

"That's not what I'm referring to."

"What, then?"

"It's a small city, Shelby. People know you. They read the paper, they hear...they hear about John, and they know you're alone."

"God, Aidan!" She laughed mirthlessly and took a swig of water from her bottle. "And I thought *Cora* was paranoid."

"It's not paranoia. I just don't think you should be on your own here."

She set the bottle down so hard on the kitchen bar that some of the water splashed out and soaked quickly into her shirt. "Aidan—"

"No, Shelby! Listen to me. It's not just that you're on your own, alone at night, living on a street that's practically deserted after 6:00 p.m. It's John, Shelby. John was *murdered*."

"So what are you saying, Aidan? That whoever killed Johnny is going to come after me now? That's a little far-fetched, don't you think?"

"It's a possibility, that's all I'm saying. And it means you're not safe."

Shelby spun away from the counter. "Come with me," she demanded.

"Where are you going?"

"I want to show you something."

When he caught up with her in the bedroom, Shelby was standing next to the elaborate wrought-iron bed. She reached for the lamp on the nightstand, and instantly the room was flooded with warm light, revealing mounds of discarded clothing, pages from Shelby's sketchbook and swatches of material. But she didn't seem at all embarrassed by the mess as she yanked open the nightstand drawer.

When she drew out the Glock semiautomatic, Aidan couldn't help thinking how unwieldy and foreign the heavy gun looked in her hands. It was John's off-duty weapon, the one, Aidan knew, John had trained Shelby to use. Aidan could remember the day John had suggested Shelby go with them to the shooting range. He remembered how vehemently she'd argued and how he'd helped John convince her it was a good idea because she lived alone and there'd been a rash of burglaries in her area.

In the end, though, it was John who'd taught her to shoot, John who'd taken her countless times to the range, and John who'd spent more and more time with her.

Yes, Aidan had been jealous. But now he was grateful; at least she could defend herself if necessary.

"I haven't been to the range in months, but I know how to use it if I have to," Shelby told him, turning the weapon over in her hands. "So are you satisfied, Aidan? Do you feel better?"

"Not much." He took the semiautomatic from her and unclipped the magazine into his palm, checking it for himself. It was full. He slid the charged magazine back into the grip and double-checked the safety before handing it back to her.

"I'm all right here, Aidan. I *have* lived alone before."

He watched her return the Glock to the nightstand

and shove the drawer closed. Then she slid her hands into the pockets of her jeans and faced him. She must have seen his concern, because she added, "What's it going to take to convince you?"

"To convince me you're all right? Or that you can take care of yourself?"

"Both."

"I'm pretty certain you can take care of yourself, Shelby. But I don't think you're all right. I think you're giving up."

"Giving up?" She pushed back her hair, revealing the furrows in her forehead.

"Yes. Giving up on life. *Your* life."

"Aidan." She raised her hands, stopping him before he could go any further. "I'm not getting into this now." She brushed past him, close enough that he could smell the faintest hint of cologne on her. John's cologne.

He wanted to stop her then, force her to tell him what was in her heart, make her acknowledge John's death. But instead, he followed her back to the kitchen and said, "Shelby, I'm sorry. I don't mean to push. I know you want to be alone. I know you miss him. Dammit, I miss him too. But I'm concerned about you. Look at yourself. You probably haven't slept in a week, and I doubt you even remember the last time you ate."

Her back was to him now, but he could see the vicelike grip she had on the water bottle on the counter.

"You have to take care of yourself, Shelby. You have to eat." He wanted to add a comment about the baby, how she needed to think about John's child, make that her priority now. But judging by the rigidity of her stance, he'd already pushed her as far as he dared.

He moved behind her and placed his hands on her shoulders, feeling the tight muscles there. "Shelby, let me take you to dinner. You need to get out of here, have a break from your work at least. What do you say?"

He waited a long time for her nod of compliance, removing his hands from her shoulders when she finally turned to look at him.

"Eduardo's?" she asked, and Aidan was touched by the faint smile that struggled to the corners of her mouth.

He returned the smile. "Anywhere you like. My treat."

EDUARDO'S PASTA restaurant was nothing fancy, but what it lacked in elegance, it made up for in food. Still, Shelby had barely touched her fettuccini.

Aidan had long since finished his pasta, and his plate had been whisked away by their waitress. Two hours ago, after agreeing to join him for dinner, Shelby had gotten changed, and Aidan had been visibly pleased. But now his expression was darkened by the same concern she'd seen when he'd first arrived at the boutique tonight.

She picked at the now cold fettuccini, wishing for Aidan's sake she had more of an appetite.

"Are you finished with that?" Their waitress seemed to have come out of nowhere, startling Shelby.

"Yes. I am." She leaned back in the window-side booth, hoping that Aidan hadn't seen her jump, that he couldn't see how on edge she was. It was lack of sleep, she tried to convince herself.

"Was it all right?" the waitress asked as she scooped up the almost untouched plate.

"It was fine. I'm just not very hungry. Thank you."

Shelby caught Aidan's gaze and guessed what was coming next. She could tell by the flexing of the muscle in his jaw as he waited for the waitress to finish clearing their dishes.

Then it came. "Shelby, have you seen your doctor yet?"

"No." She looked out the window at the wet night. A cold rain shimmered down in the lamplight and glistened off the hoods of parked cars. "I'll make an appointment for next week," she said, but wondered if she could bring herself to do it. Much easier to put it off, to put everything off, and stay at home working.

"It can't be good, your not eating. You need to be more careful"

"Aidan, I'm eating."

"That's not what Cora told me. And not what I've seen tonight."

"I'm eating. It's just keeping food down that's a problem these days." But that wasn't entirely true. Lately she'd gone whole days sometimes without opening the refrigerator, without realizing the time that slipped by. And she knew Aidan was right—she had to be more careful.

"Morning sickness?" Aidan asked.

"I suppose so."

"How's everything else?"

"You mean about the pregnancy?"

He nodded. It was the first time since he'd learned of her pregnancy that he'd said anything about it. Shelby looked out the window again, unable to meet his concerned gaze. Even with Cora, she hadn't been capable of discussing the pregnancy to any great extent. How could she when she could barely come to terms with it herself?

"It's fine, I guess," she answered him.

Beyond the window a couple huddled under an umbrella, hurrying through the rain to their car. Shelby watched the man unlock the passenger door, but instead of jumping into the car out of the rain, the woman turned to kiss him. Shelby looked away, unable to watch.

"You know I lost my father when I was twelve?" she asked Aidan finally.

"Yeah. I remember the day. You and Erin were upstairs at our house when I took the phone call. I remember my mother telling you about the accident...."

"I loved my father, Aidan."

"I know you did."

"Losing him..." She shook her head. The pain, twenty years old, was almost as keen now as it was back then. "I've never really gotten over his death. When you lose someone, someone you love, you always speculate on the future they could have had. You always think about them, as though they're still with you, and you wonder what they'd think of you now, if they'd be proud or sad. They're never really gone.

And every once in a while, when you realize that they really *are* gone, you grieve all over again. It never ends."

Aidan reached for her hand. She looked down at his strong fingers, and for a moment it was as if the past twenty years had never been, as though she'd just learned the dreadful news. Back then, Aidan, barely fifteen, had held her hand for the first time, comforting her. He'd consoled her when his sister, Erin, hadn't been able to find the words. He'd been there for her back then, just as he was now.

But Aidan had *always* been there for her.

Shelby looked up, meeting his penetrating gaze.

"I don't know which is worse, Aidan. Losing a father you love or never knowing him."

"What are you trying to say, Shelby?"

"I don't know exactly. It's just that…maybe it's better to never know than to go through the kind of pain I did when I was twelve. This baby, this child of Johnny's, he or she will never have to feel that pain—the pain of losing a father he loves. I know it sounds harsh, but…maybe it's better this way."

He squeezed her hand, but this time she pulled away. Given the harshness of her thoughts, she didn't deserve the kind of compassion Aidan lavished on her. "Shelby—"

"No, Aidan. I've thought about this a lot in the past week, and I mean it—it's probably better it happened now rather than later."

"It would've been better if it never happened at all, Shelby. Come on, you can't think like this. You can't mean it."

"Yes, I do. Johnny never would've quit, Aidan. You know that as well as I do. Any other cop would've left the force after that mess with the NYPD and Internal Affairs. But not Johnny. He came here and started all over again. You saw how he loved his work. There was no way he would've given it up. And sooner or later..." She lowered her hands to her lap so Aidan couldn't see them tremble. "Sooner or later something like this was bound to happen. All I'm saying is that it's probably best it was sooner."

"Shelby, stop."

"Aidan, I saw those children. After the memorial I saw them with their mother."

"What children?"

"Seth Cushing's. The officer who was killed. I saw his girls. Susan brought them to the memorial. And every time I looked at them, I kept trying to imagine how she told them their father was dead. I kept visualizing how she must have gone into their bedrooms that night after she'd found out, how strong she'd had to be, how she would've had to contain her own grief while she explained to them that their father was never coming home. I don't think I could do that. And I...I'm glad I'll never have to."

Aidan studied her with such fierce intensity she was forced to look away, and when their waitress brought the bill, Shelby was grateful for the interruption.

Aidan was silent for a long time after the waitress had left. Shelby knew he was waiting for her to say more, but there was nothing left to say. The bottom line was, she had to get on with her life. She had the baby to worry about, her future and the baby's, that was all that mattered now. And if that meant leaving Fairfield and everything that reminded her of Johnny, then so be it. For her child's well-being she couldn't afford to live in the past, in memories of Johnny. She had to look forward.

She wondered when she would find the courage to tell Aidan about her decision to leave.

"Shelby, listen, I know it's not easy for you to talk about this, but…how aware are you of the cases John was working on?"

"You know he rarely discussed his work with me. He knew I worried about him, and he didn't like to add to it."

Aidan, she noticed, had the same look of grim determination she'd seen in Johnny when he was working through a case in his head.

"Shelby, I want you to think about the last few weeks. Are you absolutely certain John didn't discuss any of his cases? Might he have said something inadvertently that could help us?"

"Help us with what?"

"Get whoever killed him." Aidan seemed surprised she asked, as though he believed her primary goal should be to find Johnny's killer, when instead, all she wanted was to put the past behind her.

"He didn't say anything to me."

"What did you know about the Morelli case?"

"Nothing. Except what was in the papers, and I barely even read that."

"And Feeney?"

"The same. Listen, Aidan, he didn't talk about it. The morning they found Feeney's body, when Johnny got the call from Nick, he said something about Feeney being linked to Morelli. That Feeney probably knew something he shouldn't have. But in all honesty, Aidan, I have no idea what these men were about or what angles Johnny was working. None whatsoever. He simply didn't talk about it.''

Aidan let out a long breath of frustration. He looked tired, Shelby thought, and wondered how many nights of sleep he'd lost over this.

"What about files? Could John have left any notes or paperwork at the apartment?"

"You're kidding, right? You've seen our apartment—Johnny wouldn't dare bring files into that place. He'd never find them again. No, if he'd brought any files from the office or kept any personal notes, they'd have been on the boat."

Aidan stared into his empty coffee mug, swirling the last dregs around the bottom.

"There's got to be something, Shelby. Something John might have said."

She shook her head.

"Did you know who he was supposed to have met the day he died?"

"No."

"He told me he had another potential informant. Someone who could maybe give him something on Feeney and Morelli. Did he talk to you about that?"

"Aidan—"

"The night before, he said he wanted to see me about the case, said he needed my help. He didn't happen to mention anything about that to you, did he? Maybe—"

"Aidan! For God's sake, just stop! You sound like a damned cop."

He sat back then and glanced over his shoulder. Shelby realized her shouting had drawn the attention of several other patrons.

She lowered her voice, but her whisper was still harsh. "Why are you doing this?"

"Someone murdered John, Shelby. Why *wouldn't* I do everything in my power to find out who?"

"Because it's not going to make any goddamn difference, Aidan, that's why."

"Shelby, how can you say that?"

"How? Because it's the truth! Johnny is dead. *Nothing* you do is going to change that. Nothing is going to bring him back. And even if you *do* get the murderer, Johnny's death still won't make any sense. Do you honestly think justice will be served? Do you think you'll feel vindicated or something? You won't, Aidan. You'll still feel that emptiness. It won't go away. It'll always be there. For the rest of your life. Nothing you do can *ever* take that away. He's *gone*."

"So what are you suggesting, Shelby? That we do nothing? That we sit back and let the person who did this go unpunished?" Aidan leaned across the table toward her, and if they hadn't been in the restaurant, Shelby didn't doubt that Aidan would have grabbed her shoulders and tried to shake his version of common sense into her. "You're wrong, Shelby. You *know* you're wrong."

She put a hand gently over his. But there was no placating him now.

"Of course," he continued, "finding John's killer

won't bring him back. It won't make his death any easier to accept, and it certainly won't fill the void in either of our lives, Shelby. But you can't sit there and convince me you wouldn't do whatever you could to bring John's murderer to justice.''

''Aidan—''

''That was John's work. Justice. It was everything to him. And if it was me who was killed, I'd want John to do everything in his power to find my killer. I wouldn't want him to rest until he had. And you and I both know he wouldn't. That's who he was. That's what John lived for.''

''I know.'' Shelby tried to control the waver she heard in her voice. ''I know, Aidan.''

She saw Aidan's own grief shadow his expression and knew he was right. And given the chance, she *would* do whatever it took to catch the person responsible for ending Johnny's life. For ending *her* life.

CHAPTER EIGHT

THERE APPEARED TO BE no foreseeable end to the cold that had gripped Fairfield for the past week. A constant rain had wiped away all traces of the brief Indian summer, and in its place was a damp grayness. It hovered over the city—and settled into Shelby.

She pulled Johnny's cardigan more tightly around her as her breath cast a fog on the rain-streaked pane. The street below her bedroom window glistened, and in the growing twilight she could just make out the sharp angle of the driving rain.

But the street was empty. She'd expected to see Aidan's Skylark parked across from the boutique as it had been off and on throughout the week. Even last night, after dinner, after they'd said good-night and long after she'd tried to find sleep, she'd looked out the window and seen the car. First she'd had the urge to go out and tell him to go home, that there was no need for him to watch over her. And then she'd considered inviting him in from the cold.

But she hadn't. For night was the only time she was able to be alone, the only time there were no facades to maintain or concern to deflect. So she'd drawn the blinds and tackled the unavoidable—she'd started packing.

Now, as she turned from the window to face the unlit bedroom, Shelby's gaze fell on the cardboard box she'd begun to fill last night. She hadn't gotten very far. The bedroom was still littered with Johnny's clothes. His things still hung in the closet as they had for the past week, untouched, as if she somehow expected someone else to come and take them away.

From the floor by the foot of the bed, she picked up a sweatshirt. She was about to drop it into the box when she caught the faint lingering scent of Johnny's cologne. She drew the shirt to her nose and breathed in the familiar fragrance. Closing her eyes, she could easily remember the first time she'd encountered it, the first time she'd touched him, was drawn into his embrace. She imagined she was back on the *Orion* with him, could almost feel his arms around her.

But she would never again feel Johnny's embrace.

Sitting on the edge of the bed, Shelby cast a glance at the nightstand. A shaft of light from the street lamp outside the window stabbed through the blinds and touched the framed photograph she kept there of Johnny. She could see the smile in that photo. She'd seen it enough times to know it by memory.

Only a week ago she'd contemplated fate. She remembered thinking that somehow it had played a hand for her and Johnny, that they were destined to be together. It wasn't just the pregnancy; it had been everything about their relationship. She'd come back to Fairfield to care for her mother when she'd never intended to leave New York City. As for Johnny, he'd lived all his life in New York City, and until the scandal with Internal Affairs he would never have dreamed of leaving. If they'd both stayed there, they might never have met. It took Fairfield to bring them together. Fairfield and fate.

And fate had given them this child.

But what kind of cruel fate played all those hands, stacked all those cards, only to snatch every last shred of happiness away in one blinding moment?

The phone pealed, shattering the silence of the apartment. Shelby swallowed hard over the painful lump in her throat, forcing back unshed tears.

She should have answered the phone immediately, she realized when she heard the answering machine take the call. Johnny's tape-recorded voice filled the dark apartment: "Hi. You've reached John and Shelby's. We can't get the phone right now, but leave a message and we'll call you as soon as we can."

When the machine beeped, Shelby dropped the sweatshirt into the box and released a long, trembling breath. She should have changed the outgoing message. Better yet, she should have turned off the phone.

"Shelby? Are you there? It's Cora. Please pick up. I need to talk to you."

She moved to the nightstand, her hand hovering over the receiver.

"Please, Shelby. I know you're there. You're probably working, right? Come on, pick up. It's important. Shelby? Look, I'm getting tired of talking to your damn machine all the time. Please—"

Shelby lifted the receiver. "Hello, Cora."

"Shelby." Her sister sounded relieved. "Finally. God, I thought I was going to have to call Aidan next. I've been worried sick about you."

"You've only been gone two days. Why should you be worried?"

"You haven't answered your phone."

"I've been busy."

"Right, sis." There was no fooling Cora. "So how have you been feeling? Have you seen your doctor yet?"

"I will, Cora. You can stop worrying. I feel fine. What did you want to talk to me about? You said it was important."

"I was just...I was wondering if you'd put any more thought into what we talked about."

"About my moving back to Manhattan?"

"Mmm-hmm."

"Yes, I've thought about it."

"And?"

"Look, Cora. I really need some time."

"Time to think?"

Shelby looked at the disarray of the bedroom. "No... I've already thought about it. I need time to pack."

"So you're absolutely sure about this?"

"No. I'm not sure about anything."

"Well, I need you to be."

Cora's urgent tone was more than enough warning for Shelby to know her sister had something up her sleeve.

"Why? What's going on, Cora?"

"I...I've got a lead on a place."

"Cora—"

"Come on, Shelby, I told you I was going to start looking. You know the apartment isn't big enough.

Maybe for the two of us, but with the baby...
eventually we're going to need a bigger place.''

"I wish you hadn't done that."

"Shelby, it's what we discussed."

"We *mentioned* it. I didn't commit to anything."

"So what are you saying? That you're *not* moving
here, that you're going to stay in Fairfield?"

"No. I mean, yes. I don't know. Cora, please, I
can't talk about this right now, all right? I—"

"All right. I'm sorry. I know you need time and I
shouldn't push you on this. But this is a really good
deal, Shelby. A three-bedroom. Security entrance.
There's even a small office you could use. And just
down the street are several blocks with retail spaces
for rent. I'm sure you could get a boutique set up in
no time."

"Cora—"

"And besides, Shel—" there was no stopping her
younger sister once she was on a roll "—we've been
through this. You told me you wanted to build your
career here. You said you couldn't do it stuck in Fairfield, that you wanted to get out of there."

"I know," Shelby said. She gave a resigned sigh
she doubted her sister heard.

"Listen to me, sis. I'm only telling you what you
told me the other day. You never intended to stay in
Fairfield in the first place. And now...well, what's left
for you there?"

Shelby looked at the disarray of the bedroom. In the
shadows she could see Johnny's things all around her,

each one whispering its own bittersweet memory of the love they'd shared. The love that was lost.

"You're right, Cora," she admitted at last.

"So what should I tell this guy?"

"What guy?"

"With the apartment. Do you want to come down here to look at it?"

It felt wrong. How could she consider leaving so soon after Johnny's death? How could she just let go of everything here, everything they'd shared? Then again, maybe Cora was right to push her. Maybe a push was what she needed.

"When do you have to give an answer?" Shelby asked.

"He wants to know by the end of next week."

"Then why don't we talk next week?" She could hear her own voice drag with exhaustion, and she prayed Cora wouldn't force the issue. She was grateful when her sister finally backed down.

"Sure, sis. We'll talk." The disappointment in Cora's voice was impossible to miss. "So how are you really, Shelby?"

"Cora, I'm doing all right. You can stop asking, okay?"

The other end of the line was silent.

"Okay?" Shelby said again.

"Fine. I just worry. That's all."

"Well, stop worrying—everything will work out," she reassured her, ever the older sister. "We'll talk about the apartment next week. And I'll see what I can do about getting down there to look at it." Just then she heard the buzzer for the boutique door downstairs.

"Shelby, I—"

"Cora, I'm sorry. I have to go. There's someone at the door."

"Call me?"

"I'll call. I promise."

By the time Shelby hung up the phone and reached the main floor, the buzzer had gone a second time. She crossed the dark boutique, reached for the light switches and flipped on the first bank of lights. Even though company was the last thing she wanted, she was grateful to whoever it was at the door now for rescuing her from Cora. She turned the dead bolt.

Nick DaCosta barely seemed to notice the rain that pelted down on him, soaking his thin sports jacket. He shifted his weight uneasily from one foot to the other.

"Nick."

"Hi, Shelby." He blinked and lifted a wet hand to wipe ineffectually at the rain on his face. "I thought for a minute there you weren't home. Your lights were off. I probably should have called first, huh? I hope I'm not interrupting anything."

"No." She swung the door open wider. "No, I was just on the phone. Why don't you come in out of the rain?"

He stepped inside. "I won't stay long. I don't want to intrude. It's just…well, I thought I'd bring you John's things." The cardboard box under his arm was not half as wet as Nick was, but the edges threatened to crush under the force of his hold on it.

"From his locker and his desk," he explained.

"The captain, well, he wanted to bring it over himself, but I told him I should be the one. It's my duty, John being my partner and all. And I wanted you to know, Shelby, that I'm here for you. If there's anything you need…"

"Thank you, Nick. I appreciate it." Shelby accepted the box from him, cradling it in her arms.

"I know I haven't been around as much as I probably should've in the past week to check up on you, but—"

"Nick, you don't have to check up on me."

"Right." He nodded. "Well, I want you to know I'm doing everything I can to push the investigation. To find out who killed John."

"I know you are. I'm sure John would appreciate that."

"So you're all right?"

She nodded, offering him a smile she hoped would ease his obvious discomfort. It apparently didn't. He continued to shift his weight, wiping at the rain in his face again and then toying nervously with what sounded like car keys in the pocket of his jacket. His dark eyes made a quick scan of the boutique and the loft before they settled on her again. Johnny had always described Nick as a hotshot, but she'd never seen it.

"The guys on the unit, they wanted me to give you their condolences."

"Thanks."

"We're all doing everything we can."

"Have there been any developments?"

"Nothing concrete yet. The bomb squad's still

working on what little they managed to salvage. But we'll get him, Shelby. Believe me, we'll find out who did this.''

"I'm sure you will.''

Nick's gaze flitted from hers to the boutique again, and Shelby couldn't decide if the young detective was actually looking for something or was simply too nervous to meet her eyes.

"Nick, was there something else you wanted to see me about?"

He looked at her and chewed one side of his lip. "Yeah, actually. Shelby, I hate to bother you with this, but I was just wondering if John might have had any files here.''

"Files?'' She shouldn't have been surprised.

"Yeah, files. Or notes. Anything that might be related to his work.''

"No, Nick. Johnny didn't bring his work home. At least, not home here. If he'd had anything I imagine it would have been on the boat.''

"You're sure? Not even his notebooks? Something?''

"Honestly—'' she waved a hand back at the studio "—even if there *was* something here, it would take me weeks to find it. And it would have taken Johnny weeks to find it. That's why he never kept his case files here. No, there's nothing, Nick. I'm quite certain.''

"But it could be something as simple as a receipt or a note to himself scrawled on some scrap of paper in one of his pockets or—''

"Fine, Nick. I'll look, okay? I'll go through some

of Johnny's things and see if there's anything." Her impatience had gotten the better of her. It sharpened her tone, and when she saw Nick flinch, she regretted it.

"I'm sorry to do this to you, Shelby. I know this is hard on you. If you like…I mean, if it'd make things easier, I could look through his stuff myself. Save you the trouble."

"I'll look, Nick. But thanks."

"Are you sure? I don't mind."

"No, really, I can manage. I'm in the middle of something right now, but I'll sort through a few things later. I promise."

"And you'll call me if you find anything?"

"Yes."

And then, just as Nick's intrusion had rescued her from her phone call with Cora, this time it was the phone that rescued her from more questions from Nick. When it rang, Nick looked at her as though questioning whether or not she intended to answer it.

"I should probably get that," Shelby said.

"Sure." He reached for the door.

"Thanks for bringing this over," she said, directing her gaze to the box in her arms and wondering if she could possibly bring herself to open it.

"Take care, Shelby. And call…if you need anything."

"I will."

By the time Nick had closed the door behind him and she'd started up the stairs, the answering machine had already caught the call. The sound of Johnny's voice on the outgoing message tugged once again at her heart, and grasping the box more tightly she fought back the burning in her eyes, the rising lump in her throat.

She half expected it would be Cora calling back, but there was only the hiss of empty tape and then the dialtone. The caller had hung up.

Setting the box on the already cluttered coffee table in the living room, Shelby crossed the dark apartment to the floor-to-ceiling windows. In the yellow sodium glow of the street lamps, she saw Nick's black Mustang, a plume of blue-gray exhaust swirling in the cold air behind it. There was no basis for the uneasiness that crept through her as she watched it idling, as she imagined Nick sitting there, looking at her apartment, searching the darkened windows. But not until Nick drove away did her apprehension cease.

It might have been ten minutes, fifteen maybe, by the time the phone rang again. Shelby had long since left the window and moved to the couch. She'd sat there, staring at the closed box from the precinct, unable to bring herself to open it, and when the phone's ring startled her from her thoughts, she noticed that the apartment lay in even darker shadows now.

She reached the phone by the third ring. "Hello?"

Silence.

"Hello?" She pressed the receiver harder against her ear, hearing a faint crackle over the line. "Hello?"

Only when she was about to hang up did the caller at last speak, the voice a cold monotone.

"Ms. Beaumont?"

"Who is this?"

"Ms. Beaumont?" he asked again.

"Yes. Who *is* this?"

"I'm calling about what happened." There was a hiss in the background, like tires on wet pavement, and then what sounded like a car alarm in the distance. She imagined a phone booth. "Ms. Beaumont?" the voice prompted.

"Yes, I'm here. Who are you?"

"I'm a friend of John's."

"Do I...do I know you?"

"Not yet."

AIDAN DODGED several puddles as he sprinted across the rainy parking lot of the Pier restaurant to his Skylark. There was no need to rush, though, he thought as he unlocked the car. He was soaked already, after spending the past three hours talking to everyone he could find at the yacht club who might have seen something in the days prior to last week's explosion.

And he'd gotten nowhere for his efforts.

He'd asked a lot of questions of a lot of people who had already been asked the same questions a hundred times by the investigating officers. Nothing. No one had seen anything out of the ordinary, and no one had spotted anyone suspicious around the *Orion* before or immediately after the explosion.

Aidan dropped into the driver's seat and closed the door. He shrugged off his sodden jacket and turned on the ignition. An entire week, and he was no further ahead. It was kind of ironic actually; the person he really needed right now, the one who could help him most, was John himself.

How many times in the past week had he wished he'd pressed John for information when John had asked to see him? Now he could only think that whatever John had wanted to tell him about the case had most likely cost him his life.

Aidan cranked up the car heater and flicked on the windshield wipers. Through the cleared arc he could just make out the charred remains of Pier Eight under the wharf lights. He felt the same churn in his gut now that he'd felt when he'd come down to the yacht club the morning after the explosion and seen the destruction, the debris floating on the oily surface, the salvaged remains of the *Orion* strewn across the dock. It was only then, as the crews dragged more and more fragments of the boat to the surface, that Aidan had at last started to comprehend the reality of John's death.

Even so, a whole week later, there were times it *didn't* seem real. It was only when he saw the grief and utter loss in Shelby's eyes that he recognized the truth. John was dead.

Aidan put the car into drive and steered out of the potholed parking lot. He would head to his office; there were calls he needed to make. And then he would go to Shelby's. Until they got the man responsible for John's death, she wasn't safe.

"WHY WON'T YOU tell me your name?" Shelby's grip on the receiver tightened.

"My name's not important, but the information I have is," the caller told her, and Shelby couldn't decide if the caller's voice was being deliberately muffled.

"What information?"

"Information about John's murder."

"So why are you calling me? You should talk to the police."

"I don't trust the police."

"But you trusted Johnny?"

"Didn't matter he was a cop. He was a man of his word. I trusted him for that. And I don't like what they did to him."

"Who's they?"

He ignored her question. "He didn't deserve to die like that."

"Who's *they?*" Shelby asked again. In the slight pause she heard the sound of a car passing, followed by a rustling sound as though the caller had shifted the receiver to his other ear.

"I can't talk about it over the phone."

"So why did you phone?"

"I want you to meet me."

"Meet you?" Shelby turned and stared across the dark apartment to the rain-spattered windows. "But I—"

"Look, I have information. If you want it, you'll have to meet me."

Her heart was racing and her mind was stumbling over the insane idea of accepting the caller's proposition. She wasn't a cop. She wasn't trained for anything like this. But could she afford to say no when she might be close to finding the man who murdered Johnny?

"Where?" she asked at last. "Where do I meet you?"

"Down near the train yards. You know Charlie's Bar on Marin at the end of Broadway?"

"No, but I can find it. Marin and Broadway?"

"Yeah. Be there in twenty minutes. And don't bring company. Like I said, I don't trust cops."

"How...how will I recognize you?"

There was another pause and then, "You won't have to. I'll find you."

Shelby clutched the receiver to her ear long after he'd hung up. *Don't bring company,* he'd said. But she couldn't possibly do this alone. She wasn't a part of this world—anonymous phone calls in the night, informants and snitches.

She needed Aidan. Aidan would know what to do. He was a professional. He wouldn't be seen. And then they'd have a lead. An honest-to-goodness lead.

Her fingers shook as she punched out Aidan's home number. When there was no answer, she called his office. Still nothing.

"Where are you, Aidan?" She heard the fierceness in her voice, thin and wavering in the silence of the apartment. "Where *are* you?"

Charlie's Bar at the end of Broadway. It would take her a good fifteen minutes to reach that end of the city, even if she hurried. She jogged into the bedroom.

She couldn't wait for Aidan. She'd have to do this on her own. No matter how foolish it was to rush off into the night to meet a stranger, she had to do it. For Johnny.

As she pulled open the nightstand drawer, she tried to convince herself it would be all right. At least Charlie's Bar was a public place. With witnesses, how much danger could she be in?

Still... Her hand trembled as she grasped the cool metal of the Glock semiautomatic.

CHAPTER NINE

SHELBY CHECKED her watch again and at last got up from a back booth at Charlie's. She'd waited there forty minutes, cradling her cup of tea as she watched the door. She'd avoided eye contact with the dozen or so male patrons who'd leered at her from the moment she'd stepped into the seedy bar, and still her caller had not made an appearance.

She pulled several one-dollar bills from her wallet and tossed them onto the scarred table. Tying the belt of her trench coat, she shouldered her purse. The weight of the gun inside reassured her as she made her way past the bar to the door. She nodded a quick thanks to the bartender and didn't look back.

Outside she turned up her collar and huddled under the eave of Charlie's. Several blocks away a train whistle blared, a hollow lonely sound in the wet night. Maybe just a few more minutes, she thought, watching the rain race along swollen gutters to black storm drains. She shivered, but it was more from the steadily rising uneasiness she felt than the cold damp.

A sudden flare of sheet lightning made her jump. It was followed in seconds by a low ominous growl of thunder, and Shelby wished she'd been able to have a drink, instead of just tea. Something to calm her nerves. She paced the short distance of sidewalk half-sheltered by the overhang.

Why hadn't her caller shown up? She'd come alone, just like he'd asked. She'd been on time. She'd waited. Why? What had she done wrong? Had she really been so close to finding out something about Johnny's murder only to have it slip from her grasp?

She turned and paced back toward Charlie's. Another five minutes and she was going home. The vapor from her breath caught in the blue neon glow of the bar's sign. She turned again, the click of her low heels echoing across the near-deserted street. And then a thought struck her: what if he *was* here? What if the man who'd called was here right now watching her? Maybe he didn't have information about Johnny, after all. Maybe he'd used that as a lure and was now waiting for her to walk down the block to where she'd parked her car?

Shelby searched the shadows. Nothing. A car approached the intersection and turned right, its tires thumping over the double set of railway tracks before its red taillights disappeared down Marin.

She reached into her purse. Her hand wrapped around the Glock, and one finger traced the checkered surface of the safety.

This was insane. Whoever had called her obviously wasn't going to show. She started to turn in the direction of the bar again, then froze. It could have been a play of light, a trick of the shadows, but for a split second she thought she saw the movement of a figure reflected in the dark store window across the street. Was someone on the street behind her? She spun

around. But the street was empty, only vacant buildings and storefronts, a few stacked trash cans along
the curb and a Dumpster looming in the mouth of the
opposite alleyway.

"That does it," she whispered. "I must be nuts."

Ignoring the rain that soaked her hair and whipped
coldly at her face, she headed for her car. More lightning flashed, but the accompanying thunder was
drowned by the rumble of an approaching train, its
iron wheels grinding up the track, its great weight vi-
brating the sidewalk. Shelby stopped as the gate lowered across the intersection and the warning bells
started to clang.

She took a deep breath and tried to relax, then
squinted through the rain, looking back down the
street behind her. No one was following her. At least
not that she could see. Once she could get past the
tracks, the Lexus was only a quarter of a block away.
She'd get into it, drive home, lock the doors and take
a hot bath. She was a fool to have rushed out here
tonight; she wondered if she would tell Aidan about
it.

She turned to face the train again, glancing down
the line of tank and hopper cars to the caboose. She
felt a cold drizzle trickle down her neck and drew her
collar tighter across her throat. And it was then, as she
watched the railway cars thundering past, that she saw
the man on the opposite side of the tracks.

This time it was no trick of light or play of shadow.
In the space between each car that thundered past, she
caught fleeting glimpses of the tall figure. He stood on
the other side of the train, wearing a long coat, un-

buttoned and flapping open in the wake of the passing cars. His black hair was wet and matted to his head, and the only light that revealed his rain-slick features was the red pulsing glow of the railway signals. But it was enough.

Shelby wiped the rain from her eyes. Disbelieving. But when she opened them again, she caught only a quick blur of motion between the cars. A flash of lightning revealed the sweep of his long coat, and by the time the caboose rattled past, the street was empty again.

It was as though he'd never been there. And yet, as impossible as it seemed, Shelby was almost certain of what she'd recognized. Ducking under the rising gate and almost tripping over the rails as the last of the warning signals clanged through the night, she staggered forward into the deserted intersection.

"Johnny?" Her voice cracked.

She stopped in the spot she'd seen the figure standing only seconds ago, as though it might offer her some validity of what she'd seen. Rain pounded the pavement as she looked up and down. No one was there. She turned a full circle as she scanned the area. But still no one.

"Johnny?" she called more loudly.

It was impossible. There had to be an explanation. It had been someone who looked like him. The light had played tricks. Her imagination had done the rest.

"Johnny!" Her voice echoed along the dark street and through the alleyways. It was answered by silence.

And when Shelby called Johnny's name one final time, it came out in a quiet desperate sob.

SHE COULD BARELY RECALL the drive home. She remembered sitting in her Lexus on Broadway just past the tracks for long minutes, as though expecting Johnny to appear from one of the alleyways. And by the time she finally started the car and pulled away from the curb, a numbness had settled over her.

As she parked outside the boutique, Shelby felt as though she was moving in a dream. It was raining harder now, but she barely noticed. She simply locked the car and headed for the door. She didn't even hear the other car that pulled up behind hers, and when Aidan called her name, she jumped.

"Shelby!" he called again, and she turned to see him sprinting toward her, dodging puddles and holding his jacket over his head. "What the hell are you doing out here? What... God, you're soaked through!"

He held her at arm's length and studied her for a moment. She could only wonder what she must look like, bedraggled and drenched with rain. He lifted a hand to wipe wet strands of hair from her face.

"Come on, let's get you inside and dried off." Aidan took her keys from her, but he'd barely touched the lock when the door swung open freely.

He immediately reached for his holster, casting a glance back at Shelby as though expecting an explanation. "What the hell is going on?"

"I...I don't know." Her voice sounded thin and she cleared her throat. "I left in a hurry. Maybe I forgot to lock up."

Aidan had slipped his gun from the holster and stepped into the dark boutique. "Stay where you are, Shelby," he instructed, but he might as well have been talking to the mannequins across the room. Shelby was right behind him.

The damage wasn't discernible until they moved farther into the boutique and then upstairs to the apartment. Each room showed clear signs of the intruder's destructive path: drawers had been pulled out and emptied, furniture had been overturned, papers were strewn across the floors, even clothes and boxes had been dragged from the closets and scattered. By the time they'd worked their way through the entire apartment and Aidan was certain the intruder was gone, all the lights were on and Shelby found herself standing in the middle of the living room amidst a tumble of cushions, books, papers and other personal belongings. She felt weak at the knees and grabbed the back of the couch to steady herself.

Aidan was already on the phone calling the police, but she only half heard his words as she took in the full extent of the damage. Even the box Nick had brought over earlier had been opened, its contents scattered across the coffee table. Shelby moved toward it, and it was then that she saw the small box from the funeral home.

It, too, had been torn open and cast aside. She rushed to it, a cry slipping from her lips as she knelt on the floor beside the toppled container. *Johnny's ashes.*

She reached for it, desperate to right it, when she felt Aidan's hands on her shoulders.

"No, Shelby. Don't touch it. Don't touch anything. We have to wait for the lab guys. They'll want to—"

But Shelby picked up the box, anyway, and cradled

it in her hands. After the apparition she'd seen tonight at the railway tracks, she wasn't sure what to feel. What had she seen really? Were these actually Johnny's remains? Or had she seen something else? A ghost perhaps?

She didn't believe in ghosts. So what was she holding in her hands now?

"Shelby, do you want to tell me what's going on? Where were you tonight?"

"I was down at the south end of Broadway." She placed the box amidst the clutter on the coffee table, staring at it until Aidan turned her to face him.

"Broadway? Down near the train yards?"

She nodded mutely.

"What the hell were you doing down there at this time of night?"

"I received a phone call."

"A phone call?"

"From a man. He said he had information about Johnny's murder."

"What? Someone called you here? About John?"

She nodded again. Disbelief and concern twisted Aidan's features as he listened to her description of the call, her drive down to Charlie's Bar and her subsequent wait.

"So he never showed?"

"No. I waited forty minutes and gave up."

Aidan shoved a hand through his damp hair, then shook his head, finally fixing her with the sort of stare she would have expected from an older brother. There was a time when she'd cherished that older-brother look from Aidan, but right now she almost resented it.

"God, I don't believe this, Shelby. What were you thinking? Some stranger calls and you fly off into the night? Just like that? Have you lost your mind?"

"Everything but." She drew off her wet trench coat and brushed past him to hang it on the coat tree. It, too, was toppled and she had to right it first.

"Shelby, don't. Please! Don't touch anything else."

She hung up her coat, ignoring him.

"Shelby, listen to me—" he followed her as she headed to the bedroom and rummaged on the floor for a sweatshirt "—what you did tonight... Look, if this guy makes contact again, you have to call me."

"I *tried* to call you, Aidan."

She struggled with the buttons on her shirt, her growing anger making the task more difficult. And when finally she peeled the wet shirt from her bare skin, Aidan cast his gaze down until she'd pulled on the sweatshirt.

"Then you should have waited," he said, following her to the kitchen this time.

"I couldn't afford to wait. I wasn't about to pass up the opportunity to get information on Johnny, and you can't tell me you wouldn't have done exactly the same thing."

"But how do you even know this guy was legit, for God's sake? Look around you, Shelby! Whoever trashed this place wasn't in any hurry. Don't you see what's happened here? There *was* no information. There *was* no informant. Whoever called you tonight told you whatever they had to in order to get you out of the apartment."

"You can't know that for certain."

"No. But it's a damned better theory than someone calling you anonymously with information about John's murder."

"Why is that so far-fetched, Aidan? Why *wouldn't* someone call me?"

"Because they'd call the police first."

"He said he didn't trust the police."

Aidan shook his head with frustration again. "There's no getting through to you, is there?"

"I believe the caller."

"Why?"

"Just a feeling, okay?" She took a bottle of water from the fridge and caught Aidan's censoring gaze. "Please, Aidan. I hardly think they're going to find the guy's prints in the fridge."

"So if this caller was legit, why didn't he show up?"

"I don't know. Maybe something scared him off."

Like maybe Johnny scared him off, she thought. But she didn't dare tell Aidan about that right now. He was already deaf to her reasoning, already thought she was nuts.

"Listen, Shelby, I'm sorry for coming down so hard on you. But you could have been hurt tonight, and—"

"And you promised Johnny you'd look out for me," she finished for him.

"To hell with Johnny!" Regret immediately showed on Aidan's face, and he lowered his voice. "Look, this has nothing to do with John, all right? Shelby, I care about you. I...I always have. And I could never forgive myself if something happened to you."

The way he looked at her then was new to Shelby. She couldn't remember ever seeing him so upset, and when, suddenly, he turned away from her, she wondered what exactly she'd seen in those clear blue eyes of his.

She studied him from behind, wondering if it had been fear she'd seen there. Aidan had suffered a loss, as well—his best friend. And now he feared he would lose her, too.

That was it. That was the reason behind Aidan's upset, his flare of anger. It couldn't be anything else. Could it?

"Aidan?"

"Just be careful, Shelby, all right?" he said at last, turning to meet her gaze once more.

She nodded slowly. "Sure, Aidan. I'll be careful."

"And listen, I don't think you should tell anyone else about your phone call tonight. Not until we know more—if there *is* more to know."

"THE LAB GUYS are just about through for tonight," Dan Barnes said, crossing the living room to the sofa where Shelby sat, wrapped in a blanket, her legs drawn up beneath her.

The captain sat down next to her and patted her knee. "Whatever else they need from the place, I told them they can get tomorrow morning. Just try not to touch a lot of stuff downstairs if you can help it."

"Thanks, Dan." She was grateful for the control he'd taken of the situation. "Thanks for everything."

"Are you sure you want to stay here tonight?" he

asked for what had to be the tenth time. "I can make arrangements."

"No, I'd rather stay here, Dan. Thanks."

She knew he was going to say something about it not being safe and was grateful when Aidan interrupted.

"I'm going to camp out here for the night, Captain. Keep an eye on things."

"Good idea. But I'm still going to have a patrol car posted out front."

He didn't have to state the obvious—that he, like the rest of the officers in the apartment, suspected a connection between tonight's break-in and Johnny's murder. So far they hadn't found anything missing, and since many items of value had been passed over, it was obvious that whoever had broken in had been looking for something very specific.

Dan gave Shelby's shoulder a quick squeeze before standing up. "All right, guys, we're done for now."

In a matter of minutes the officers and technicians had cleared out, leaving the apartment in a vacuum of silence. Shelby glanced around the place. Not only was it a mess because of the break-in, there was now a trail of black powder left behind by the lab guys.

Aidan seemed to read her thoughts. "I'll give you a hand cleaning up," he offered.

But before he could move from where he stood at the back of the sofa, Shelby caught his hand. "Leave it for now, Aidan," she said quietly. "I need to talk to you."

She waited for him to sit next to her. Then she stared at her hands, unable to meet his troubled gaze.

She had to tell him. As insane as it was going to sound, she had to tell Aidan. She could still see Johnny's face, his eyes, staring at her between those train cars tonight, and the more she thought about it, the surer she was that somehow it had indeed been Johnny. That somehow he'd been watching over her.

"What is it, Shelby?"

"I…" She twisted a tassel from one of the pillows between her fingers. "I…I think I saw Johnny tonight."

Aidan said nothing until she finally turned her gaze on him.

"Shelby." He took her hand in his and stroked it soothingly. "You've gone through a lot this past week and—"

"What? You think I'm just seeing things?"

"No. I'm merely suggesting that you've been through so much and perhaps you mistook someone else for—"

"No. I *saw* him, Aidan. Down on Broadway and Marin. Tonight. At the intersection. A train passed between us, but I saw him. He was watching me. We just stood there, staring at each other. I know it was him."

"So what happened to him, then?" She heard the challenge in Aidan's tone.

"He…disappeared."

"Come on, Shelby. You saw someone who looked vaguely like John, and it's understandable that in your state—"

"No! That's not what happened." She stood, the blanket falling to the floor. "I know it sounds crazy, but think about it, Aidan. What if...what if Johnny somehow...survived the explosion?''

"Shelby—"

"What if he *did* survive? Admit it—it's possible. He could have been thrown clear. How are we to know he's not out there somehwere?''

"Because we'd know, Shelby. He'd *let* us know."

"But what if he's...confused? What if he has amnesia or something? I know it sounds crazy, but be honest—it's not impossible, is it?''

"Shel—"

"It's *not* impossible, Aidan. It's not." She could hear the desperation in her raised voice, and she struggled to calm herself. "I won't believe he's dead, Aidan. I can't. Not after what I saw tonight. He could be out there right now and—"

"Shelby!"

Aidan stood and grasped her by the shoulders, steadying her, forcing her to look him in the eye. "Shelby, why are you doing this to yourself? Johnny's dead, all right? He's dead. They found his body. What more proof do you need?''

The part of her that had no fight left, the part that had wanted to die when Johnny had, was ready to fall into Aidan's comforting arms and believe there was no hope, no future, her life was over. But with the memory of what she'd seen tonight, Shelby found a lingering reserve of strength. What if she was right?

"Maybe it wasn't him on the boat, Aidan. What then?''

"For God's sake, Shelby. Will you stop? You can't go on like this.''

She tore away from his grasp, putting space between them. "Who's to say it wasn't someone else on the boat?"

"I'm not going to listen to this. Do you hear what you're saying?"

"Yes, I hear exactly what I'm saying, Aidan. *I saw Johnny tonight.*"

"And it was Johnny you saw on the boat! Shelby, you're not making any sense."

"No, I'm making perfect sense. It's the rest of you—you and Dan and Nick and the rest of the police force—who aren't making any sense, who can't see the possibilities here."

"Dammit, Shelby! There *are* no other possibilities!"

"Dental records."

"What?"

"Dental records. What about Johnny's dental records? Did they—"

"Shelby, stop!" Aidan tried to grab her shoulders again, but this time Shelby was too quick. She stepped back from him, almost tripping over a toppled dining-room chair. He started to help her, but immediately she bent down to right the chair and use it as a barricade.

In all his years of knowing Shelby, Aidan had only once before glimpsed the kind of sorrow that racked her face now. Even then, years ago, at the news of her father's death, she had managed to keep her darker feelings carefully hidden from the world, as though she saw these as a sign of weakness. But when that dam of hers had finally broken all those years ago it was Aidan who'd seen it, Aidan who'd been the one holding the pieces together for her.

And tonight Shelby's dam was breaking again.

As she stood her ground, he saw her knuckles whiten on the chair she held between them. Her eyes were wide, and in them he saw a fierce desperation as though she was hanging on by only a thread. Her last thread. Her last hope.

"Shelby, please—"

"Did they *prove* it was Johnny, Aidan? Did they check his dental records?" Her voice possessed a cold angry edge that sounded painfully foreign coming from her lips.

"No! They didn't check, Shelby. They couldn't. There wasn't enough..."

He could see her shaking now. "Don't do this, Shelby. Please. You have to be strong. For yourself. And for the baby. You have to get on with your life."

"I think you should leave, Aidan." Her voice was flat now.

"You shouldn't be alone."

She backed away from him and retrieved his jacket. When she offered it to him, Aidan could see that she was holding herself together this time, reaching within and finding her own strength. She didn't need him. She didn't need anyone. Not tonight.

"I won't be alone," she said. "You heard Dan. There's a patrol car out front."

Aidan crossed the living room and took his jacket from her. "Shelby—"

"Good night, Aidan."

He didn't move, only stood in front of her, waiting

for her to meet his gaze. And when she finally did, Aidan couldn't remember if he'd ever seen her resolve so strong. "I'll talk to you in the morning, then."

"Sure."

He didn't dare argue or try to convince her to let him stay, nor did he attempt to touch her. Instead he let himself out, waiting on the front step listening for her to turn the dead bolt. A moment later he heard her give a muffled sob, and the sound tore him apart.

The rain had let up. Across the wet street, Aidan saw no sign of the patrol car. Obviously, with the changeover to the night shift, backup hadn't yet arrived. He would wait for the black-and-white to show up. And maybe he'd stay even longer, keep an eye on the place himself.

He zipped up his jacket and was about to go to his car when he heard a scuffle in the alley. It could have been a stray dog or a cat seeking shelter amongst the trash cans farther back. But Aidan's training would not allow him to dismiss other possibilities readily, especially not after tonight. He drew his gun, releasing the safety and bringing it up before he'd taken the first step into the dark mouth of the alley.

With more time to think about it, he might have gone to his car for a flashlight, but if someone *was* back in the alley, someone who shouldn't be there, he had no time to waste. Rainwater dripped from rusted fire escapes, drumming against sodden boxes and aluminum trash cans, and what little light came from the street cast long shadows ahead of him. Aidan breathed in the musty stench of rotting cardboard and dirty water.

It wasn't until he'd inched his way halfway down the alley that he heard another sound—a single footfall on the wet pavement. This time, however, it was directly behind him. He whirled, bringing his gun to chest level in one fluid motion. Backlit by the street lamps, a figure, that of a man, was lined up perfectly in his sights.

"I wouldn't take another step if I were you," Aidan warned, his grip on the revolver tightening. "Bring your hands up where I can see them. Slowly."

Aidan watched as the man raised his arms, and only then did he see an object glint faintly in one of the man's hands.

"Drop your weapon," he commanded.

"It's not a weapon." There was a faint click, and Aidan found himself squinting directly into the beam of a flashlight.

"Who are you?"

"A friend."

And when the man redirected the beam of light onto himself, Aidan gasped in shock. "John?"

CHAPTER TEN

JOHNNY GAZED through the rain-spattered windshield of Aidan's Skylark to the second-floor windows. Her lights were still on, and as he had every night for the past week, he waited and prayed to catch a glimpse of Shelby.

"I don't believe this, John. I can't believe you're here. How...?"

Johnny turned to his friend. Aidan had been expressing his disbelief for the past ten minutes, ever since he'd lowered his revolver in the narrow confines of the alleyway. It wasn't as though he'd expected Aidan to greet him with open arms, but when he'd finally stood before him, Johnny had seen fury in Aidan's features, and he'd half expected Aidan to deck him.

Seconds later a patrol car had pulled up and parked in the street out front. Aidan had left the alley, brought his car around to the loading docks behind the boutique, and Johnny had climbed in. It was then that Aidan had confirmed Johnny's suspicion—someone *had* broken into the apartment. He'd thought so when he'd seen the black-and-whites and then the crime-scene unit's van. In fact, he'd almost *expected* the break-in. He'd known all along that whoever was behind the Morelli/Feeney murders and the bomb would eventually attempt to cover his tracks, and that included destroying any shred of evidence Johnny might have lying around the apartment.

That was why he'd been watching out for Shelby.

"So are you going to tell me what's going on?" Aidan said.

"How's Shelby?"

"You have to ask?"

Johnny felt the familiar stab of guilt. He stared at his hands, twisted his academy ring around his finger a few times. Still he didn't answer Aidan's question.

"What was she doing down on Broadway tonight, Aidan?"

"Looking for your killer. Why else would she risk her life in that part of town in the middle of the night?"

"What are you talking about?"

"She got a call tonight. Anonymous. Someone saying he had information about the explosion. My hunch is the call was nothing more than a way to get her out of the apartment. John, what the hell is going on here? What happened? Talk to me."

With one finger Johnny traced the three-inch gash along his right cheek where a piece of shrapnel from the explosion had caught him before he'd hit the water. It was still tender. He closed his eyes, remembering.... It had been a week, and without Shelby, the week seemed like an eternity.

"John, they found remains. Who was on the boat?"

"A snitch by the name of Robert Logan."

"A friend of Feeney's?"

"An associate. After we found Feeney's body down at the waterfront, I cashed in one last chip and latched on to Logan. We'd been wanting him for some petty stuff, nickel-and-dime, really. But I was lucky. He'd witnessed what happened to Feeney the night before. And recognized the guy who shot him."

"So he gave you the shooter's name?"

Johnny shook his head. "He was going to. That's why we were on the boat that afternoon. He'd agreed to meet me, but didn't want to come into the station, so I suggested the boat. We were belowdecks less than ten minutes when I smelled fumes. I figured there was a leak in the fuel line, so I went up top to check the pump. And that's when I found the bomb. I lifted the hatch and it was just...there. It happened so fast. One moment I'm looking down at this thing and seeing the last few seconds ticking away, and the next I'm shouting to Logan and jumping overboard. There was no time for anything else."

"So why didn't you come in, John? You could have asked for protection."

"No. I couldn't come in. Someone tried to kill me, Aidan. I barely escaped with my life that afternoon. I was dazed and disoriented, but I knew damn well I couldn't go home. It wasn't safe."

"So where did you go?"

"Up to your cabin. I thumbed a ride part of the way. Hiked the rest. I took a day to regroup and then I got that old Dodge of yours in the garage running."

"You know Shelby was in the hospital?" Aidan's tone was filled with accusation.

"Aidan, I *know,* all right? Dammit! You don't think I'm aware of what I've put her through?"

"No. I don't think you are, John."

"Look, I don't need this." Johnny reached for the door and opened it. He hadn't disclosed himself to Aidan to receive yet another dose of guilt. He already had more than his share of that.

"Wait, John." Aidan caught his sleeve, stopping him.

"No, Aidan. I came to you because I need help. Because I trust you. I thought *you* of all people would understand there's no other way I can do this. You don't think this is killing me? What I'm doing to Shelby? I *love* her. But there's no other way. I thought you'd see that. Obviously I was wrong."

"John, close the door. Let's talk about this."

If he hadn't needed Aidan's help, if Aidan wasn't the only person he could turn to, Johnny would have left. Instead, he pulled the door shut and looked again to the lit windows of the apartment. What he wouldn't give to hold Shelby in his arms. Just imagining it made his heart feel as if it was being squeezed by a fist.

"So what about this Logan guy?" Aidan asked. "Did you get anything out of him before the explosion?"

"Only that it was someone on the force."

"So take that to Internal Affairs. Have them start up an investigation. They'll protect you, John. They'll protect Shelby."

"No! They can't, Aidan. They can't protect us. More importantly they can't protect Shelby." The thought of someone hurting Shelby was more than he could bear. "No, if there's one thing I learned through that whole mess down in New York City, it was that you can't count on Internal Affairs. IAB is the *last* place I can go right now. And besides, there's no way of knowing how deep this thing reaches."

"You have to trust someone, John."

"I trust you."

A silence fell between them and Johnny looked up again at the apartment. She'd turned off most of the lights now; the only lit window was the bedroom. He imagined being with her there....

"So what do you need me to do?" Aidan asked, interrupting his reverie.

"I've got nothing, Aidan. No leads. The only thing I can hope for is that the guy trips up. I've been watching Shelby, in case he makes a move on her. That's all I've been able to do. There's no way I can dig up any dirt, not while I'm supposed to be dead. And I realize there's not much you can get, either, since you're not with the department. But I know that someone on the force is taking bribe money, and I have a hunch who."

Aidan knew how good Johnny's hunches were. "Who, John?"

"Nick."

Aidan didn't seem surprised.

"He's been off ever since he joined the FPD. Too eager. Too restless," Johnny explained. "He had complete access to everything on the Morelli case. He could have searched through my desk and figured out the connection to Feeney. Logan told me he recognized the cop who killed Feeney, and I know that Nick was the arresting officer on Logan's last charge. Also, Nick knew I was going to be on the boat that afternoon. I don't think he knew I was meeting with Logan, but maybe he did. And maybe he hoped to get rid of both of us.''

"And now he has access to Shelby. As your partner, he can come and go as he pleases around her without raising suspicion.''

It was that knowledge that had sent a hot wave of fear snaking through him every time he'd seen Nick come anywhere near Shelby over the past week.

"That's where I need you, Aidan. You have to convince Shelby to leave. To get out of Fairfield.''

"That's not going to be possible.''

"Why?''

"*Why?* Why do you think, John? Because she saw you tonight, that's why. Now she's convinced you're alive—which of course you are.''

Johnny looked up in time to see Shelby pass by the window. It was only a brief glimpse, but it was enough for that fist around his heart to squeeze harder.

"Then you have to *un*convince her.''

"John—''

"Her life depends on it, Aidan. Please. I'm begging you.'' He wondered if his ex-partner could hear the desperation he struggled so hard to keep from his voice. "Listen to me, if Nick *did* guess I was meeting with an informant on my boat, if he knew about Logan, then no doubt he's probably wondering why there was only one body recovered from the debris. If he even suspects that I survived that explosion, he'll target Shelby next, use her to get to me. He'll hurt her, Aidan, in order to flush me out.''

"All the more reason to let Shelby know you're alive, John. Let her know the danger she's in.''

"No. I can't risk that. I don't know for certain that Nick suspected my meeting with Logan on the boat. If he *didn't* and if Shelby knows I'm alive, it'll be written all over her face. And Nick will see it. He'll use her to get to me. I can't take that risk. I won't put Shelby's life on the line. No, Aidan, she has to believe beyond a doubt that I'm dead.''

In his peripheral vision Johnny saw Aidan shake his head again. Damn. He should never have gotten out of the car tonight after he'd followed Shelby down to the bar on Broadway. But after she'd been in the bar for twenty minutes and he'd watched several customers come and go, seen the type of crowd Charlie's catered to, he'd gotten nervous. And when finally Shelby had come out, he'd watched from down the street, figuring she'd head straight to her car. Instead, she'd paced the sidewalk, and his uneasiness had mounted. He thought for sure someone was going to come after her; that was the only reason he'd risked stepping into the street when the train thundered past.

It had been a mistake.

Lifting his hands to the back of his neck, he undid the chain from which hung his father's old St. Christopher medal and withdrew it from under his sweatshirt. Then he removed his Police Academy ring. When he reached across and placed them both in Aidan's hand, it was obvious that his friend understood his intentions.

"Convince her, Aidan," he said, wishing there was another way. "Convince her I'm dead."

"Oh, man, no. You can't do this, John. You're killing her. You realize that? Shelby's dying inside. Hell, until tonight, until she saw you, she *wanted* to die. I saw it, John. For this past week I've seen it in her eyes. There's no life left in her. Without you she doesn't *want* to live. And now she finally has hope again. Hope that you're alive, that you'll come back to her. And you want to do *this?*" Aidan held out the medal and the ring as if to hand them back to Johnny.

"I have no choice."

"This is going to kill her."

"You have to get her away from Fairfield. Away from Nick. Convince her, Aidan. You're the only one who can."

This time when Johnny reached for the door handle, Aidan didn't try to stop him. He stepped out into the wet night, closed the door behind him and tapped the roof. Aidan took the signal and started the car. Drawing the old trench coat tighter around him, Johnny watched the Skylark reverse out to the street before he slipped farther into the shadows of the alley. From there he watched Shelby's windows.

SHELBY HADN'T MANAGED to sleep more than three or four hours all night. On the few occasions she had dozed off, she'd been haunted by images of Johnny and the explosion; her waking images were just as disturbing. Over and over she saw Johnny, as if on some ragged piece of film, standing on the other side of the tracks, the train rushing by between them. And over and over she questioned what she'd seen, searching for an explanation. Could Aidan be right? Could it have been a stranger, and could she have so desperately wanted it to be Johnny she'd thought it was him?

But he'd just stood there, as she had, staring between the passing boxcars, not as a stranger would, but as Johnny would. And there had been a feeling—something she couldn't put her finger on.... But there had been a sense, a recognition, pass between them. She was certain. She'd even gone as far as allowing herself to toy with the idea of angels—guardian angels—and ghosts.

The light of morning hadn't offered any answers, but at least it had given her something to do other than toss and turn. She'd been up at dawn, tackling the exhausting chore of cleaning the wrecked apartment. She'd called Doreen to inform her of the break-in and tell her she shouldn't bother coming to work. And then she'd cleaned some more.

By nine the police technicians had shown up to finish their dusting for prints in the studio and the boutique, and by ten Shelby was alone again, and grateful for it. As she sank into the cushions of the sofa and felt every muscle sag with exhaustion, her thoughts returned to Aidan's words last night.

Unconsciously she dropped a hand to her belly as she stared at the small box sitting on the coffee table.

You have to be strong, Aidan had told her. *For yourself. And for the baby. You have to get on with your life.*

She knew he was right—she had to move on. Move

to New York City—that was her plan, wasn't it? But how could she if there was even a chance, however slim, that Johnny was alive?

Shelby drew herself to the edge of the couch and reached for the box as though it might somehow hold an answer. As she cradled it between her palms, she felt nothing. If this was Johnny, if these were his remains, then shouldn't she feel something? Anything?

The buzzer at the front door sounded and Shelby put the box down. She went down to the door and opened it to Aidan.

In the gray light of midmorning, he looked exhausted. It was obvious she hadn't been the only one tossing and turning last night.

"Looks like you could use some coffee," she said as he followed her upstairs.

"Sure could. Thanks."

Shelby filled a mug at the kitchen bar and watched Aidan lower himself into the wing chair next to the sofa. "Did you get any sleep last night?" she asked him.

"Not really. But then, it doesn't look as though you did, either." She saw him glance around the apartment. "Were you up cleaning all night?"

"No, but I got an early start on it."

"So the lab guys were already by this morning?"

"Mm-hmm. There's another mess waiting for me in the studio."

Shelby moved into the living room and handed Aidan his coffee. Then she sat on the corner of the sofa nearest him and reached over to place her hand on his.

He stared at it for a long moment, and she knew he was looking at the engagement ring.

"Aidan, about last night...I'm sorry for yelling. And for kicking you out like I did. That was wrong of me. I know what Johnny meant to you and that this is as hard for you as it is for me."

"Shelby, there's nothing for you to apologize for." He gave her hand a quick squeeze before withdrawing his. "I should be the one apologizing for coming down so hard on you."

"Maybe we should just call a truce, then?"

"Sure."

Her smile, fragile as it was, was enough to give Aidan hope for her. And at the same time John's words flitted through his mind: *Convince her, Aidan. You're the only one who can.* It made him sick to his stomach when he thought about why he was really here this morning.

"So is anything missing?" he asked.

"Not that I've been able to tell."

"Maybe we frightened the burglar off when we walked in."

"Or maybe it wasn't a burglar," she suggested.

"What do you mean?"

"Come on, Aidan. I'm not stupid. No burglar rips a place up like this and doesn't find at least *something* to take. You said yourself last night that whoever it was had a lot of time. Obviously he was looking for something specific."

Aidan had hoped she'd draw this conclusion. He wanted her to realize for herself that staying here wasn't safe. Then maybe, just maybe, if he could convince her to leave, it wouldn't be necessary for him to give her John's ring and the St. Christopher medal.

"Do you have any idea what they might have been looking for?" she asked.

"My guess would be notes. Files or something."

"Johnny's notes, you mean."

Aidan nodded. "Listen, Shelby, I don't want to frighten you, but there's every likelihood that what happened here last night is directly related to Johnny's murder, and I...I don't think it's safe for you to stay."

"What? You think I should go to some hotel? Come on, Aidan. This is my studio, my boutique. My work is here. I can't just up and move to a hotel."

"Actually I wasn't suggesting you move to a hotel, Shelby. I was referring to Fairfield in general. I think it would be a good idea if you left town."

"Left town? No. That's insane. I can't leave."

"Maybe only for a while, Shelby. Until all of this blows over. You could go down to New York City. Stay with Cora. You know she'd love to have you."

"Aidan, I'm not leaving Fairfield. Not now."

"Why *not* now? This is as good a time as any. There's nothing for you here, Shelby. Go to New York—"

"What do you mean, there's nothing for me here? There's Johnny."

Between last night and this morning, he must have gone over it a million times in his head: how he would tell her what John wanted him to and what he could say to convince her. But he had prayed that with the light of day Shelby would have come to believe that what she'd seen last night had been nothing more than her imagination. Obviously his prayers hadn't been answered.

"I can't leave, Aidan. Not if there's a chance Johnny's alive."

"Johnny's dead, Shelby." God, how it hurt to say those words! Knowing the truth and knowing how much his lies would crush her.

Last night in the car he should have told John about the pregnancy. He'd wanted to, battled with the idea for some time, knowing it wasn't his place to tell John and at the same time wondering if knowledge of Shelby's pregnancy would change John's mind. No, Aidan thought now; if he'd told him, John would only have been more adamant that Aidan convince Shelby to leave Fairfield—for her safety *and* the baby's. So he *had* to convince her.

Shelby shook her head, and for a moment he was certain that last night's argument was about to play itself out once again. But Shelby was spent, the fight knocked out of her.

"I saw him, Aidan. I saw him." Her voice was strained.

"Shelby, you saw a figure in the shadows. You were distraught. You were frightened. How can you be certain of what you saw?"

"I'm certain. In fact, I think we should talk to Dan about it. I think the police should start looking for him, because if he's alive, if Johnny's out there…"

Aidan set down his mug and clasped Shelby's hand in his. Again and again he silently cursed John. He saw the pain flicker in those dark eyes of hers, and he wanted to charge out into the back alley and find John.

He wanted to drag him up here and force him to trust Shelby with the truth.

"Aidan, what is it?"

"I know you hope that what you saw last night was real. I know you want to believe John's alive, Shelby. But you can't. You have to get on with your life. You have to think about your baby. It's not safe for you in Fairfield right now, can't you see that?"

She shook her head again and withdrew from him.

She has to believe beyond a doubt that I'm dead.... Convince her, Aidan.

He reached into his shirt pocket and withdrew the ring and the chain with the medal.

"Look, I realize this won't be easy, but I knew you'd want these." He heard her quiet gasp, and when he lifted his gaze, he could see how badly she was shaken. Johnny had known what he was doing, that was for sure; he'd known Shelby would recognize the significance of the two items.

"I...I had them cleaned for you. That's why you didn't get them before," he lied. But there was no need for him to explain or make anything up; Shelby wasn't listening.

She reached out, catching the ring and medal between her fingers, and when he dropped the chain into her palm, Aidan could see how violently her hands were trembling.

Johnny had let her see him last night and had given her hope, and now he was leaving it up to Aidan to crush that all over again.

Shelby stared at the ring and the medal glittering on her palm and said nothing. Eventually her fingers closed around them, and when she brought her tear-filled gaze up to his, Aidan realized he'd never seen Shelby cry before. He felt helpless; there was nothing he could do to ease her pain.

Through her quiet tears, she searched his face as though she still didn't want to believe.

"He's really dead, isn't he, Aidan?" Her ragged whisper seemed wrenched directly from her heart.

He only looked at her, unable to answer or even nod. But when she moved toward him, he opened his arms and held her, rocking her gently while her body shuddered with sobs.

In time they ceased. Aidan brought his hands up to her shoulders and pushed her away gently so that he could see her face.

"You're going to be all right, Shelby." He wiped at the tears on her cheek, waiting for her gaze to lift. "*Everything's* going to be all right."

Nothing could have prepared him for what happened next. First there was only Shelby's dark anguished gaze. And then, in an almost fluid motion, her mouth was on his.

Her lips tasted salty from her tears, and when she pressed herself against his chest, Aidan could feel the heat from her body and the racing of her heart. Her hands slid to the back of his neck, drawing him deeper into her kiss, stealing his breath—and his heart.

But there was no love, no real desire in the kiss. Aidan knew that. Instead, there was only wild desperation. Shelby, too, must have realized that because seconds later she pulled apart from him and leaped up from the sofa.

She turned away, obviously too ashamed to look him in the eye. "God, Aidan, I...I'm so sorry. I shouldn't have—"

"Shelby, it's okay." He stood, as well, and moved behind her, touching her shoulder.

"No, it's not okay. I took advantage of you. It was wrong. I let my emotions... Aidan, I shouldn't have done that to you. You and Kate." She shook her head. "I'm sorry. I should never have put you in that position."

"It's understandable, Shelby."

"But it's not excusable."

"It never happened," he whispered, and gave her shoulder a squeeze.

He saw her hands shake as she lifted them to her face and dried her tears, apparently trying to gather what shattered reserves of strength she might have left. But when she spoke again, her voice was as tremulous as ever.

"I just miss him so much, you know? I can't...I don't know what to do without him."

"I promise you, Shelby, it won't always be like this."

"And, Aidan, I know this'll sound crazy and horribly selfish. It's not like it was his fault, but sometimes...sometimes I really hate Johnny for leaving me. For leaving our child."

CHAPTER ELEVEN

"I TOLD YOU BEFORE, John, I have no idea. You know what Shelby's like. She won't do something until she's good and ready."

Johnny caught a definite edge in Aidan's voice. Aidan had turned in the driver's seat of his car to glare impatiently at him where he was slouched down out of sight in the back. He'd left the old Dodge on the side street catercorner to the boutique, and fifteen minutes ago, when Aidan had parked at the end of the block, he'd been able to sneak into the Skylark.

The patrol car was still parked out front. With the dome light on and the *Fairfield Chronicle* spread across the steering wheel of the black-and-white, the posted officer hadn't even noticed the second occupant in Aidan's car. Now that dusk was falling, there was even less chance of anyone spotting Johnny.

"So she didn't agree to leave," Johnny said, following his ex-partner's gaze to the lit windows of Shelby's apartment. "Damn."

"No, but she didn't say she wouldn't."

"Then I'll stay until she does."

"Sure." Aidan's voice was flat, detached almost, as he stared out the windshield. Yes, there was definitely something bothering his friend, Johnny thought.

"How did Shelby take it when you gave her the ring?"

"What do *you* think?"

"Okay, Aidan. I give. What's wrong?"

"I honestly have to spell it out for you?"

"Yes. Please."

"*This*, John!" Aidan waved his hand toward the boutique and then turned again to glare at Johnny. "This is wrong. All of it. You lying to Shelby, hiding from her. And then making *me* lie to her. It made me *sick* to give her your ring. Do you have any idea how upsetting that was for her?"

"I'm sorry, Aidan. It had to be done."

"Yeah, well, I don't know about you, partner, but I'm not sure how much longer I can keep up the lies."

"You think it's easy for me?"

But Aidan didn't answer that. Both of them looked at the boutique as Shelby passed by one of the lit windows. Johnny noticed she had a box for packing in her arms, and again he wished that Aidan had been able to convey more urgency when he'd talked to her about leaving Fairfield. She should have left today. Better yet, she should have left a week ago.

The day after the explosion, he'd considered going to Shelby, convincing her to leave, to stay with Cora. But then he'd thought about the bomb, Morelli's murder, Feeney's murder. Whoever was behind all of these was intent on covering his tracks carefully. They wouldn't leave any stone unturned. If they suspected Shelby knew something, they'd come after her to New York City, anyway, maybe only to ask questions, but that was all it would take. They'd be able to tell by her reaction or by her expression that he was alive. And then, for sure, they'd use her to flush him out. After that...they'd both be killed.

He knew Shelby was going through hell believing he was dead. But ultimately it was a small price to pay for her life.

So he'd stayed hidden for the past week and watched over her. He'd been there, always. He'd seen her leave with Aidan for the memorial service, and then he'd seen her return. She'd worn the black dress she'd designed specifically for the banquet they'd gone to seven months ago when he'd been awarded with a commendation. They hadn't stayed long at the banquet, sneaking out early and going home. Johnny remembered how he'd taken that black dress off Shelby that night and remembered the passionate love they'd made once it had fallen to the floor. Never had he imagined Shelby wearing that same dress to mourn his death.

Seeing her now, moving by a window, Johnny could almost imagine her touch, her voice, her smell. God, how he longed for those things—her laughter, her smile. And last night, when he'd been so close to her, when he'd held her gaze, he'd wanted nothing more than to call out her name, to run to her and take her into his arms.

But instead, he'd left her standing in the middle of that dark wet street, calling his name. He'd had to. It was the only way he could uncover the corruption on the force and find out who had tried to kill him. And it was the only way he knew of to keep her safe.

"You know something, John?"

"What?"

Aidan didn't take his eyes off the apartment. "You don't deserve Shelby. What you're putting her through—no one should have to go through that."

Johnny was still picturing Shelby as he'd seen her last night. Maybe Aidan was right. Maybe he *didn't* deserve her.

"She'll never forgive you," Aidan said. "You realize that? Once this is all over she's never going to forgive you for what you've done."

"That's a chance I'm going to have to take, Aidan. Because right now, Shelby's forgiveness isn't what's important. Her safety is."

Johnny studied Aidan's profile for a moment, wondering if his ex-partner could understand, if *anyone* could understand, his love for Shelby—a love so great he would risk everything, even losing her love, to ensure she remained unharmed.

"So what's your next move, then?" Aidan asked.

"I'm sticking with Shelby. I don't trust her life in the hands of some underpaid rookie." He nodded to the patrol car. "I need you to talk to a couple of guys for me, Aidan. I'd do it myself, but if wind of it gets around and anyone even suspects I'm alive, they'll go right for Shelby." He handed Aidan a piece of paper with two names and addresses on it. "These guys might know something. Logan gave me their names, said they were taking heat from someone on the force. It's the closest thing I've got to a lead."

Aidan stuffed the slip of paper into his shirt pocket. "What else?"

"After that, I don't know. Other than to keep an

eye on Nick. See where he goes, who he talks to and—"

Johnny swallowed his words the second he saw Nick's black Mustang turn onto Jefferson Street and stop in front of the boutique. A hot surge of rage licked through him as Nick climbed out of the sports car.

"What the hell's *he* doing here?"

"He's your partner, John. He's probably checking on Shelby. See how she's doing after the break-in."

"I don't like this."

"Hang on. Let's just see what he does. And for God's sake, stay low."

Johnny slouched down farther.

"He won't try anything as long as the radio car's out front."

But even as Aidan said this, they watched Nick lean into the window of the black-and-white and speak to the officer. When Nick stood back from the car, Johnny expected the officer to drive off. If Nick was up to something, he'd at least get rid of the patrol car.

But the officer returned to his paper. The car didn't move.

Nick started for the front door of the boutique, pausing to cast a glance down the street.

"Do you think he recognizes your car?" Johnny asked.

"I doubt it."

Nick stepped up to the storefront and rang the buzzer. In moments the light mounted overhead came on and Shelby opened the door.

Even at a distance Johnny could see the wind ruffle

her thick hair and tug at the thin material of her pant-suit, hinting at the painfully familiar curves beneath. He recalled how easily that same outfit had slid from her shoulders that last night they were together, and how ravenous their union had been. He'd survived this past week on those memories alone. He remembered how different their lovemaking had been that night. It had been frantic, almost savage, as if it might have been their last time in each other's arms....

In the light from the overhead lamp, he recognized Shelby's forced smile as she greeted Nick. How she braced herself against the doorjamb, obviously reluctant to allow him inside.

And then, as though she'd subconsciously heard Johnny's inner voice warning her, Shelby lifted her gaze. She looked down the street directly at Aidan's car, and Johnny thought his heart might stop. He knew it was too dark and the distance too great; she couldn't possibly see him. Yet he felt as though Shelby's eyes gazed directly into his.

"I'M SORRY I haven't been by sooner, Shelby." Nick didn't seem put out by her failure to invite him in, but twice he'd peered over her shoulder into the boutique as though he suspected she was entertaining someone. "I didn't hear about the break-in until I came on shift this morning, and then we got swamped with calls. How are you doing?"

Shelby only nodded and managed another brief smile. She hoped the light over the door wasn't bright enough to reveal that she'd been crying.

"The captain said that whoever it was did a real

number on your place. I thought maybe you could use a hand cleaning up.''

"I've got things under control. But thanks, Nick.''

Again he squinted into the dark boutique behind her.

"I, um…I stopped by the lab before I left the precinct today. You know they didn't come up with any prints.''

"I heard. Dan called a while ago to let me know.''

"The captain says nothing was taken.''

"No, not that I can tell.''

"And you still haven't found any notes or anything of John's?''

"No.''

"Well, just checking. You know we're trying every angle on this thing.''

"I know.''

"It's just that…if there's anything John may have had here that might help us with this case—''

"I'd call you, Nick.'' Although now Shelby began to wonder if she would. It could have been because she was tired, but there was something about Nick that troubled her. It wasn't anything she could put her finger on, but he seemed so *eager*.

"Are those John's?''

Shelby was momentarily confused by Nick's question until she realized he was eyeing Johnny's ring that hung from the chain around her neck, along with the St. Christopher medal.

"Yes,'' she answered quietly, curling her fingers around them.

Nick stared at her hand for a moment as though

hoping to catch a glimpse of the ring once again, but when she didn't uncurl her fingers, he eventually nodded and said, "All right, then, I guess I'll leave you. I don't want to keep you from your work. I'll talk to you later, Shelby."

She waited in the doorway, watching him climb into his Mustang and start up the engine. When his taillights disappeared, she looked toward Aidan's car again. He'd been out there for a good thirty minutes, and she had half a mind to walk down the street and tell him to go home. But she doubted he'd stay long; he hadn't last night—no doubt because of the patrol car. The officer in the black-and-white gave her a quick wave, which she returned before closing the door.

After she'd locked up, Aidan still preyed on her mind. She wondered if she should go out and invite him in for a drink. But finally she decided not to. Not after this morning, not after she'd kissed him. Even now she wasn't entirely certain where that urge had come from; her only excuse was grief. Still, what she'd done was unforgivable. No apology was enough to make up for the awkward position she'd put Aidan in.

But that wasn't the only reason she didn't want Aidan here tonight. She was tired. She'd spent the day packing, preparing for the eventuality of her move to New York City. She had no doubt now that her future lay there. There was nothing for her in Fairfield. And nothing for their child. It was time to leave.

She would call Cora in the morning and tell her sister to expect her by the end of the week. She'd drive

down to New York City and look at that apartment.
They could spend a couple of days going over details
and maybe even check out a few retail spaces for the
new boutique. She would call her New York contacts,
make arrangements with distributors, have lunch meetings and see what kind of help was available. She
could only hope that Doreen would consider making
the move with her.

In the bedroom Shelby shoved a cardboard box under the bed. She couldn't pack any more tonight. It
had been only a halfhearted attempt, anyway, but at
least it was a start. She would hire movers to take care
of the rest of the apartment, but Johnny's things...she
needed to pack those herself.

She climbed into bed, curling herself into the tangle
of sheets and the duvet, and drew Johnny's pillow into
her arms. All lingering traces of his scent were gone.
She hugged the pillow more tightly and stared at his
photo on the nightstand.

Maybe it sounded corny, but from the moment
she'd first seen that smile and looked into those eyes,
she'd felt as if she'd come home after a long journey,
as if she'd at last found the one thing she'd searched
for all her life. And she hadn't even been searching.
But now that she'd found him, he'd been snatched
cruelly away.

All that was left of him was their child. And their
child would be her life now, she resolved. Johnny's
child. She recalled her words the other night, when
she'd told Aidan she was glad this child would never
have to go through the pain of losing Johnny. The pain
she was going through now.

She closed her eyes. In her heart of hearts she *knew* that Johnny would never have quit the force and there would always have been the worry. The waiting, the wondering. Never knowing if the next phone call would be the one...

Exhaustion swept through her, both physical and emotional, and with images of Johnny flitting through her head, she drifted off.

She wasn't certain how long she slept, but when the phone woke her, the bedroom was dark. She groped for the bedside lamp, squinting at the warm yellow light, and reached for the receiver.

She cleared her throat. "Hello?"

"Ms. Beaumont?"

Instantly she recognized the man's voice on the other end of the line. She sat bolt upright, her heart racing.

"Why didn't you show up last night?" she demanded, glancing at the alarm clock. She'd only been asleep an hour. "I waited in the bar. I was alone, like you asked, and you didn't show."

"It wasn't safe."

"Please, can't you give me your information over the phone?"

"No."

"Is it money you want? Is that it?" Shelby got off the bed and carried the phone to the window. In the dark street below there was only the black-and-white patrol car. No sign of Aidan. "Look, I can get you money, if that's what it is."

"It would help. But I'm leaving town, so it's gotta be tonight."

"What kind of information do you have?"

"I told you, I'm not getting into this over the phone. Either you meet me or you don't. I'm doing this as one last favor for John, and then I'm outta here."

"Okay, okay. Where?"

"Down at the docks."

"The docks? But why there?"

"'Cause it's quiet down there. Safe."

Shelby worried her bottom lip between her teeth. She didn't like this. The docks would be practically deserted at this time of night. She'd be a fool to go there to meet someone she didn't know. And what if Aidan was right about the first call, that it hadn't simply been a way to get her out of the apartment?

"Not the docks," she said at last. "Someplace with a few people around, or the deal's off."

He grunted a laugh. "The way I see it, *I'm* the one doing the favors here. I don't think it's up to you to call the shots."

"*Do* you want money?"

"I don't need it that bad."

"So what's it worth to you to meet me at Charlie's?"

"You couldn't pay me enough. Look, it's the docks or nothing. A half hour and then I'm outta here for good."

Shelby moved back to the nightstand, and when she did, she looked at Johnny's photo again. She had to do this. Had to take the risk. For Johnny. It was her last chance to get information on his killer—if there *was* information.

"Okay," the caller barked into the phone as she

hesitated. "Let's just forget about it. Forget I ever called."

"No, wait! Wait." She heard a clattering sound and for a sickening moment thought he'd hung up. And then she heard his breathing. "The docks are fine," she said at last. "I'll meet you at the docks. Thirty minutes. Where will I find you?"

CHAPTER TWELVE

THE RAIN HAD STARTED only moments after Nick left the front step of the boutique and gotten into his car. Aidan hadn't needed any prompting. He'd started the Skylark and popped it into drive almost before Johnny had had a chance to get out the back door and duck into the side street.

"I'm going to see where he goes," Aidan had said, and as Johnny watched the taillights of the Skylark disappear around the same corner Nick's Mustang had, he'd felt a familiar rush, remembering the old days. They'd made a good team, he and Aidan. All those years it was as if they could read each other's mind.

He missed that, Johnny thought now as he looked through the rain-blurred windshield of the Dodge to Shelby's windows. He missed sharing an unmarked car with Aidan, working the streets with him, but mostly he missed the thrill of solving a case with him. And now, after everything that had happened, after everything he'd put Shelby through, he was starting to wish he'd taken Aidan up on his offer of partnership in O'Neill Investigations. If only he'd been able to put his selfish goals aside long enough to realize that Shelby was far more important to him than his career as a cop, he might have quit before any of this had happened.

He continued to stare at Shelby's windows. For almost an hour there was no movement, and then the bedroom light came on and he saw her come to the window. Despite the dark and the rain, he was pretty sure she was on the phone.

After that, her light went out and all seemed quiet again. Johnny shifted in his seat, trying to stretch his legs. He scratched at the day's growth of stubble along his chin. The night before, when it was apparent Shelby was in bed and the patrol car was stationed plainly out front, he'd dared to slip away for a couple of hours. There hadn't been much likelihood that whoever had broken into the apartment would make a second move the same night, so he'd driven to Aidan's cabin, showered, shaved and changed, and sped right back.

He wouldn't be doing anything of the sort tonight, not after seeing Nick nosing around. He wondered if he had any food left in the back seat of the Dodge and was about to check when the door of the boutique swung open.

Johnny sat up, already reaching for the keys in the ignition when he saw Shelby step out. Her hair was pulled into a ponytail that barely cleared the turned-up collar of her trench coat, and when the edges of the coat blew back in a sudden gust of wind, he noticed she hadn't changed her outfit. Dread trickled down his spine. It appeared she was in a real hurry to get somewhere.

"Come on, Shelby," he whispered as he watched

her lock the boutique door. "Tell the patrol where you're going. Let him know. Come on, Shel."

But she didn't. Instead, she gave the officer little more than a glance before she sprinted through the rain to her Lexus. Johnny saw the officer roll down his window and shout something, most likely asking her what she was up to, but Shelby pretended not to hear. She was clearly flustered, even dropped her keys as she got into her car, and in the dim illumination of the dome light, he could see her struggle with the seat belt. In seconds her car's headlights gleamed through the rain.

Swiftly Johnny ducked below the steering wheel and at the same time switched on the Dodge's ignition. Only after the Lexus accelerated down the street past the nose of his car, did he dare sit up again. The rookie in the patrol car cranked up his window, then made a sharp U-turn and followed Shelby.

Johnny left his headlights off for the first few blocks, flipping them on only once the three-car convoy had left Jefferson Street and was swept up in the southbound traffic. Using what few vehicles there were as cover, Johnny managed to keep up with the patrol car, but he knew he couldn't rely on the officer's ability to keep up with Shelby. He had to tail her himself. Her driving was erratic, weaving in and out of lanes, passing slower-moving traffic and gunning the engine through every amber light. It was clear that no matter how closely the black-and-white rode her tail, she intended to lose the officer. And if anyone could do it, Shelby could.

No wonder Aidan hadn't been able to convince her

to leave Fairfield. She was too damned headstrong. Johnny loved her for that—loved her tenacity and her fearlessness. But right now that stubborn bravery of hers was going to get her in trouble—or worse, get her killed.

"What are you doing, Shel? Where are you going?" Johnny flipped his wipers on high and used the back of his hand to wipe away the fog accumulating on the inside of the windshield.

Four cars ahead, at the front of the left lane, the Lexus idled at a red light. If he didn't know Shelby as well as he did, Johnny wouldn't have been prepared for her next tactic. Before the light had even switched to green, the Lexus lurched forward and over to the right lane, speeding west. If the rookie behind the wheel of the patrol car hadn't flashed his lights once to stop traffic, neither he nor Johnny would have managed the turn after her.

Johnny took the intersection more slowly, edging the beat-up Dodge in front of another right-turning vehicle, whose driver blared his horn impatiently. Heading west now, Johnny held back as far as he dared while still keeping the taillights of the Lexus within view. She could lose the patrol car—Johnny didn't care about that. But if she lost *him*... No, he wouldn't even consider that possibility.

"Dammit, Shelby." His grip tightened on the steering wheel, and he leaned forward to peer through the downpour. "What the hell are you up to?"

THE PATROL-CAR OFFICER was certainly dogged, Shelby had to give him that. She squinted against the glare of headlights in her rearview mirror. Even when she'd cut across the intersection a few blocks back, she hadn't managed to lose him. One more stunt like that and he'd probably pull her over. In fact, she was surprised he hadn't done so already. She'd have to make her next maneuver count, she thought, tucking a loose strand of hair behind her ear.

The Lexus dragged severely to the right as the tires plowed through a gutter filled with rainwater. Shelby corrected the steering, her hands tensing around the wheel. Again she looked in her rearview. The officer hadn't eased up at all.

She watched the street signs. Two more blocks and she'd be able to lose the patrol car, she was certain. Dark storefronts and vacant buildings slipped past her. The headlights of an approaching car fragmented across her rain-covered windshield, and then...the traffic light she'd been looking for. Taking one last glance at the patrol car in her rearview, Shelby laid her foot on the gas and gunned the engine. The light turned from green to amber, then red as she barreled the Lexus through the intersection and into the middle of the opposing traffic.

She cranked the wheel sharply to the left, barely missing a southbound car, and felt her own car threaten to slide out of control. Its tail skimmed across the slick pavement, and then shuddered as the tires found purchase again. Horns blasted, and when she glanced into her rearview she saw only a jumble of lights.

Frantically she searched for the alleyway she knew was there, and when she saw its dark narrow entrance, the first wave of relief swept through her. The second wave of relief came after she'd swung the car in through the opening, killed the ignition and the lights, and locked the doors. Twisting around in her seat, she peered through the fogged-up back window. Seconds later she saw the patrol car speed past, a blur of black and white.

She let out a long breath and turned in her seat again. She checked her watch: eight-forty-five. She would wait one minute, no more. She couldn't be late, but she also couldn't risk leaving her hideout too soon in case the patrol looped back.

She had Johnny to thank for this one, she thought, staring out the streaked windshield into the looming shadows. This wasn't her first time here in this dark alleyway sitting in a car. Almost a year ago she'd been in the very same place, only Johnny had been driving.

It had been on their third or fourth date. They'd been headed for the waterfront when she'd noticed Johnny checking the rearview mirror and seen the ominous expression on his face. She'd asked him what was wrong, but he'd remained silent. Seconds after she'd turned in her seat and seen the car tailing them, Johnny had sped through the same intersection Shelby had only moments ago. He'd parked in the same alley, turned off the engine and the lights, and they'd both watched through the back window as their tail had sped past the entrance to the alley.

He'd suggested it was nothing other than his suspicious nature and tried to convince her that the car had probably not been following them. Then he'd leaned over to kiss her, to ease the concern he no doubt had seen there. But Shelby had known better. And from that night on she'd been distinctly aware of the danger inherent in Johnny's line of work, the risks and the threats.

Shelby lifted a hand to wipe a stray tear from her cheek. Sitting here in this same alley, she remembered the feel of that kiss, the taste of his lips, as he'd tried to quell her apprehension. And the memory gave her the determination she needed now to start the Lexus and head back out to the street. She would do this for Johnny, for the love they'd shared. And when this night was over, she would give Aidan whatever information she got from her anonymous caller and leave Fairfield and all of its painful memories forever.

GRAVEL GROUND beneath the tires of the Lexus as Shelby pulled up to the storage house at the end of Pier Twenty-seven and parked. She gazed through the windshield at the crude sign over the wide loading doors. Two of the three bulbs mounted above the sign were burned out, and she'd almost missed the building because of it.

She'd seen no other cars near the pier. Either her caller hadn't arrived yet or he'd parked behind the storage warehouse out of sight and was already waiting inside.

Shelby drew a deep breath. She didn't like this. Even in the relative safety of her locked car, she felt her stomach twist into a tight knot of nerves. Again she thought of Johnny, and again his memory gave her the strength she needed. She took her purse from the passenger seat and opened it. The cold metal of the

Glock semiautomatic against her palm was only a slight reassurance, but at least it was something.

The rain had tapered off to a cold drizzle by the time she stepped out of the car. Pulling her coat more snugly around her, she breathed in the damp foggy lakeside air, the smell reminding her of Johnny, of the explosion. She struggled to keep those images from her mind. She couldn't give in to either fear or grief right now. She needed to be strong.

Across the bay she could hear the blast of a horn. The clang of buoy bells echoed between the low warehouses along the wharf like an eerie orchestra of chimes, keeping rhythm with the gentle slapping of waves against the pier. Shelby glanced back over her shoulder. The pier was empty.

I wish you were here, Johnny, she said silently, and promptly realized how ridiculous the thought was. If Johnny weren't dead, she'd have no reason to be here in the first place. She'd be safe at home or, more likely, safe in bed with Johnny.

Checking the gun in her purse a second time, she reached for the steel handle of the storage building's side door half expecting—half hoping—it would be locked. It wasn't. The door swung freely open, and taking one last look down the empty pier, Shelby stepped inside.

The silver luminescence of the night behind her spilled through the doorway. Long fingers of pallid light reached across the floor ahead of her and into the inky blackness. A gust of wind slammed shut the door, and Shelby gasped at the sudden darkness. She waited for her eyes to adjust, but the storehouse was a labyrinth of shadows and phantom shapes. Down the wide center aisle, between hulking outlines of boats, several thin columns of light from the wharf lamps outside filtered in through dingy windows.

Shelby walked toward the shafts of light, searching the shadows for any possible movement, straining to hear the slightest indication of another person in the building with her. The structure creaked and groaned under the burden of the wind outside. The only other sound was the hollow echo of her low heels on the cement floor.

It was pointless to call out; if he was waiting for her somewhere in all this darkness, he already knew she'd arrived. And with each step she took, she became more and more certain that he *was* here, watching her. The knot of fear in her stomach tightened. She slipped her hand into her purse again, this time gripping the semiautomatic and—

Shelby didn't see her attacker. He burst from her left, slightly behind her, out of the shadow of a boat. There was no time to draw the gun from her purse and no time to slip free before a muscled arm locked around her throat and dragged her back against the solidness of his body. And when she struggled, his arm became more vicelike, threatening to cut off her air completely.

With one hand she clutched at the arm. With her other she fumbled for her purse, desperately searching for the Glock. For one hope-filled moment her fingers brushed the cold steel. But before she could grasp the gun, the purse was torn from her and cast to the floor. She thought she heard the gun clatter out, then skitter across the cement as if kicked, but there was no way of seeing where.

Frantically gulping air, Shelby struggled to free herself. She twisted, bucking against her assailant and flailing for a hold on anything. She tore at his clothes, wrestling his superior strength even as the arm around her throat constricted further until she thought she might black out.

Johnny's face flashed before her mind's eye. Only a couple of days ago she'd believed that life without Johnny wasn't worth living. And yet now she was fighting for her life—and fighting for her child's life.

It was only when she felt the smooth muzzle of a gun press coldly against her temple that she surrendered. Her body slackened, and in response, her assailant's arm eased by a degree. But it was enough. Delicious air rushed into her lungs.

"What do you want from me?" Her words came out in a painful rasp.

"Where is he?" It could have been the same voice she'd heard over the phone, but she wasn't certain.

"Where is who?"

She craned her neck, trying to glimpse her assailant's face, but to no avail.

"Where is he?" her attacker demanded again, pushing the gun more firmly against her temple.

"I don't know who you're talking about!"

"Stop playing games. You can't protect him. Just tell me where he is or—"

"*Who?* I've no idea who—"

A gunshot exploded through the building. As the echoes of the blast ricocheted into the darkness, she realized it hadn't been her assailant's gun that had discharged.

If the door to the storehouse had been opened during her struggle, she hadn't heard it. But obviously a third party was in the building with them. Still pinned in her attacker's throat lock, she peered down the cavernous passageway. She thought she saw a shadow move fleetingly, and then she heard his voice—steady and clear.

"Police. Drop your weapon."

The next few seconds were a blur. Shelby expected her assailant to return fire, but instead, he hurled her to the floor. Skinning her hands on the cement, she frantically scrambled away. She ducked behind the keel of a boat, gasping for air, and when she looked behind her, her attacker was no longer in sight. She could hear the sound of running feet, then a pause, then more running. Twice she thought she saw movement deep in the shadows between the looming outlines of boats and packing crates.

She crawled across the floor, searching for the Glock. She found it just as a door slammed shut on a far wall. There were more rapid footfalls, then the door again. She flinched at the sound of gunshots.

Her fingers wrapped around her own weapon and she gave a small whimper of relief, then scurried back to the cover of the boat. Crouching beneath its hull, she breathed deeply in and out, trying to steady herself.

Beyond the walls of the building, she now heard the roar of a car starting up, and then gravel flying under spinning tires. Now was her chance to leave. Run from the building, jump into her own car and get the hell out of here.

Taking one last calming breath, she abandoned her cover and stepped into the silent main passageway. Her legs were shaking and her nerves were frayed. And when she thought she heard a footfall behind her, she froze.

Silence again. And then another footfall.

Shelby whirled, both hands gripping the semiautomatic. She could see nothing.

"Don't come any closer," she demanded.

But whoever it was, concealed by shadow, continued his approach.

Shelby's finger found the curve of the trigger. Her elbows and wrists locked; her shoulders ached from the strain. And finally, about twenty feet beyond the barrel of the semiautomatic, Shelby saw the figure—a tall man in a long coat. Silhouetted by a shaft of dingy light, he took another step closer.

"I said stop! I swear, I'll shoot." Her arms shook and she wondered if she'd be able to do as she threatened. Her heart was pounding in her ears, and her palms were damp. She took a long even breath, then released it, just like Johnny had taught her. Breathe in, release, breathe in...

And that was when she saw the faint glint of the gun in *his* hand, hanging at his side.

"I swear," she said, "if you don't stop right there, so help me—"

CHAPTER THIRTEEN

"IT'S ALL RIGHT, Shelby." The voice, low and soft, slipped gently through the darkness, but Shelby took no comfort in it. He knew her name.

"Who are you?"

"Shelby—"

"Who *are* you?"

"It's all right, Shel. Just put the gun down."

Johnny's voice. And yet...it couldn't be. It wasn't possible!

"Shel."

"Show yourself, dammit!" She fought to control the tremor in her voice, her hands tightening around the Glock. "Show yourself, or I swear I'll—"

"It's me, Shel."

He stepped from the shadows into a shimmering column of light. It pooled around him, glistening off his wet hair and accenting the chiseled features she knew so well.

"Johnny?"

Shelby stopped breathing. She lowered her gun, her grip instantly slack. She was shaking even before he closed the gap between them and stood in front of her.

She shook her head, still disbelieving. It couldn't be true. After everything she'd gone through, it wasn't possible that he was standing here...now...just like that.

She was looking at a ghost. There was no other explanation.

She was vaguely aware of him reaching down and sliding the semiautomatic from her grasp. And when she felt his hand brush hers, she could no longer suppress the sob that hung in her throat.

"Is it...really you?" she managed.

He only nodded.

"It's really... Oh, my God...you're real?" Her hand trembled as she lifted it, reaching toward the vision before her. And for a moment she didn't *want* to touch him, afraid that he *was* an apparition, that she would reach out and find only empty space, and then he would be gone forever.

But when at last she did touch him, when her fingers fluttered against his cheek, she felt his warmth, his life, beneath her palm.

"Johnny. Oh, my God, Johnny."

She said his name again and again, as if doing so would convince her he was real. She searched his face, met that dark all-consuming gaze she'd longed to look into ever since the explosion. She caressed every angle of his face, tracing the lines she knew so well.

Silently he lifted his hand to lay it over hers against his cheek.

"So I'm not imagining this?" she asked. With her other hand she touched his mouth, tracing the curve of the smile that struggled to his lips.

He shook his head. "I'm here, love."

The sound of his voice was enough to tear another

cry from her throat. "Oh, my God!" And then she was in his arms. Just as she'd prayed for all those days and nights of grief. She clung to his solidness, his familiarity, his reality, afraid that if she let him go again he would vanish like some figment of her desperate imagination.

But he wasn't. He was here with her now. He'd stepped out of the shadows as though nothing of the past week and a half had even happened.

Eventually, though, Shelby took a step back, looked once more into his eyes and murmured, "You're alive."

"Yes, I am."

"You son of a bitch!" Shelby cursed, and swung at him with all the hurt and rage in her heart. Her hand met his jaw with such force that her palm came away stinging. And still, it wasn't enough.

"Shel—"

"How *could* you? How…?" She was shaking, but now it was from anger.

She watched lines of distress crease his forehead and a look of abject apology soften his face. But it didn't come close to extinguishing the pain she'd suffered.

She raised her hand a second time.

JOHNNY'S JAW THROBBED from Shelby's first blow. He was prepared for the next one and caught her wrist in midswing, gripping it tightly. There was a fury in her eyes he'd never imagined possible from the Shelby he knew and loved. Nonetheless it was a fury he should have expected.

She tried to tear her wrist free of his grasp, but Johnny held fast.

"Shelby, listen to me." He pulled her to him, hoping to hold her and ease the pain he saw swimming in those wide dark eyes. He wanted to take her in his arms as he'd yearned to for the past week and a half, to clutch her to him and end her grief.

But she only fought harder.

"Listen to me—"

"I don't want to hear anything you have to say!" she said, finally freeing her wrist.

He watched in amazement as, despite her wild anger, a tear slipped down her cheek. But he didn't dare reach out to wipe it away.

He knew Shelby, and he knew she needed space.

"I'm sorry," he said.

"Sorry? You're *sorry?*"

"Shelby, please—"

"How could you do this, John? How could you let me...all this time...and you...you just let me believe you were dead?"

"I can explain, Shel. Please. I—"

"No, John." She held up her hands and took another step away from him. "There's nothing to explain. I think I know exactly what's going on here."

"No, you don't, Shelby. You have *no* idea what this is about. Just hear me out, that's all I ask. You owe me at least that much." But the second he said it, Johnny knew he'd made a grave error in his choice of words.

"*Owe* you? Do you honestly think that after all this I somehow owe you something?"

"Shelby, no. That's not what I meant." He reached for her again, but caught only a handful of her coat as she jerked back from him.

"What do you want from me, John?"

"I love you, Shel."

"Damn you." Her voice was low, intense. Any tremor that had been there before was gone. "Damn you, John Spencer."

He saw it coming, but didn't try to stop her. When her hand met his cheek, the blow was far harder than the first one. But Johnny didn't even flinch. He deserved it—and a hell of a lot more.

In seconds she'd turned and was marching through the dark storage house to the front doors.

"Shelby, wait."

She ignored him. The tap of her heels echoed through the building, and in each shaft of light she passed through, Johnny could see how her fury stiffened her stride.

"Wait!" He ran after her. "You can't go, Shel."

"Watch me," she shouted over her shoulder.

"Shelby, for crying out loud." He caught her arm and spun her around. She wrenched her arm free and stood there, staring at him.

"You can't just leave," he said.

"No?"

"It's not safe."

She was silent for a moment, appearing to weigh her options. And then she spun around again, heading for the door.

"He might come back, Shelby." Johnny followed

her. "Whoever it was, he might be waiting for you. Or he could be at the apartment."

Shelby swung open the door and stepped outside. Rain lashed at her clothes and dragged at her already ragged ponytail. She seemed completely oblivious to the elements.

"Look, Johnny—" she turned to face him again, raising her voice over the wind and rain, and he could see the fine line she was walking between anger and anguish "—I think I can take care of myself. I have for the past ten days."

"Right, Shel," he said. They were standing just inches apart. "Like you took care of yourself tonight? Racing out here on your own, without Aidan, without backup, to meet someone in the middle of the night? You could have been killed!"

"Oh, yeah? Well, it's too bad I wasn't!"

"What's that supposed to mean?"

"Because then maybe *you'd* get to go through the same hell I have ever since that explosion, Johnny!" It wasn't just the wind she was shouting over now; it was the torment he'd made her suffer. Johnny heard it loud and clear.

He tried to reach for her again, and again she twisted away. It had become a dance.

"Shelby—"

"No!" The rain streamed down her face, and she wiped the water from her eyes with an angry motion. "You always have to be such a goddamn hero, don't you, Johnny? John Spencer, Super Cop. The police force before everything else, isn't that it?"

"That's not what this is about, Shel. You don't know—"

"Yes! I *do* know! I know that whatever damned case it is you're working on is far more important than anything or anyone else in your life. Everything is expendable for the sake of the case, isn't that right, John?"

"No! That's not right!" He grabbed Shelby by the shoulders, his fingers digging hard into the wet trench coat so that she couldn't pull away. "You're wrong, Shelby. You are *so* wrong."

He couldn't tell if it was the physical contact or the fact that she actually allowed herself a long-enough look into his eyes then, but suddenly Johnny could feel her resolve begin to crumble. When she brushed aside the strands of hair that clung wetly to her face, he could see her hand shake. And then he saw her bite her lower lip. Biting back her tears.

"Come on," he said softly, taking her hand in his. "We can't stay here. It's not safe."

THE LIGHTS OF FAIRFIELD had slipped behind them into the night more than half an hour before. Johnny checked the rearview mirror again. There was only blackness. If they had been followed from the waterfront, he'd managed to lose the tail before he and Shelby had left the city limits.

Back at the pier Johnny had emptied the Dodge of all his personal belongings, anything that might link Aidan's car to him, and locked up. He'd ushered Shelby to the passenger side of her Lexus, and she'd complied without argument. But now, after forty minutes of silence, Johnny wished she would say something.

He looked across at her. In the meager light from the dash, the lines of stress on her face were painfully evident. She stared straight ahead, seeming mesmerized by the winding road illuminated in the car's high beams.

For the first few minutes of the drive Johnny knew she'd sneaked frequent glances of him, perhaps still not believing. But now it had been some time since she'd looked at him. She seemed to have fallen into her own dark reflections, and he could only guess at what rolled through her head as they sped through the night.

She'll never forgive you, Aidan had warned him. Johnny had recognized the insight behind his friend's words, and now, enduring Shelby's relentless silence, he worried that Aidan's warning held far more truth than his heart could bear.

What if she couldn't find it in her soul to forgive him? What then? Johnny had thought he'd been prepared for that. He'd convinced himself that Shelby's forgiveness was secondary to her safety. But now, sitting only inches away from her in the confines of the Lexus, the thought of never touching her again was unbearable.

Lowering his hand from the steering wheel, Johnny reached over and laid it over hers, where it rested on her lap. He half expected her to pull away, to retreat again. Instead, she allowed him to put their entwined hands on *his* lap, and when she squeezed his fingers, Johnny felt his heart hitch. He looked over at her again and saw her take a deep breath, but she didn't return his gaze.

It would take time, he told himself, but there was hope. And he counted himself lucky to have at least that.

The thought of how close he'd come to losing her tonight sent a cold shudder through him. If he hadn't recognized her tactic at that last intersection before she'd eluded the patrol car, she might be dead now. But as soon as he'd seen her accelerate through the red light at Westminster and Baker, he'd known what she was up to.

He'd slowed the Dodge as he passed the entrance to the side alley, and he'd spotted the tail end of the Lexus and the faint plume of exhaust lingering in the air behind it. Halfway up the street he'd turned his car around and parked at the curb. As he waited for her, he'd admired Shelby's spunk and ingenuity. But at the same time he knew it was that very spunk that could have easily gotten her killed. Now that he had her safe, he vowed she'd never be out of his reach again.

Johnny steered the car off the main road onto the narrow tree-lined drive that led to Aidan's single-level log cabin. The place wasn't anything fancy, but it was certainly inviting. Definitely more inviting than it had been all week, Johnny thought. But that was because Shelby was with him.

He'd left the porch light on, and when he parked by the front steps, Shelby's face was illuminated. He studied her profile as she glanced from the cabin to their entwined hands. She looked exhausted. He couldn't recall if he'd ever seen her look so drawn. There was no life in her eyes, no spark.

"Shelby?"

She closed her eyes and didn't respond.

"Come on, Shel." He gave her hand a gentle squeeze. "Let's go inside. We'll talk."

He wanted to lean over and kiss her, just as he'd so often imagined kissing her for the past week and a half. But he didn't dare.

"Please, Shel?"

She nodded silently and reached for the door handle.

Johnny circled the car to join her. The rain had stopped, and the wind was only a whisper in the uppermost branches of the trees. They could have been a million miles away from the city, he thought as he stood beside Shelby, a million miles away from everything that had happened.

He followed her gaze to the small lake. Its glassy surface reflected the three-quarter moon that had struggled through the scattering clouds. Still, she said nothing and her continued silence worried him all the more.

"You should get out of those wet clothes," he told her, and took her hand to lead her up the cabin steps.

Shelby knew her way around Aidan's cabin. In fact, she and Johnny had used it more than Aidan had in the past year. Without a word she shed her wet coat, hung it by the door and headed to the bedroom.

He watched her go. Only when she closed the door of the en suite bathroom did he turn his attention to the living-room fireplace. In a matter of minutes a small blaze sparked to life in the hearth, taking the edge off the dampness in the cabin.

The second fireplace in the bedroom required a little more effort, and as Johnny positioned the kindling and poked at the struggling flames, he listened to the shower running. He watched the starving flames lick at the logs and wondered if Shelby was truly in the shower or if she'd turned it on only as a cover.

Satisfied with his handiwork, Johnny took a fresh shirt and jeans from the extra clothes hanging in the closet and changed into them. When he left the bedroom, the shower was still running.

In the kitchen he set a kettle of water on for tea, reached for the phone and dialed Aidan's office. His ex-partner answered on the first ring.

Johnny told him about the events at the waterfront, then reassured him: "She's fine, Aidan. She's with me now up at the cabin. You might want to make up some story about the Dodge. I had to leave it there. Pier Twenty-seven."

"Don't worry. I'll take care of it. Did you know Barnes is ready to send out half the force to find her? He called just a while ago asking if Shelby was with me. He said the patrol unit lost her down on Westminster."

"She pulled the old duck-and-hide." Johnny cast a glance down the hall to the bedroom. The shower had been turned off. "Call Barnes back. Tell him she's all right. Tell him she's gone to visit friends out of town for a couple of days."

"Okay, John."

"Where did you end up when you followed Nick?"

"Nowhere. After he left Shelby's, I tailed him to the precinct. He stayed there for half an hour maybe, and then he just drove around."

"He didn't go anywhere?"

"I think he got suspicious, John. At one point he pulled over, made a call on a pay phone, and that was it. I lost him after that. Sorry, partner."

"It could have been him tonight, then," Johnny said, keeping his eye on the bedroom door. "If you lost him an hour or so after he left Shel's, it could have been him down at the waterfront."

"What the hell was Shelby doing down there, John?"

"She hasn't told me yet, but I'd guess she thought she was meeting an informant."

"And he tried to kill her?"

Johnny felt the same sickening coil in his gut he'd felt when he'd seen Shelby in her attacker's grasp. "He had a gun to her head, Aidan."

"God."

"And I didn't get the bastard."

"But you have Shelby, John. She's safe. That's the main thing."

He could hear her moving around in the bedroom now. "Look, Aidan, I gotta go. You can take care of Barnes?"

"Yeah. And I'll keep an eye on Nick when I can. I'm going to take some time tomorrow to track down those names you gave me."

"Will you meet us up here?"

"If the coast's clear, I'll come up late afternoon."

"We'll be here," Johnny said, then hung up, praying he'd be able to convince Shelby to stay.

When she came into the living room at last, she was wearing thick wool socks and a heavy terry robe. He watched her cinch the sash around her slim waist and draw her legs up beneath her as she sat on the couch. She didn't look at him where he stood in the kitchen doorway.

Johnny poured the water for tea and loaded up a tray, but before he headed to the living room, he grabbed a couple of tumblers and a bottle of scotch.

In the flickering glow of the fire he could see that Shelby had been crying, although she didn't meet his gaze directly.

He joined her on the couch, making a deliberate effort to give her space. She needed to come to him, he knew. It had to be on *her* terms, or else there'd be no winning her forgiveness.

"Have a drink, Shelby. It'll warm you up," he said, pouring a shot of scotch into a tumbler and offering it to her.

She raised a hand. "No, thanks."

"Come on, Shel. Drink it. You're wound so tight. It'll help you—"

"I said no."

She got up from the couch, crossed to the fireplace and stood there staring into the dancing flames. She tucked her damp hair behind her ears and crossed her hands over her belly.

It was only then that Johnny spotted the engagement ring on her finger.

A wave of realization washed over him, as he

watched the diamond sparkle in the glow of the fire. It all made sense. Through an anonymous call he'd placed to the hospital a week and a half ago, he'd discovered that Shelby had been down at the pier when the *Orion* had exploded. At the time he hadn't understood why she would have been anywhere near the waterfront that afternoon, but now he knew. She'd decided to accept his proposal, and given her impulsive nature, she'd wanted to tell him immediately. She'd probably driven to the precinct and found out he'd left early for the docks and so had gone there to find him.

Johnny lifted his glass and tossed back the scotch. He eyed the other tumbler, then stood.

He expected her to tense when he came up behind her, but she didn't. Nor did she withdraw when he touched her shoulders. She lifted her own hands to his and drew his arms around her, easing back into his embrace.

"Oh, Shelby," he murmured into her ear. How he'd longed for this—breathing in her scent, feeling her warm body against his. He wanted to bury his face in the curve of her neck, wanted to kiss that one spot he knew would make her melt with desire and elicit the moan that always—no matter how many times he heard it—sent an answering desire raging through him.

"I never meant for it to be this way," he whispered.

She turned within his arms and looked into his face. Her eyes glistened.

When she brought up one hand, he saw it tremble. She gently touched the gash on his right cheek.

"From the explosion," he started to explain. "I...I saw the bomb and—"

But Shelby placed her fingers over his lips, silencing him. She didn't want an explanation, Johnny realized. Not right now. Maybe never. Because *no* explanation would be good enough. No explanation could ever erase what he'd put her through.

"I've missed you, Johnny." Her voice trembled, and when a tear slipped down her cheek, he wiped it away.

Her hand dropped to his waist, and she held his gaze, unmoving but not unwilling, as he traced the lines of her face with his fingertips—her perfect cheekbones, her strong jaw and her defiant chin. He brushed one stray wisp of damp hair behind her ear, and from there his fingers followed the line of her neck to the low V of her robe. He never took his eyes from hers, even when he slid his hand beneath the heavy terry cloth and cupped one satiny breast. He heard her catch her breath and hold it. And when he slipped his other hand inside the robe, forcing the sash to fall open, Shelby let out her breath with a small gasp. She blinked, her eyes wide and unfathomable in their depth.

His hands moved downward, molding every familiar contour, every curve, traveling over her rib cage and abdomen to her hips. And when he reached around to the small of her back and drew her more tightly against him, he could see in her eyes that she felt his arousal, knew that he wanted her...needed her.

He lowered his mouth to her neck and pressed his lips to the sensuous curve below her jaw. Shelby tilted back her head and another small gasp escaped her throat.

But her hands never left his waist. Her body moved against his, but she wouldn't caress him. Johnny wondered if she was afraid to.

He drew back to search her face, wishing there was some way to calm the tumult of emotions he saw there. He took her hand in his and lifted it to his mouth, brushing a kiss into her palm. He waited for her to touch him. And when she did, her fingertips whispered across his face, tracing his mouth, his cheekbones, his forehead, caressing each angle as though she had to "see" him with her hands, unable to believe her eyes alone.

At last she spoke, her voice trembling. "I...I thought I'd never see you again." She brought her other hand up, framing his face. "All that time...I would have given anything, Johnny...my own life... just to hear your voice, to feel your touch one more time."

"I'm here, love." He brushed away another tear. She wanted to be with him as much as he wanted to be with her. He could see it in her eyes. He could feel it in the heat of her skin.

But he wasn't fooling himself. This wasn't forgiveness. It was not going to be this easy.

He knew Shelby was going to kiss him even before she tangled her fingers in his hair and brought his mouth to hers. What he hadn't been prepared for was the desperate hunger in that kiss.

All those nights of watching Shelby, standing outside her window, not being able to go to her... He'd survived solely on his memories, but none of them had come anywhere near this reality, having her in his embrace at last.

He slipped his hands beneath her robe again, gliding them over her smooth skin. He pulled her hips tightly against his again—but he wanted more. He wanted to feel her nakedness against his own. He needed to feel her body move with his, to consume him with the love and passion he knew still blazed between them. Nothing could take that away. Nothing—not all the pain or all the lies in the world—could douse the passion that had been there from the moment they'd first looked into each other's eyes.

WHEN JOHNNY LIFTED her into his embrace, Shelby locked her legs around his waist, her arms around his neck. And as he carried her to the bedroom, she didn't stop kissing him. She couldn't. For the past ten days she'd wanted nothing more than to be with Johnny again, and now that he was here, alive, holding her in his arms, she was powerless to pull away. She couldn't dwell on what he'd done to her, what he'd forced her to endure. She needed him too desperately now.

He lowered her to the bed, then straightened, standing at the side of the bed and looking down at her. In the flickering light of the fire she saw the remorse in his expression. She sat up and cupped his cheek with her palm.

But this was not the time for words or explanations or apologies. With deft fingers, she undid the buttons of Johnny's shirt. Her breath caught in her throat at the sight of his muscled torso, at the mere anticipation of feeling his flesh against hers.

As his shirt dropped to the floor, she trailed her hands over every ridge and angle of the body she knew so well and had truly believed she would never touch again. She pressed her cheek to his firm stomach, breathing in his warm male scent, and when she kissed his skin it tasted faintly of salt.

Johnny lowered himself onto the bed with her, brushing back the edges of the robe so that she lay naked before him. As he raked his gaze over her, she wondered at the tears she saw glistening in his eyes.

"God, you're beautiful, Shel," he whispered, and lowered his lips to her neck. His kisses burned a trail to her breasts, pausing to suck each nipple in turn, and swept down past her ribs, the hollow of her stomach and lower. Johnny's mouth had always worked unparalleled magic on her, but tonight the magic was beyond anything she'd yet experienced. She opened herself to him, feeling the first fervent shocks of desire lick through her, as hot and desperate as his kisses. And when his name trembled from her throat, she reached for him, drawing his mouth to hers again, certain she would shatter from longing.

She drank in his kiss, which grew steadily more urgent as he answered her seemingly unquenchable hunger. She wanted more of him. All of him. She wanted him to surround her completely, to consume not only her passion but the anguish in her heart.

Yet even as he kissed and caressed every inch of her, and despite her desire for him, Shelby wondered if she could ever forgive him. And it was just that uncertainty that made her want him even more now, for there was a good chance that after tonight, she might never be able to let Johnny touch her again. It had been too much, what he'd made her suffer. Not only was it unforgivable, but after such calculated deceit, how could she ever trust him again?

For now, though, their passion drove these fears from her thoughts. Her hands glided down Johnny's back to the waist of his jeans, and she slid one hand between their bodies so she could feel his erection straining against the denim. Another shock of anticipation surged through her. She fumbled with his belt and held her breath as she unzipped his jeans. And when at last she slipped her hand beneath the material to caress his rigid length, Shelby heard Johnny's low urgent moan.

His mouth barely left hers as he stripped off the jeans, and in moments he lowered himself to her again. When he propped himself on his elbows above her, Shelby met his gaze.

He brushed her hair from her forehead and murmured, "I love you, Shelby."

She watched as the firelight danced across his face. "I know you do," she whispered.

When she felt his erection hot against her thigh, a molten longing flooded through her. She shifted beneath him, their gazes unbroken, and brought her hips up to meet his.

And finally he moved into her. Slowly. Exquisitely. As though wanting to savor every delicious second. In each quivering muscle along his shoulders and back, Shelby could feel his restraint. But at last she pulled him hard into her, all the way, needing to feel him deep inside.

There was an urgency then, unlike anything she'd ever shared with Johnny before, spiraling them to new heights. And somewhere between ecstasy and desperation, Shelby cried out his name. His thrusts deepened further still, every muscle straining until she felt his body go rigid. And when her own white-hot release ripped through her, when she felt him fill her, she heard him call her name. It was a sound, she was certain, that came from his heart.

CHAPTER FOURTEEN

SOMETIME IN THE EARLY hours of morning, the fire in the hearth had flickered out, leaving only dimly glowing embers and the cabin gripped by a damp chill. But Johnny hadn't wanted to leave Shelby's side to restoke the fire. Even now, with the first light of dawn slipping through the shutters, Shelby slept, tucked tightly in his embrace.

Johnny luxuriated in their closeness—the heat of flesh on flesh, the lingering scent of their passion and the feel of every familiar contour pressed snugly against him, whispering memories of what they'd shared last night. After they'd made love, Shelby had curled against his body and stared at the hearth while he stroked her hair. He'd hoped they might talk then, in the light of the fire and the afterglow of their lovemaking. There was so much they had to discuss, so many things he wanted to explain. But Shelby had fallen silent. And eventually she'd fallen asleep. He'd lain awake most of the night, holding her close and trying to come up with a way to tell her why he'd done what he had, a way that would ensure he wouldn't lose her.

Carefully he propped himself up on one elbow and gazed down at her. In sleep there was a kind of peace about her. He suspected she hadn't found the peace sleep brought since the explosion.

Shelby moaned quietly in her sleep. He watched her forehead tighten and the corner of her mouth turn down slightly as she nestled further into his embrace.

No. He couldn't lose her. He couldn't live without her. And still, he had no idea what it was he could say to gain her forgiveness.

The only thing he knew for sure was that he had to finish this case as quickly as possible. Last night had proved that. Whoever had attacked Shelby at the waterfront had been serious. There was no telling what the guy would have done had Johnny not arrived on the scene when he did. He only wished he'd been able to catch a better look at the fleeing assailant. But the building had been too dark, and then, after almost losing the man in the maze of shipping crates in the back of the building, he'd been too late finding the side entrance. All he'd seen of the attacker's speeding car were the rapidly receding taillights.

But it could have been Nick. The more Johnny thought about it the more it fit. Aidan had said he'd seen Nick stop at a phone booth just before he'd lost him. And Johnny had spotted Shelby at the apartment window on the phone moments before she'd left for the waterfront. It could have been Nick calling her.

His only hope now was Aidan. Maybe his ex-partner would get some information from the men whose names he'd given him.

God, he needed answers. He needed to put this case behind him, to get on with life—his life with Shelby. If she'd still have him.

He pressed a kiss to her temple, the warmth of her skin sending a fresh wave of longing through him. He buried his face in the curve of her neck, kissing her again and breathing in the heavenly familiarity of her scent.

"Morning, love," he whispered.

At last Shelby stirred. She turned in his embrace, accepting his kiss. But when he looked into her eyes, he saw that last night's confusion and uncertainty had returned.

Yes, they had to talk.

She withdrew from his embrace, wordlessly shoving back the covers and reaching for her robe. When she stood, Johnny drank in the beauty of her nakedness for that brief moment before she threw the robe over her shoulders. She wouldn't look at him, even when he got out of bed, too, and pulled on his jeans.

She cinched the robe around her waist and glanced around the room for her clothes. From the chair next to him, Johnny picked up her pantsuit.

"Your clothes are still wet, Shel."

She looked at him finally from across the room, her expression almost instantly clouding with trepidation. Something so simple, and she seemed at a complete loss as to what to do next.

"I'll get you something," he told her, heading to the closet. "We've still got the extra clothes we brought last time."

He rummaged for a moment, and when he returned with a pair of leggings and an oversize flannel shirt, Shelby was standing at the window next to the bed, her back to him and her arms folded across her chest.

Johnny came up behind her, and the second he placed his hands on her shoulders, he felt her stiffen.

"Don't, Johnny." She pulled away.

"Don't what?"

"Don't touch me," she said, turning to face him and holding up her hands as though to ward him off. "Just…please, just stay away, all right?"

Johnny took a step back. He sighed and shoved his hands into the pockets of his jeans.

"Listen to me, Shel. I respected your desire not to talk last night, but we have *got* to discuss this. The case. I know what you've been through, and—"

Her bitter laugh cut him off. "No, Johnny. You have absolutely *no* idea what I've been through. What you've put me through."

"Shelby—"

"You died, Johnny." She raked a hand angrily through her hair, her eyes almost black with rage. "I saw you. You died that afternoon when I saw the boat explode. You have *no* idea what that's like. You *can't* know. I went to your memorial service. They gave me your medal of honor, whatever the hell that means. I have your goddamn ashes on my coffee table at home, Johnny! So don't you *dare* stand there and tell me you know what I've been through."

When she brushed past him, Johnny tried to catch her wrist, but she was too quick.

"Shelby, listen to me. Please. At least let me explain."

She turned and crossed her arms over her chest again. "Fine, Johnny. If it's going to make you feel better, if it'll ease your conscience, then go ahead. By all means, explain.''

She held her ground, standing there in the middle of the bedroom, waiting. And the quiet rage never left her eyes.

He told her about meeting with his informant, Robert Logan, on the boat, and how Logan had confirmed his suspicions of corruption on the Fairfield force. He explained that he'd seen the bomb and jumped ship, that the remains they'd found were Logan's. He told Shelby how he'd watched over her, how there was nothing else he could have done, knowing his killer might make a move on her. Then he told her he feared the killer might be Nick.

''I was worried about your safety, Shelby,'' he said, taking a step closer to her at last. ''And yes, what you said last night about me playing Super Cop...well, maybe that *is* partly true. Maybe I *do* take the job too seriously, and maybe my cases *are* more important to me than the average cop in this town, but I would *never* put a case ahead of you, Shelby. Never.''

''So you're saying you did all this not because of the case, but because of my safety?''

''Yes.''

She released another bitter laugh. ''Well, Johnny, the way I see it, all of your hiding out, all this cloak-and-dagger stuff of yours, was for nothing. I mean, I'm still in danger, right? That's what you're implying, isn't it?''

He didn't have an answer for that, not a good one, anyway. Everything he'd rehearsed in his head, everything he'd wanted to say to her, had just been squashed by her fury.

He could only stand there, watching as she stripped off the robe and reached for the clothes he'd set out. Her movements were angry, as though she could release that anger through the simple task of dressing. If nothing else, it seemed to calm her. When she spoke again, her voice was steadier.

"Why can't you take this higher up, Johnny?" she asked, buttoning the flannel shirt.

"Because it might *not* be Nick. I can't take this anywhere until I have something concrete. Besides, right now there's no way of knowing how high up the corruption might reach. It might not stop at Nick. And until I know, I can't trust anyone on the force."

"What about Internal Affairs?"

Johnny started shaking his head.

"You should have taken it to them in the beginning," she said.

"I couldn't."

"Why not? Because of what happened in New York City?"

"Partly."

"Johnny, that was New York. This is Fairfield. Why do you assume that everyone's out to screw you? That only *you* can handle this case?"

"Because I *have* been screwed before, Shelby. I was screwed out of a career and a life back in New York. And I learned the hard way that the only person I can count on is myself."

The cold look she gave him went straight to his

heart, and it was in that moment that he recognized he'd lost her.

"Well, it's very reassuring to know you think that way, John." She spun on her heel and gathered her things, then strode to the bedroom door.

"Where are you going, Shelby?"

"Home."

"Shel, you can't. You can't go back there. Not on your own."

"Watch me."

"It's not safe." He followed her, snatching her arm before she reached the door.

When she tore herself from his grasp, she fixed him with another glare. "I can take care of myself," she said.

"Like you did last night?"

"Last night? Last night, Johnny? I wouldn't have gone anywhere *near* that storehouse last night if I'd known you were alive! I went down there because of you, John. Because I thought you were dead!"

"So what are you saying, Shel? You thought I was dead and because of that, there was no reason for you *not* to risk your own life? Not to get yourself killed?"

"You don't get it, do you?"

"Get what?"

"I went down to the waterfront because I *thought* maybe I would find out who supposedly killed you. If it hadn't been for you, Johnny, if it hadn't been for your lies, I would never have put my life at the risk I did last night."

"Shelby—" he was pleading with her now, could hear the desperation in his voice "—I know it was wrong, what I put you through. I'm sorry. What else can I say?"

Her voice was low, steadier than it had been all morning, and its assuredness worried him. "Nothing, Johnny. You don't have to say anything else."

Her clothes balled under her arm, she spun out of the room, too quickly for him to stop her.

"Shelby, wait! Let's talk."

"No, Johnny. There's nothing to talk about. I can't do this. I can't be with you right now."

"So what was last night?"

"Last night…" She paused, and this time there was no mistaking the grief in her eyes. "Last night shouldn't have happened."

AIDAN SWALLOWED the last dregs of his coffee. Dan Barnes had handed him a cup when he'd stepped into his office about fifteen minutes ago.

"I wouldn't have thought this stuff could get any worse." Aidan grimaced.

"Hey, that's the *good* stuff. First pot of the morning. You're just not used to it anymore." The captain winked. "Another reason for you to come back to the detectives' squad."

"Now if that isn't incentive." Aidan got to his feet, tossed the paper cup into the garbage and began to pace the floor of the small office. "How's your wife, Dan?" he asked, noticing the photos on the desk.

"Barbara's fine," Dan said with a shrug. But his face indicated differently—deep lines of fatigue and stress made him appear years older than he was.

"How's she doing with her treatment?"

The captain's face sagged with defeat, and Aidan guessed he'd hit the nail on the head.

"She's doing as well as can be expected, I guess. The chemo—it takes a lot out of her, you know? It's hard. And if that wasn't bad enough, the medical bills are starting to stack up. You know the kind of coverage we get on the force. And she still worries."

"I'm sorry, Dan."

The captain shrugged again, dismissing the topic as he did most topics of a personal nature while in the office.

"So how did the bomb squad make out with the last battery of tests?"

"Nothing." Dan seemed grateful for the change of subject, even though it wasn't a positive change. "Hit a dead end."

"So what now?"

"I don't know. We've got nothing, Aidan. Unless you have some leads you haven't told me about."

"Sorry, Dan."

Past the glass enclosure of the captain's office, Aidan saw Nick at his desk. The younger detective appeared to be studying a file, but it was clear to Aidan that his senses were tuned to the goings-on in the captain's office. No doubt he was itching to hear their conversation.

"What about Nick?" Aidan asked.

"What about him?"

"He was working with John on the Morelli and Feeney cases. So doesn't he have any ideas on what leads John might have been following? Any theories of his own?"

"Aidan, Nick was John's partner. You know I can't authorize him to assist on the investigation."

"Come on, Dan, if that was me, you know I'd be all over that case no matter what the policy is. You're telling me he's not at least sniffing around?"

Dan sighed and leaned back in his chair. He laced his fingers behind his head and said, "Okay, fine. I'll admit, Nick's checking out a few things."

"Like what?"

"I don't know, Aidan. All I know is that he's been working hard to clear his own cases, as well as some of John's. And on his own time maybe he's working a few angles here and there. So far, he hasn't brought anything to me. But it's on *his* time. I can only make him account for his hours on duty. If he does find something, he'll bring it to me."

"So basically you've got nothing."

"Basically, yeah. Look, Aidan, as much as I hate to even suggest it, not all cases go down. You know that. And this might be one of those."

"Right, Dan." Contempt sharpened Aidan's voice as he reached for the doorknob. This was not going to be one of those cases. It couldn't be. It *had* to go down, because if the man who wanted John dead wasn't flushed out, John would never be safe. And neither would Shelby.

When he crossed the detectives' wing, Aidan made a point to avoid Nick. There were other people he needed to talk to right now, starting with Corky McNair. The ballistics expert also had an expert ear—if there were any rumors to be heard around the precinct, Corky almost always heard them.

"WHAT DO YOU MEAN, last night shouldn't have happened?"

Shelby dragged her gaze from Johnny and cast it frantically around the living room. She needed to find her purse. She needed to get out. Get as faraway from Johnny as she could, because right now she knew that if he so much as touched her, her resolve would crumble. Like it had last night.

"What do you mean, it shouldn't have happened?" he repeated, and started across the cabin toward her.

No. She couldn't let him near her. She could barely hang on to reason when he looked at her, and if he touched her... Being in his arms again had almost erased the dark memories of her life since the explosion. And while making love with him last night she'd actually believed that things could go back to the way they were, that she could pretend nothing had happened.

"Shelby, why shouldn't last night have happened?" he demanded again, and she was grateful when he stopped several feet away, giving her the space she needed.

"I don't know, Johnny. It...it just shouldn't have. I'm not ready for this. I'm not ready for *you*. We can't just pick up where we left off and pretend that what you did—the lies and... I can't pretend it never happened, okay?"

He inhaled deeply and dug his hands into the pockets of his jeans. His shirt was hanging open. Seeing him like this, seeing the body she'd made love with so passionately last night, Shelby knew she was going to have difficulty maintaining her resolve.

She blamed herself. She was the one who'd initiated their lovemaking last night. She should have listened to that warning voice in her head, because now, once again facing the reality of what Johnny had done to her, there was no question in her mind that she had to leave him. And it would have been far less confusing and painful if last night had never happened.

"Shelby, I love you," he told her. "Don't you think this was hard on me, as well? I *wanted* to tell you. I wanted to be with you. Do you think it was easy for me to watch you go through everything you have in the past week and a half?"

"And since you suffered, too, that makes it all right?"

"No!"

"Then what are you saying?"

"I'm trying to make you understand why I did what I did. I'm trying to tell you that if there'd been any other way I could have done it, I would have. In spite of what you think, Shelby, I *didn't* put the case before you. And I did not deliberately set out to hurt you."

"No?"

Her hand moved to her throat and caught the chain that lay half-hidden beneath the lapels of the flannel shirt. She watched Johnny's expression tense as she drew it over her head; and then she saw the hopelessness in his eyes as she let the St. Christopher medal and his academy ring dangle from her fingers.

The sorrow that had devastated her when Aidan had given them to her the other day would stay with her forever, its memory fixed in the dark reaches of her heart. When he'd laid Johnny's ring and the medallion in her hand, Shelby had thought her life was over. And more than anything, she'd *wanted* her life to be over.

"So why this, Johnny?" she asked him, shaking her head and fighting back the tears in her voice. She thrust the chain toward him, wishing he would take it.

He kept his hands in his pockets.

"Why, Johnny? You didn't think I was hurting enough? Is that it?"

"Shelby—"

"Did you think I wasn't putting on a good enough show as the grieving girlfriend? My performance wasn't up to par, so you figured you had to twist the knife that was already buried in my heart?"

"Yes. No! God, Shelby, I *had* to make Aidan give you those. Don't you understand? After you saw me the other night, at the tracks..." He shook his head, struggling with his words—something, Shelby realized, she'd rarely seen him do. "I tried to get Aidan to convince you to leave town, but he told me you thought I was alive. I had to...I had to convince you, Shelby."

"And how long has Aidan known? You told him, but you couldn't tell me?"

"Aidan's only known since the other night, Shel. I swear."

"But the point is, you trusted him."

This time when she thrust the chain at him, he caught it between his fingers.

"You should have trusted me with the truth, Johnny. You should have had faith in *me*."

When he looked at her, his eyes seemed to beg for

her forgiveness, for her understanding. But she was beyond any understanding now.

"You shouldn't have done this," she told him flatly, coldly.

"I had no choice."

She clenched her fists at her sides and stayed silent.

"Shelby, please. Understand. *I had no choice.*"

"No, Johnny. You *had* a choice. You had a choice and you made it. And then *I* had to live with it!"

"Shel."

"No one makes choices for me, Johnny. You should know that. You had no right to decide what I should and shouldn't know, what I could or couldn't handle. You had no right to control and manipulate my emotions the way you did. And you had *no* right to make that choice. This is *my* life."

"And this is *mine*, Shelby. For God's sake, I'm a cop."

"You think I don't know that? Come on, Johnny! Every single day you left for work, I never knew if that would be the day somebody would knock on my door and tell me you were dead. Every time you were late, every time the phone rang, I wondered, Is this it? Is this the call? And I had to live with that." She paused and shook her head despairingly. "But I was willing to accept it. For the rest of my life. I was prepared to live with your job and with my fears. But now—" she shook her head again, forcing back her tears "—I'm sorry, but I can't forgive you for this. You went too far, John. Way too far."

At last he nodded. Then he shoved the chain into his pocket and crossed the living room to stand right in front of her. She tensed, steeling herself for his touch. But he only looked at her.

"So what are we going to do now?" he asked.

"It's your case. You're the cop."

"I mean us, Shel. What about us?"

"Honestly?"

He nodded again, and when she saw the misery in his eyes, Shelby wished she could lie just so she could make it go away. But she had no energy left for lies. There could only be truth now.

"I don't know about us, Johnny. I only know that *I* can't do this. I can't be with you."

She'd never seen such resignation, such utter defeat, in Johnny's face before, and it pained her to see it now. She was grateful that he didn't move closer, that he didn't try to hold her. For she was hanging on by a thread.

Johnny must have sensed this.

"All right, Shelby," he said at last. "I understand. But I beg you, don't leave on your own. Wait until Aidan gets here this evening. Then he can be with you when you drive home. I need to know you're safe."

Shelby only nodded, realizing it was going to be one of the longest days of her life.

CHAPTER FIFTEEN

FOR JOHNNY, time moved too slowly, each hour, each minute seeming longer and more difficult than the last. He and Shelby had exchanged barely a dozen words during breakfast, and as soon as they'd finished eating, he'd gotten busy clearing the table to escape the awkward silence. Shelby had gone outside and sat on the front porch. He'd watched her through the kitchen window as he washed the dishes, and he'd racked his brain for anything else he could say to her.

But everything had already been said.

Morning had ebbed into afternoon, and throughout, the silence had persisted. Then, as daylight waned and the sun was dropping behind the distant ridges, time began to move too quickly. Darkness was already settling over the small lake, which meant that Aidan would arrive soon. And Shelby would leave shortly afterward.

Johnny couldn't stand the thought of her leaving. Even if they weren't speaking, at least they were together—in a sense.

From where he'd been sitting on the front steps of the porch for the past hour whittling a stick, he looked beyond the clearing to the small wooden dock and the lake. In the dying red-orange glow of the sunset, he watched Shelby pace the narrow span of shore. She'd been out there most of the afternoon, pacing, skipping stones across the lake's still surface, sitting and gazing at the distant shoreline.

He watched the wind play at the folds of the over-size shirt she wore, revealing her lithe figure beneath and setting off another low ache of longing in him. He saw her wrap her arms around herself and didn't doubt she was getting cold. The wind that danced across the lake's surface carried a hint of frost. But he knew she wouldn't come in. Not for a while, anyway. Maybe not even until Aidan arrived.

He was grateful she'd seen reason and agreed to wait for Aidan before heading back to the city. Aidan could keep her safe. And now that she realized the potential danger, Johnny doubted she would need much convincing to leave Fairfield until this case blew over.

She turned just then and looked back at the cabin, as though sensing his gaze. Either that, or she was checking to make sure he was still sitting there on the porch. She'd done that a lot during the day, Johnny had noticed—checking on him, as if she still didn't quite believe that he was here, that he was alive.

Earlier in the afternoon she'd looked pale and drawn, and he'd convinced her to take a nap. It was a good two hours before he saw her again. He'd been out behind the cabin, stacking firewood, when Shelby had burst through the back door. That was the only time all day she'd allowed Johnny to touch her. She'd thought he'd left, she told him shakily, and he'd placed steadying hands on her shoulders. The most she would admit was that she'd had a bad dream, woken up and found him gone. She'd been almost frantic with worry by the time she found him behind the cabin. In seconds, though, Shelby had pulled herself together and retreated, her composure intact. But since then, she seemed to have kept a visual tab on him throughout the day.

Johnny met her gaze now. Even across the distance of the clearing, he could see the strain in her face. He wished he could go to her, take her into his arms and hold her. He watched her pick up a stone from the shore. She turned her back to him again and skipped the stone across the water.

No, he couldn't go to her. She needed to work things out for herself. Even then, there were no guarantees. He'd realized that this morning.

I can't forgive you for this, she'd said. *You went too far, John.*

He thought he'd prepared himself for the possibility Shelby might not forgive him. And he'd convinced himself the risk was worth the guarantee of her safety. God, if there was any way he could do things over...

But there wasn't. The damage was done. All he could do now was make sure Shelby was safe and flush out the corruption on the force. Only then could he concentrate on rebuilding their relationship—if there was anything left to rebuild by the time this mess was over.

He directed his gaze to his whittling, watching the shavings fall to the littered steps around him. Even though it meant she'd be leaving, he hoped Aidan would arrive soon. Maybe with Aidan here, she'd come around. Her silence was unsettling, and he was beginning to wonder how long it could go on.

He thought of his mother and the silence into which she'd retreated when his father had been killed. Back then, the silence had seemed unending. His mother hadn't spoken for days, weeks.

So why should Shelby? He'd put her through exactly what he'd seen his mother go through twenty years earlier, exactly what he'd vowed never to put anyone through. Only...this was worse. He'd deliberately made Shelby suffer.

He heard Aidan's car turning into the drive and was already on his feet by the time the Skylark pulled up to the cabin. He looked toward the lake again, half expecting Shelby to rush up and demand Aidan take her back immediately. She didn't. She only picked up another stone and skipped it over the water.

Aidan turned off the engine. He climbed out of the car and headed for the cabin where he joined Johnny on the steps of the porch.

"How's she doing?" he asked.

"She's pissed off," Johnny told him, throwing away the stick he'd whittled down to nothing and pocketing his knife. "But that's an understatement."

"And how are you?"

"Not so good." Another gross understatement, he thought.

"Did you find out any more from Shelby about last night? Did she get a look at the guy?"

Johnny shook his head. "It was too dark. And she won't talk about it, anyway. Hell, she won't talk at all right now. The only thing I managed to get out of her was that she'd received another anonymous call demanding that she go to the waterfront," he said, remembering their very short conversation over lunch. "And...that whoever jumped her probably already believes I'm alive."

"What? How?"

He shrugged. "She said he kept asking, 'Where is he?' And told her that she couldn't protect him."

"You think her attacker was referring to you?"

"I don't know who else."

"So why do you figure he ran?"

"You mean, instead of shooting me right then and there?"

Aidan nodded.

"If it *was* Nick, I don't think he even recognized me. Shelby didn't right away. And besides, if he'd opened fire, he would have had to kill both of us. I don't think that's his intention." He watched Shelby turn once again to look at them. "No, if he's going to make a move, Aidan, it's going to be on me. I don't think he's keen on making the body count any higher than he has to."

"So what next?" Aidan lifted a hand and returned Shelby's wave.

"I'm not sure right now. But I have to convince Shelby to get out of here, out of Fairfield. She wants to go back with you."

Shelby had stopped skipping stones and was making her way toward them.

"I might have something of interest to you," Aidan said, and kicked at some of the wood shavings on the bottom step. "I haven't gotten anywhere yet with those names you gave me. Can't locate either of the guys. But there's something else, John. I don't know if it's related.''

"Let's talk about it later, Aidan," he said, nodding at Shelby. "Like I said, she's not too happy with me."

"I told you this would happen, John."

"I know you did, partner." Johnny sighed miserably. "I know you did."

IT WAS ALMOST like old times, Shelby thought—the three of them sitting around the cabin, a fire in the hearth, some light jazz playing on the stereo. Johnny had given her a quizzical look when she'd turned down his offer of a drink just before dinner, and she'd been thankful he hadn't questioned her about it. Now, as they sat in the living room, full from the Chinese food Aidan had brought, it was almost as if the past week and a half had been nothing more than a bad dream.

With Aidan's arrival the tension had eased considerably, but it was still there—hanging in the air between her and Johnny, lingering in every shared glance, prickling along her skin every time they got close.

"Well," she said, "I'm going to put away some of that food." But the truth was, she didn't give a damn about the food congealing in the containers on the kitchen counter or the dishes stacked on the table. It was obvious Johnny was waiting until she was out of earshot to discuss the case with Aidan, as though he could protect her from the harsh reality of what still had to be done.

Standing up from the couch, she gave them a quick smile and headed to the kitchen. As she started clearing the dishes, she realized she could just make out their words.

"I had a chat with Dan Barnes this morning," Aidan was saying.

"And?"

"Bomb squad's come up with zip. I don't think they've got a single lead at this point. Dan says Nick's working his own angles, but it's all off the record, and as far as he knows, Nick's got nothing yet."

"And we've got nothing on Nick." A pause. "So what else, Aidan? When you got here, you said you might have something."

"Well, after I talked to Barnes at the precinct, I went downstairs to look up Corky. I figured that if there were any rumors floating around, Corky would have caught them."

"Anything?"

"No rumors, but I did find out something of interest."

When Shelby stepped through the kitchen doorway, Johnny must have sensed her presence. He'd gotten up from the couch and now he turned to face her.

"It's all right, Johnny," she said before he could object. "I'm as involved in this as you two are. I'd like to know what's going on."

He shared a quick glance with Aidan.

"Come on, Aidan," she prompted, taking up her position on the couch once again and drawing her legs up beneath her. "What were you going to say? You were telling Johnny you talked to Corky...."

Johnny let out a breath of frustration and gave Aidan a nod. His uneasiness, however, was apparent as he took a brisk swig from his beer bottle and started pacing.

"It's about the armed robbery from a couple weeks ago. The one where Seth Cushing got shot."

Johnny lowered his beer. "Yeah?"

"Well, the day after…after the explosion it seems that the perp arrested at the scene finally gave up the name of his accomplice in the heist."

"You mean, the guy who shot Seth Cushing."

"Yeah, well, that's where it gets interesting. See, they picked up this second guy, the accomplice, and they recovered his weapon."

"A .357 magnum."

"Right. The same caliber as the gun that killed Cushing."

"What are you talking about, Aidan? Of course it was the same caliber."

"But it wasn't the same *gun*, John. According to Corky, the riflings on the slug they took from Seth Cushing's body don't match up with this felon's gun at all. And from what Corky's heard around the place, the crime-scene technicians came up with absolutely nothing to put this guy anywhere *near* that rooftop from where the shot was fired."

"It was raining that night, Aidan. Any evidence was probably washed away."

"Yeah, except that when Corky got around to running the tests on this guy's gun, it hadn't even been fired recently."

"So you're telling me Seth Cushing's death had nothing to do with that armed robbery?"

"In all likelihood...no."

Johnny stared into the fire. From where she sat, Shelby could see his expression darken. She could almost imagine reaching out her hand to smooth away those lines of stress.

"Did Corky say what model of gun the slug might have come from?" he asked.

"No. I think he figured he'd already told me too much."

When Johnny lowered himself onto the couch beside Shelby, she fought the urge to touch him. His hands rested on his thighs, and she found herself studying them—the wide knuckles and long strong fingers. Loving caring hands, she thought, remembering how they'd felt on her body last night....

She looked up and caught him staring at her. In that dark fleeting glance, Shelby could tell that Johnny didn't want her to hear what he was about to say. But he had no choice.

"So maybe *I* was the target, right, Aidan?" he asked, turning to his ex-partner.

Aidan nodded. "Yeah, maybe. You told me you were within a foot of Seth Cushing when he was shot."

Shelby's spine stiffened. Johnny had said nothing to *her* about being next to the officer when the man was killed.

"Where was Nick during all this?" Aidan asked.

"He was with us. On the street. I'm almost positive."

"Well, you see, that's the part that doesn't fit. I mean, if your hunches about this case are right, John."

"Maybe he hired somebody."

"How likely is that?" Aidan asked.

Johnny seemed surprised when Shelby suddenly reached over to place her hand in his. She wondered if he could feel her hand tremble.

"Or maybe there's more than one person who wants you dead, Johnny," she suggested, and his hand tightened around hers.

No one spoke after that. Aidan picked at the label on his beer bottle and Johnny stared into the fire. Shelby watched him, seeing a muscle in his jaw flex periodically. He was obviously mulling over the case and deciding what to do next.

It wasn't until the logs in the fireplace settled, sending up a rush of sparks, that Johnny moved. He gave her hand a gentle squeeze and then stood from the couch.

"I'm going to get more wood," he said, but Shelby guessed it was air he needed. And space. At home Johnny would go for a run whenever he wanted to think through a case. Now he was getting wood.

When the back door closed behind him and Aidan and Shelby were alone, Aidan turned to her and said, "Listen, Shelby, I'm sorry about this. About not telling you when I knew."

"Aidan—"

"And giving you John's ring and medallion. I realize how upsetting that was for you."

She felt her cheeks grow warm with embarrassment when she remembered the kiss she'd forced on Aidan yesterday afternoon. She found it difficult to meet his gaze now.

"It's not your fault, Aidan. I know Johnny made you give me those things."

He lowered his voice and asked, "Have you told him yet?"

"Told him what?"

"About the baby."

Shelby looked away. All day she'd grappled with the question of whether or not to tell Johnny. And if so, when? How? With emotions already running as high as they were...

Aidan frowned. "So you haven't, have you?"

"No..."

"I think you'd better. You owe him—"

"I *owe* him?" Shelby's tone was harsh. "I don't owe Johnny anything, Aidan. Not after all this."

"It's his child, too, Shelby. He has a right to know."

The look Aidan fixed on her then with those cool blue eyes was enough to sharpen the twinge of guilt she already felt at not telling Johnny. But after what she'd heard tonight, about people wanting Johnny dead, about his being a target and the dangers he faced—not just now, but always—Shelby was surer than ever that she couldn't tell him about their child.

"You're *not* planning on telling him, are you." Aidan's voice held disbelief.

"I don't know. There are a lot of things I have to consider before making that decision. I have to think about our child—and what's right for its future."

"So what are you going to do? Just leave Fairfield without ever telling him?"

"Maybe."

"Shelby, you can't!"

"Look, Aidan, I don't know what I'm going to do yet, okay? The only thing I'm sure of is that I can *never* go through this kind of hell again. Can you understand that? And I am *not* about to put our child through it, either."

Aidan crossed the room and sat on the edge of the coffee table in front of her. Taking her hand in his, he waited for her to look at him before he spoke.

"Shelby, listen to me. Johnny loves you. You know that, don't you?"

"Aidan, I appreciate your concern. Really, I do. And everything you've done, being there for me through all of this, but I don't need to hear this right now." She tried to pull her hand away, but he held it fast.

"Yes, Shelby, you do. You *do* need to hear it. Johnny loves you. He loves you so much he was willing to lose your love to ensure you were safe. He realized you weren't likely to forgive him for what he put you through, but he knew he had to take that risk. Because he loves you, Shelby."

Fresh tears welled in her eyes. All day she'd been on the verge of crying. She tried to blame the pregnancy, her hormones, but the truth was, she wasn't sure how much more she could handle.

"I can't believe I'm defending him," Aidan told her. "I think what Johnny did was wrong. But if it was me...I'm not sure, Shelby, if it was me, I might have done the same thing.''

"Aidan, please." She pulled her hand from his grasp. "I'm not telling him. Not right now. Can't you respect my decision?''

He looked at her long and hard then. And when at last he stood, he shook his head and said, "This isn't right, Shelby."

"Please. Don't argue with me on this, Aidan. Just promise me you won't tell him."

But Aidan didn't have the chance to make that promise. Because at that moment the door opened and Johnny walked into the living room, his arms laden with logs.

JOHNNY HAD STOOD on the back step of the cabin for some time, breathing in the crisp night air and mulling things over. Again and again he tried to recapture that rainy night almost two weeks ago—the night Seth Cushing had been killed. And the more he replayed the scene in his head, the more uncertain he was of Nick's whereabouts at the actual time of the shooting. He was there afterward, once the paramedics had removed the dead officer from the street, but Johnny couldn't remember his partner's location before that. There'd been too much confusion.

Maybe Shelby was right, Johnny decided by the time he'd loaded his arms with firewood and pushed open the back door. Maybe he should have gone to Internal Affairs, as soon as he'd suspected police corruption in connection with the Morelli homicide. At the very least he might have taken it to the captain.

Together, he and Dan Barnes might have been able to get to the bottom of this mess long before it had reached this stage.

He would talk it over with Aidan first. And then maybe…maybe he'd go to IAB. For Shelby; he'd seen how disturbing hearing the details of the case had been for her. She didn't need any more of this.

When he stepped into the living room, he saw that she looked more troubled than ever. "Are you all right?" he murmured as he passed the couch with his armload of wood.

She nodded and smiled slightly. As he dumped the logs into the wood box, he thought how "All right" had definitely become a relative term these days. And he knew he'd interrupted Shelby and Aidan in some conversation; no doubt they'd been discussing their imminent return to Fairfield.

Johnny squatted before the hearth and stoked the embers, wondering if there was any way to convince Shelby to stay with him here. He remembered the softness of her hand in his only moments ago and the hope he'd derived from that contact.

"Well, those dishes aren't going to do themselves," Shelby said at last, and started to rise from the couch.

Johnny rose, as well, and that was the moment everything cascaded into a blur of commotion.

He saw Shelby sway suddenly, then stumble as though she might faint. And in that same split second, as Johnny and Aidan both rushed forward to catch her, a gunshot rent the night, along with the sound of shattering glass.

Instinct and training kicked in. Johnny dragged

Shelby down to the floor beneath him. Aidan must have turned off the single lamp, because when Johnny looked up, the living room was in darkness. The glowing embers in the hearth cast just enough light for him to see Shelby's face.

Her expression was terrified.

He had no idea which had come first—Shelby's near collapse or the gunshot.

"Were you hit?" he asked, his hands already frantically searching her body for injuries.

She shook her head, seemingly speechless.

"What happened?"

"I don't know," she gasped. "It was just a dizzy spell, and then..."

Still he searched her, expecting to find blood.

"Johnny! I'm fine."

Just then there was a loud click. Aidan, Johnny realized, had switched off the power in the cabin, including the outside porch lights.

"Aidan," Johnny called softly, "do you know where the shot came from?"

"The west side, I think."

"Do you have your gun?"

"Yeah."

Still in a crouch, Johnny drew away from Shelby. Instantly her hand caught his shirt.

"Where are you going?"

"Just stay here, Shel. And stay down," he instructed.

"But where are you going?!"

"To check things out. I need you to stay here." He

left before she could argue further, crawling across the dark floor toward the front door to get his gun.

Aidan was already there, and together they stepped cautiously outside onto the porch.

They both listened, straining to hear. Johnny tapped Aidan's shoulder once, indicating he would go first. Stealthily he inched around the side of the cabin, using the porch for cover.

The night was black. Clouds had completely obliterated the moon and stars. Johnny stopped to listen to the sounds of the forest, his hand tightening on the grip of his gun.

Suddenly off to his right, Johnny heard the sound of something—or someone—thrashing through the deep underbrush.

"Come on, Aidan," Johnny called as he sprang into action. "He's making for the road."

This time he was not going to let the assailant get away, Johnny swore as he plunged into the dark forest. Above the sounds of his hammering heart and his own crashing through the undergrowth, he could hear the other man's progress. He was headed for the road.

Johnny was vaguely aware that he couldn't hear Aidan behind him. But he didn't have time to check. He forged on, plowing through brush and shrubs, his eyes still not adjusted to the darkness. He stumbled over rocks and roots, slipping on wet leaves, but still he didn't break pursuit.

"No!" he shouted when he heard a car door slam and the roar of an engine. He still tore through the forest toward the road, but he knew he was too late, especially when he heard the sound of tires spinning on the sandy shoulder of the road.

"Son of a bitch." He stopped running and lowered his weapon. Then he watched as twin pinpricks of red shimmered fleetingly through the trees and disappeared.

"Aidan!" he called, turning back toward the cabin. "Aidan, get the car!"

He knew it was slim, but there was still a chance they could catch up with the fleeing shooter.

"Aidan?"

No response. Aidan should have been right behind him. And that was when Johnny noticed the blood on his hand. In the dark it was nothing more than a black smear on his left palm, but its sticky warmth was a giveaway.

It wasn't *his* blood on his hand, he was sure of that. "Shelby!" A million images shuttered through his mind as Johnny plunged back through the undergrowth. "Shelby!"

And when he broke through into the clearing in front of the cabin, he saw Shelby and Aidan huddled on the drive. She was kneeling beside Aidan, partially lifting him from the gravel. And Aidan was letting forth a string of expletives.

Johnny joined them, realizing now that it wasn't Shelby who'd been shot. "What the hell happened?" he asked.

"I lost my footing," Aidan muttered. "Slipped on the damned gravel."

"You were shot!" Shelby exclaimed.

Aidan grunted. "Yeah, that, too." Johnny heard the pain in his voice.

"How?" Johnny asked. "I thought you were okay."

"I just didn't feel it at first," Aidan explained. "Figured I'd hurt my shoulder when I hit the floor."

"We've got to call an ambulance, Johnny." Shelby's voice trembled. "He's bleeding."

"Hang on. Let's take a look. Where, Aidan? Where are you hit?"

"It's just a flesh wound, John."

"Where, for God's sake?"

"Left shoulder." Aidan sat up now, pushing away any assistance as though determined to stand on his own. Still, he visibly winced at the pain.

Johnny opened the passenger side of the Lexus and guided his friend into the seat. In the glare of the domelight he could see the crimson stain on Aidan's shirt.

Aidan winced again when Johnny pulled back the torn fabric. Then he groaned as Johnny inspected the wound in the top of his shoulder.

"Oh, God!" Shelby gasped. She was right behind him.

"It's all right, Shel. It only looks bad. But I don't think the bullet exited, Aidan."

Shelby raced into the cabin then and reemerged moments later with a towel. "You're going to be okay, partner," Johnny told him, pressing the towel to the wound, then let Aidan do it himself.

"But, Johnny, he's—"

"Shelby, he's going to be fine. Aidan's right, it's just a flesh wound."

"He needs an ambulance."

Johnny was already reaching for the seat belt and pulling it around Aidan's chest. "No. It'll be faster to drive him. Run and get your purse and car keys."

She didn't argue and raced into the cabin again.

"How are you doing, Aidan?" Johnny adjusted the towel.

"Well, it hurts like hell." Aidan managed a crooked smile.

"Yeah, I bet it does. But at least you can rest easy."

"How do you figure that?"

"I think when they get that slug out of you, you'll find my name on it."

"Yeah, you're probably right."

"I'm sorry I dragged you into this, Aidan." He could hear Shelby coming back down the porch steps. "Listen, I'll check in with you later."

Aidan nodded, then shifted in his seat to grope into the front pocket of his jeans. He withdrew his set of keys and handed them to Johnny. "You'll need these for the Skylark."

"Thanks, Aidan. You hang in there. And take care of Shel for me?"

"I will."

Johnny closed the passenger-side door and faced Shelby.

"Don't worry, Shel." He guided her to the driver's side of the Lexus. "He's going to be fine."

Then he opened the door, holding it for her to climb in. "Just get him to Fairfield General and—"

She looked at Johnny in surprise. "Me? What... what about you?"

"I can't go with you, Shel."

"What? No!" She reached for him, grabbing a handful of his shirt. "No, Johnny, you—"

"Shelby, I can't go with you."

"Johnny—"

"Whoever shot Aidan...he's after me, Shel. Not Aidan. Not you. And as long as I'm with you, I'm putting both your lives at risk."

"I can't...I'm not just leaving you here! You can't do this. *Please*, don't do this." She was shaking her head, her eyes never leaving his, begging him. "Don't leave me again, Johnny."

She threw her arms around him and clung as if she'd never let go.

"Shelby, you have to take Aidan to the hospital," he told her quietly, wishing with all his heart that there was another way that he could keep her with him. "I want you to stay there with Aidan. Do you hear me? I don't want you to go home. Not tonight. Promise me."

He waited for her nod and soft, "I promise."

"Just stay at the hospital. You'll be safe there."

When at last she eased out of his embrace, he could see the shimmer of tears in her eyes. He took her chin in one hand and, tilting her face, pressed an urgent kiss to her lips.

"Don't worry about me, Shel." With the back of his hand he wiped the tears from her cheek.

"I can't just leave you here!" she said again, as though there was still a chance of convincing him.

"You have to."

"I already lost you once, Johnny."

"Shelby—"

"I can't lose you again."

"You're not going to. Believe me."

He lowered his mouth to hers once more and kissed her, tasting her fear. When he drew away and looked at her, Shelby cast her gaze downward, perhaps hoping he wouldn't see her cry.

"Where are you going to go?" she asked him.

"I don't know yet. But I'll contact you, Shel."

When she brought her gaze back up to meet his, Johnny knew that, for as long as he lived, he would never forget that look in her eyes—a haunted combination of fear and love.

"I love you, Johnny," she whispered at last.

"I know you do." He gave her a quick smile he hoped would reassure her.

But there was no answering smile on her lips as she got into the Lexus and started the engine. She looked at him through the window one last time, and then pulled away.

Johnny stood in the drive watching until the tail-lights disappeared completely.

CHAPTER SIXTEEN

SHELBY MANAGED the forty-minute drive from the cabin to Fairfield in thirty. Aidan was silent in the passenger seat for most of the ride, only commenting from time to time on her speed and assuring her there was no need for it.

When she swung into the emergency-entrance driveway, Aidan calmly instructed her to park in the regular lot, instead. And he refused to get out of the car until Shelby agreed on their story. They couldn't tell the truth, he told her, or else the police would be all over the cabin by morning, and if Johnny was still up there...

She helped him to the ER entrance then, filled in the appropriate forms and paced the corridor as they took Aidan to surgery. Even before the doctor had finished patching him up, two officers arrived to take her statement. She was grateful she knew neither of them; it made lying easier. Still, they didn't seem to buy her story about a drive in the country and a hunter's stray bullet. Eventually they left, assuring her they'd be back later to question Aidan.

When Aidan was at last assigned a room, she sat in the vinyl-cushioned chair next to the bed and watched him sleep off the painkillers the doctor had given him.

Visiting hours were long over, but Aidan had cleared with the staff earlier that she was to stay with him. Now she drew her knees up and wrapped her arms around them, listening to his low breathing. But her thoughts were on Johnny.

Her last sight of him had been in her rearview mirror as she'd driven off into the night. She knew it was completely illogical, but with that image of Johnny locked so firmly in her mind, she began to fear it might be the last time she'd see him.

"He'll be all right, Shelby."

She started at the sound of Aidan's voice, dropping her feet from the edge of the chair and pulling herself closer to his bed. He gave her a groggy smile.

"Hey," she whispered, trying hard to return it as she reached for his hand. "How are you feeling?"

"Like hell. What time is it?"

Shelby checked her watch. "Just after 1:00 a.m."

He winced as he craned his neck to scan the room, assuring himself they were alone.

"You should ask them to give you a bed, Shelby."

"I wouldn't be able to sleep anyway." She shrugged. "The doctor says you're going to be as good as new."

"He does, does he?"

"Well, almost," she amended. "He says you should be able to get out of here by tomorrow." She paused. "I paged Kate."

Aidan groaned. "I wish you hadn't. You know how crazy she gets with worry. What did you tell her?"

"That you're okay. And that she can pick you up

tomorrow afternoon.'' Shelby gave him a quick smile, but she wasn't fooling Aidan. He knew her too well.

"John's going to be all right, Shelby," he said again.

She nodded.

"He's like a cat."

"Oh, yeah?"

"Yeah. He's got nine lives."

"Well, I don't think I want to be around to see all of them."

"So what are you going to do, Shelby?"

She stood and, crossing her arms over her chest, began to pace. From the corridor she heard a cart clatter by the closed door.

"Do you want to know the one thing that's become clear to me now, Aidan?"

"What?"

"Johnny will never leave the force."

"You can't say that for certain."

"Yes. I can. His job is everything to him. It's his life. It was his father's life. He's got it in his head that he's taken over where his father left off, like it's somehow his legacy to make a difference on the force because of what happened twenty years ago."

"Have you thought of asking him to leave?"

"A million times. But I don't dare. I can't. If I even suggested it and he *did* quit, eventually he'd resent the decision. He'd resent the relationship, but most of all he'd resent me."

"If you think that, then you don't know John."

"Aidan, come on. This job, it's…it's what Johnny lives for."

"Maybe if he had other things to live for—"

"No!" She held up a hand to stop him. "No, Aidan. Don't do this."

"Do what?"

"Don't even suggest that if I told Johnny about our child, he'd just give up the force. It's more complicated than that. You know that."

Aidan lifted a hand and pinched the bridge of his nose between his thumb and forefinger before looking at her again.

"So what *are* you going to do?"

Shelby resumed pacing. She couldn't look Aidan in the eye because for sure he wouldn't approve of her decision. After being with Johnny again, the decision to leave him and Fairfield was, without question, the most difficult one she'd ever made. But in the long run, leaving Johnny was for the best. For the good of their child. And in the long run, Shelby hoped, she would get over the emptiness of life without Johnny.

"Shelby?"

"I'm moving to New York, Aidan."

"What?"

"I've already made all the necessary arrangements with Cora. She's found us a place, even a retail space for a boutique."

"And all of this is definite?"

She nodded, feeling guilty for the partial lie, but knowing that a single phone call to Cora would make her last statement true. "What other choice do I have?"

"You have to think about this, Shelby."

"I *have* thought about it. For almost two weeks now

I've thought of little else but the future of my child. I don't know what else to do.''

''Well, I'll tell you what I know, Shelby, and that is that Johnny loves you. More than the job. More than anything. But this isn't just about the job, is it?''

''What do you mean?''

''If it was just the job, then your answer would be simple—either John quits and you two have your life and your family together, or he doesn't quit and you go off to New York City to raise your child on your own. But there's more to it than that, isn't there?''

She cursed Aidan then—for knowing her so well and for being able to see exactly what it was she worked so hard to hide from the world.

''You're afraid you'll lose him again, right, Shelby? Whether John's on the job or not. Because even if he quits, there's going to be that one day when you lose him—and you just can't live with that. In fact, you'd rather live without him for the rest of your life just so you don't have to suffer the pain again of losing him.''

''Yes. All right? Yes, I'm terrified of losing him again. You don't know what it was like, Aidan. You don't know what I went through.''

''I think I have an idea.''

The look he gave her then stopped her. Of *course* Aidan knew what she'd gone through. He'd witnessed it firsthand, been there for her throughout, and he'd put up with her grief when he too had been suffering.

''I'm sorry, Aidan. That was unfair of me. You *do* know what it was like. So you must understand all the more then that I can't go through that again. More importantly, as I told you once before, I will not put our child through that.''

"You'd rather have your child grow up and never know his father?"

Coming from Aidan's lips, it sounded insane. When she heard it in her own heart, however, it made all the sense in the world.

"Yes," she answered him. "Yes, I would."

ONCE AGAIN, Shelby resumed her pacing, as though needing to put distance between herself and the challenge of Aidan's words.

Aidan watched her. He worried about the exhaustion he saw in her face. He knew that her reasoning was the result of the emotional impact of the past week and a half and not of any kind of rational thinking. On the other hand, John *had* pushed her too far. And the more he pushed her, the more Shelby would listen to her heart and not her head.

Any other woman, Aidan thought, wouldn't have the strength to leave. And Shelby's stubborn determination would ensure that she stayed away. Forever.

"Shelby, you can't just run from this."

But when she faced him at last, he could see that her resolve was fixed.

"No? Why not, Aidan? What's so wrong with running away?"

"Nothing, I guess. I'm just…surprised. I've known you almost all my life, Shelby, and I've never seen you back down or give up or run from anything."

"Well, maybe I'm tired, Aidan. Maybe I need to back down this time. Maybe I need to run, instead of fight." She closed her eyes and let out a long breath, and when she opened them again, he watched her force a smile for his sake.

"Listen, are you okay on your own for a few minutes?" she asked. "I'm just going to pop out and see if I can find something to eat."

Aidan nodded and watched her leave. Trying to ignore the low throb in his shoulder, he worried about Shelby. Her complexion had been almost ashen, her expression drawn. And then he worried about the pregnancy—if Shelby had to endure any more on top of what John had already put her through, there might not *be* anything for her to tell John.

He was just beginning to doze off when he heard the door of his room creak open. He opened his eyes, expecting to find Shelby in the doorway.

THE CAFETERIA was closed, but Shelby had found a vending machine in the corner of a deserted waiting lounge. She sat tensely on the edge of one of the couches and unwrapped the sandwich she'd bought.

She'd barely managed a couple of mouthfuls before she put it down, leaned back against the understuffed cushions and stared at the pay phone on the opposite wall. It had been at least fifteen minutes since she'd last called to check her answering machine for messages. Maybe Johnny had called since then.

He'd said he'd contact her. And he knew she checked her messages frequently. But she wondered if he'd risk leaving a message if he *did* call. Yes, she decided. He knew that Doreen never touched the answering machine since the number was both business and personal.

He'd call; he'd leave a message. He'd tell her where he was so that she could go to him. And then she would have to decide, once and for all, whether or not to tell him about their baby.

"JOHN, YOU SHOULDN'T BE here."

"I had to see Shelby."

"She just stepped out for some food. She'll be right back."

John set Aidan's apartment keys on the table. "Figured you'd need these to get into your place. How are you doing?"

"Holding my own."

"What about the police? They been around yet?"

"Two officers apparently. Shelby's not sure they bought the story she gave them, but we've got it covered. The cabin should be safe."

John glanced around, grateful Aidan had a private room. He'd debated the risks in coming to the hospital. In fact, he'd sat out in the parking lot for the past hour, turning Shelby's engagement ring over and over in his hand, thinking about it.

It wasn't until earlier that night, after Shelby had driven off with Aidan and he'd gone back into the cabin, that Johnny realized she'd taken off the ring. He'd found it on the dresser, as though she'd left it there deliberately. As though she was telling him it was over.

"I think she's leaving me, Aidan," he confessed at last. Hearing the words actually spoken frightened him. He reached into his pocket and rubbed the smooth band of the engagement ring.

A long silence fell between them, neither seeming to know what to say. But at last Aidan spoke.

"John, you know how you're always asking me why Kate and I don't get married? And how I'm always telling you that we're not ready or that Kate's got her career or that the business is too hectic?"

"Uh-huh."

"Well, none of that's the truth. The real reason I haven't asked Kate to marry me, John, is because of you and Shelby."

"What are you talking about?"

"Well—" Aidan sighed "—I've been envious from the day you first asked Shelby out. If any two people belong together, it's you and Shelby. And seeing your love it's just... I'm not sure Kate and I *have* that kind of love. At least not yet."

"Why are you telling me this, Aidan?"

"Because, if you don't do something, Shelby *is* going to leave."

"I know. That's what I just said."

"No. I mean *really* leave. She's...Shelby's planning on moving to New York City. She told me tonight."

"Well, that's it, then, isn't it?"

"John—"

"I can't stop her, Aidan. You know how determined she is and what her career means to her. There's nothing I can say that'll convince her to forgive what I did to her, so there's nothing I can do to persuade her to stay. I can't blame her, really. I should've expected

this. I knew the sacrifices she'd made for our relationship even before any of this happened. I should never
have asked her to marry me." His fingers clenched
almost painfully around the engagement ring in his
pocket. "No, Aidan, if Shelby's determined to leave,
she'll leave. I can't stop her."

"There's more, John."

"What?"

Johnny could see that his ex-partner was struggling
with the wisdom of imparting whatever information
he had.

"Aidan, what is it?"

"Shelby's pregnant, John."

It was as if someone had slugged him, as if the wind
had been knocked out of him. Nothing could have prepared him for that news. And yet, it made sense now
that he thought about it. It wasn't just Shelby's refusal
of alcohol or the dizzy spell; it was her whole emotional state. There'd obviously been far more on her
mind than just their relationship when they'd been together at the cabin, when they'd argued about their
future. All along Shelby had held back her secret. All
along she'd been thinking about her own future with
their child, not *their* future together—as a family.

"Listen to me," Aidan implored. "You know how
headstrong Shelby is. And you know how upset she's
been. She's thinking with her heart right now, not her
head, and what she needs, what she *really* needs, is
you, John. Don't give up on her."

Johnny didn't know what to say. He felt anger and
a sense of resentment and betrayal.

"Promise me you won't give up on her."

"Shelby's going to do what she's going to do, Aidan," he said coldly and started for the door. "I can't convince her otherwise. You know that."

"Where are you headed?"

"I don't know."

"Talk to her, John."

"I can't, Aidan. I can't see her right now." He swung open the hospital-room door, caring only about getting outside. Getting away from Shelby.

SHELBY CHECKED her answering machine one more time before leaving the lounge, even though she knew there wasn't likely to be a message from Johnny. She threw out most of the sandwich she'd bought from the vending machine and then took the elevator up to the fourteenth floor, wishing she could blame the sandwich for the nausea she felt. But she knew better. She was worried sick about Johnny.

Aidan was sitting up in bed when she pushed open the door to his room.

"You should be trying to sleep," she scolded him, crossing the room.

"Says who?"

"I don't know. But I'm sure the doctor would if he was here. It's a hospital. You're supposed to rest." She reached out to brush a lock of hair from his forehead.

"And what about you?"

"What about me?"

"You look like hell, Shelby."

"Thanks." She managed a smile. "Maybe you

should just keep your compliments to yourself and concentrate on getting better, hmm?''

"So did you eat something?"

"Yes. One of those gruesome hermetically sealed numbers from the vending machine downstairs, so you can lay off the big-brother routine. I also checked my answering machine a couple of times in case he called. Do you think I should try the cabin?"

"John's all right, Shelby."

There was something in Aidan's expression, in the way his eyes flitted away from hers, that tipped her off.

"Aidan?"

When finally he met her gaze, she knew.

"Johnny was here, wasn't he? When I went out, he—''

"Shelby."

She didn't even need to see the set of keys on the side table—Aidan's keys, the ones he'd given Johnny.

"He *was* here! Aidan, when? When did he leave?"

"A couple of minutes ago. But…"

Shelby was already rushing to the door. Aidan called after her, but she was well down the corridor by then, punching the button for the elevator.

CHAPTER SEVENTEEN

IT BEGAN TO SNOW, the huge flakes illuminated by the shafts of light from the parking-lot lamps, when Johnny strode across the pavement to the Skylark. The first snowfall—normally he would have taken a moment to appreciate it; tonight he barely noticed it.

Aidan's words spun through his mind. *What Shelby really needs is you. Don't give up on her.* But wasn't it Shelby who'd given up on him? By not telling him about their child and now with her plans to leave Fairfield, wasn't *she* the one who was giving up on their relationship?

He'd come here tonight, risking detection, because he'd wanted to see her, talk to her. During the drive from the cabin, he'd actually thought he might convince her to let him put the engagement ring back on her finger.

And now this.

On the one hand, he couldn't blame her for wanting to raise their child on her own, if that was her intention—especially after what he'd put her through. But on the other hand, her even considering keeping it from him—that was unforgivable.

She's thinking with her heart now, John, Aidan had told him.

Well, what about him? What about *his* heart?

He thought he heard her call his name just then, the sound faint in the cold dark parking lot, then shrugged it off as just his imagination. Seconds later, as he unlocked the car, he heard her call again and knew it hadn't been his imagination.

He spun around and watched her sprint past the last few rows of cars. As she came nearer, a smile of relief lifted the corners of her mouth. But she must have sensed that something was wrong, because by the time she stood in front of him, her smile faded.

"Why didn't you wait for me?" she asked, taking a step back from his obvious anger and wrapping her arms around herself. "Johnny?"

"You should have told me, Shelby."

She shivered. Lines of confusion furrowed her forehead.

"Told you what, Johnny? What are you talking about?"

"The baby, Shel. What else?"

For a moment she just stood there immobile. Eventually she dropped her gaze to the pavement. She took another step away from him and anxiously raked her fingers through her hair.

"Yes, Shelby, Aidan told me. And thank God he did because if he hadn't, I might never have known." He paused. "Isn't that right?"

"Look, Johnny—"

"No, *you* look, Shelby. You had no right to keep this from me. What were you going to do? Just leave without saying anything? Raise our child on your own and never even tell me?"

"I don't know."

"And what were you going to tell our child, Shelby? Hmm?"

"I don't know."

"Were you going to tell him I didn't exist? That I'd run off or something? Or maybe that I simply didn't give a damn?"

"Or maybe I could have told him you were dead, John."

Shelby watched Johnny's gaze darken. Never had she seen this kind of rage in him before.

"Just one damn second." He was practically shaking with fury. "This is an entirely different situation, Shelby. *Entirely* different! Don't you *dare* compare what I did to this."

"And why not?"

"The fact that you were even considering having this child and never telling me about it. *Our* child, yours *and* mine, Shelby. What I did isn't forgivable. I know that. But it does *not* compare to this."

"How, John? You let me believe you were dead. For a week and a half you hid in the shadows and watched me suffer. And when that wasn't enough, you dug the knife a little deeper and twisted it, didn't you? By making Aidan give me your ring. So how? How is that any less unforgivable?"

"I did what I did for your protection, Shelby."

"And maybe I was doing this for our child's protection! Did you stop to think that maybe I don't want our child to go through the kind of living hell you put me through? *No* child should have to go through that. At your memorial service, I saw Seth Cushing's children. Four and six, John—that's how old they are.

Four and six years old. They're devastated. Their father is gone. The world they knew has ended. The few years he was able to give them—were they worth the anguish they're suffering now? How fair is that?''

"Life doesn't come with any guarantees, Shelby.''

"No, you're right—it doesn't. But it comes with even fewer guarantees when your father's a cop, doesn't it.''

He didn't have an answer for that, Shelby realized as she held his silent stare. She fought back the urge to touch him. She wanted to throw her arms around him and tell him they would start over, put the past week and a half behind them and get on with living. With loving. But it wasn't that easy. There was too much between them. Too much pain. Too much anger.

"Come on, Johnny,'' she said at last, shivering from the cold. "You lost your father when you were fourteen.''

"And you lost yours when you were twelve, Shelby. And he wasn't even a cop. So what's your point?''

"Don't you remember how much that hurt? Don't you remember what it felt like when you found out? And then the bitterness, the anger, at him for leaving you. All those unshared years, Johnny. I want you to be there for our child's life. Not just for a few games of catch in the park on a sunny afternoon or a couple of camping trips on summer vacation. I want you to be there for *all* of it, Johnny. Like our fathers couldn't be.''

"But you're grateful for the few years you had with

your father, aren't you? That you at least *knew* your father. You weren't even going to give our child that, were you, Shelby?''

"I don't know what I was going to do. I hadn't made any decisions. I—''

"You have. You're planning to move back to New York—Aidan told me. And what was all that talk about choices? What was that you said about me making choices and then forcing you to live with them? Seems to me that's exactly what you're planning on doing. You've made your choice. You've decided that maybe I shouldn't know about this child and that's that, right? I've simply got to live with your choice. Were you *ever* going to tell me?''

"I didn't know what to do, Johnny." She was shivering even more now, but it wasn't from the cold.

"You didn't think I'd want to know you were carrying my child? You didn't think it would be important to me?''

"I thought you were dead!''

"Well, I'm not, am I, Shelby?''

One second he held her gaze with a look of dark accusation, and the next, he'd spun around and flung open the car door. As he climbed in, Shelby pleaded with him. "Johnny, don't leave like this. Let's talk.''

"I've got nothing else to say!'' he snapped, then slammed the door. Through the closed window, she watched him turn the key in the ignition. As the Skylark rumbled to life, Johnny leaned back in the seat and stared out the windshield. For a long time he simply sat there, and for just as long Shelby stood beside the idling car, watching him.

When he rolled down the window, she reached inside and pressed her palm to his cheek.

"Johnny." She wished he would look at her and prayed that if he did she'd find forgiveness in his eyes. "Johnny, I love you," she whispered.

He didn't look at her when at last he spoke. But Shelby could hear the hurt in his voice. "You know something, Shelby?" he said, and shoved the car into drive. "Maybe it *is* better if you move to New York City."

"Johnny, wait!"

But there was no stopping him. He revved the engine and pulled out of the parking spot, and as Shelby watched him drive away, she could no longer contain her tears.

"Johnny." She leaned back against the fender of a parked car and watched the Skylark career out of the lot. She shoved a hand through her snow-covered hair, shivered again. "Dammit, Johnny."

SOMETIME IN THE EARLY hours of morning, the snow had turned to rain. The sky over Fairfield looked permanently bruised, as though no amount of sunshine could ever heal it. From the rain-blurred fourteenth-floor window of Fairfield General, Shelby had watched the parking lot, not really expecting to see Johnny return, but wishing nonetheless. She'd seen the hospital night shift filter out and then the daytime staff come in. Through the closed door, she heard the activity in the corridor rise steadily, and through it all, Aidan slept.

Shelby rubbed the back of her neck and shoulders,

trying to massage away the stiffness that had settled there. She'd spent most of the night curled up in the chair by Aidan's bed.

After Johnny had driven off and she'd finally come in, she hadn't been able to bring herself to face Aidan and the apology she knew he'd offer. Instead, she'd sat on one of the hard vinyl chairs outside his room, needing time to think, time to collect herself. When she'd slipped into his room almost an hour later, Aidan had been asleep.

Only once had he awoken, groggy on painkillers, and reached out to take Shelby's hand. He'd apologized then, as she'd known he would.

"It's okay, Aidan," she'd assured him. "Johnny had a right to know."

"But you should have been the one to tell him."

"That's true. But I know you were afraid I might not. It's okay, Aidan. Really."

Of course *nothing* was okay. After hearing the hurt in Johnny's voice before he'd driven off last night, Shelby doubted he'd ever want to see her again, anyway, baby or no baby. So many things had gone wrong between them she could hardly imagine where to begin repairing the damage.

Aidan had tried to convince her that Johnny would come around, and he'd mumbled something about Johnny's love for her. But Shelby had put little faith in Aidan's words in those wee hours of the morning. And even less faith in them now.

She couldn't blame Johnny if he didn't see his future with her. In fact, that wasn't the thing that worried her most. More troubling was the fact that if Johnny figured he didn't have a future with Shelby and their child, he would take greater risks for the sake of his case. She doubted he would think twice about putting his life on the line—if that was what it would take to bring his case down.

Behind her she heard Aidan stir. By the time he opened his eyes, she was at his bedside.

"Well, at least someone got a good night's sleep." She managed a smile as he eased himself up with a groan.

"You've been here all night?" he asked.

"Just like the good detective ordered."

"Did John come back?"

She shook her head.

"And you checked your machine for messages?"

"Nothing. Look, Aidan, I'm going home."

"Shelby, I promised John I'd watch out for you."

"Would you stop worrying? I've already called Doreen. She's agreed to come in today even though it's the weekend. She's probably at the boutique already. And besides, it's only for a few hours until I come back here to pick you up unless, of course, Kate beats me to it. I need a shower, Aidan, and a change of clothes. And I need to get some work done. Then you can be my bodyguard, all right? Even though I don't know how good you'll be with that bum shoulder." She gave him another smile before she leaned over to place a kiss on his cheek.

"I'll check in on you a little later."

She gave him a wave goodbye at the door, ignoring his frown, and headed for the elevator. She hadn't lied; she *did* want to get some work done. At the very least it would take her mind off this nightmare—if that was possible. But she also clung to a slim hope that maybe Johnny would try to see her or call. And if he did, she wanted to be there.

Her drive through Fairfield to the north end of the city was a blur. Her mind wandered constantly to Johnny, to his final words to her. *Maybe it is better if you move to New York City.* She tried to tell herself that he hadn't really meant it, and that he'd be able to forgive her for even contemplating not telling him about their child. It had been his anger speaking, she reasoned, and his hurt. But by the time Shelby pulled onto Jefferson Street, she still hadn't managed to convince herself Johnny had been anything but honest last night.

It wasn't until she'd gotten out of the Lexus that she realized how absorbed she'd been with her thoughts. Not only hadn't she noticed the sedan right on her tail, but she hadn't even seen Dan Barnes climb out of it until he called her name.

She spun around, startled. "Dan." A thin mist of rain dampened her hair and clothes as she waited for him to join her.

"I was actually on my way to see you and Aidan at the hospital," he explained once they were sheltered under the front-door awning. "I figured you might still be there, but when I saw you pull out of the parking lot, I decided to chase you down and talk to you first. How's he doing?"

"He's going to be all right. The doctor says he can go home this afternoon."

"So are you going to tell me what happened,

Shelby? Or are you still sticking to that bogus story you gave the officers last night?" The captain followed the question with the kind of playful knowing look Shelby might have expected from a father.

But it was Johnny's words, as outrageous as they seemed now, that warned her. *There's no way of knowing how high up the corruption might reach. It might not stop at Nick. And until I know, I can't trust anyone on the force.*

"It wasn't bogus, Dan. Honestly. We really *were* just out for a drive in the country."

"Uh-huh. And Aidan got out to retrieve something from the trunk?"

"Actually, no. I think he went out to, you know, relieve himself. He was gone a few seconds, and then there was this shot. Out of nowhere. Aidan and I assume it was a stray bullet from a hunter or something."

Dan Barnes exhaled loudly and shook his head. "Right, Shelby. I saw the slug they took out of Aidan's shoulder. I don't think you'll find many hunters who use .357 magnum rounds."

"Then I guess it'll be that much easier to catch the guy, huh?" As she turned to unlock the door, she knew she wasn't fooling him. "Look, Dan, maybe you should talk to Aidan, you know? I was upset. I don't remember much about last night."

He seemed to relent, probably realizing he wasn't going to get anywhere with her. Shelby was grateful; it was hard enough to lie, but to Dan Barnes it was almost impossible.

"You should have told me you were back in town,

Shelby," he said. "I would have made arrangements for a patrol car again. Of course, after giving the last one the slip the way you did, I'm not sure there'd be much point."

"I'm sorry, Dan. Really. I was in a hurry. I wasn't even thinking about—"

He held up a hand. "That's all right, Shelby. I don't suppose I'd want some cop on my ass day and night, either."

Perhaps it was the heavy grayness of the day, Shelby thought, but suddenly Dan looked very old.

"Would you like to come in for a coffee?" she offered. "I think you're probably even wetter than I am."

"That'd be nice, Shelby" he said, reaching for the door and holding it for her.

Doreen was already a flurry of activity before Shelby even stepped inside. In her arms she cradled two large garment bags as she scurried across the boutique to one of the tables. She cast Shelby a frazzled glance and laid the bags out before reaching up to work a couple of stray red curls back into her restrained mop of hair.

"Has it been nuts?" Shelby asked her, not needing Doreen's eye-rolling gesture to know so.

"It's been insane, Shelby. I called Peter to tell him we'd be working today and the next thing I know he's sending all these samples over he wants you to look at. Then I figure I'd better make some room so we can spread out, and the doorbell goes off, and I'm thinking it's the samples already, right? But it's not. It's Detective DaCosta looking for you, and—"

"Nick? What did he want?"

"Didn't say. Well, he didn't get a chance to, really. I mean, he was barely in the door when Peter's delivery kid comes around, so I ask Detective DaCosta to wait, and then this kid is dropping stuff left, right and center, in the pouring rain no less. So I go out and help him, and then the phone's ringing, and I'm thinking it's probably Peter. You know how paranoid he is about deliveries. So the phone's ringing and this kid's dropping everything and I'm helping him, and before I can even tell him you'll be here shortly, Detective DaCosta just takes off. Practically *flew* out of here. You just missed him, in fact."

"Who was on the phone, Doreen?" But a sick feeling was already growing in the pit of Shelby's stomach.

"I don't know. I was outside getting these samples, so I let the machine pick up."

Shelby raced for the stairs.

"Dan, I'll be with you in a minute," she called.

Before she'd hit the top step and crossed the hallway to the answering machine, the sick feeling had worked its way up to her throat. And when she checked the volume dial on the machine, her worry escalated to hot panic.

For the past week and a half, she'd screened her calls. The volume had been turned up—definitely enough for someone downstairs in the boutique to hear. Not Doreen. No, she'd been outside bringing in the samples. But Nick...Nick could have heard just before he'd rushed out.

Shelby lowered the volume. If her worst fears were

accurate, she already knew the voice she'd hear when her finger touched the play button.

"Shel, it's me. Look, we should...I think we should talk. I, um, don't want to tell this all to the machine, but you're right, Shel. The decision *is* yours and I have to live with it. I'll respect whatever you decide to do. Just, please, let's talk about this. Call me...at the cabin. I love you."

The beep marking the end of the message sounded, and still Shelby stared at the machine. Long fingers of dread curled around her chest. She knew why Nick had rushed out the way Doreen described—he must have returned to the cabin last night, seen that Johnny had left, and given up. But now he'd overheard the message. He knew Johnny had gone back to the cabin. And at this very moment, while Johnny waited for Shelby's call, Nick was already on his way there.

She had to warn Johnny.

Snatching up the receiver, she punched out the cabin's number. But with each unanswered ring, her grip tightened on the receiver. How could he not be there? Was he out back chopping wood and couldn't hear the phone? Or maybe he was on the dock?

She had to get up there. Johnny needed her.

She flung the receiver into its cradle and closed her hand over her car keys. When she spun around to leave, she let out a startled gasp.

"Dan!" How long had he been standing right there behind her? What had he heard?

"That was John." He pointed to the answering machine, a look of confusion rippling across his features. "What's going on, Shelby?"

Johnny's warning meant nothing now. If Nick was on his way up to the cabin, she needed help. She had to trust someone. It might as well be Dan.

"Shelby, unless you start giving me some answers right now—"

"Johnny's alive, Dan. But there's no time to explain. We have to go. Now."

"Where?"

"To Aidan's cabin. That's where Johnny was calling from. Nick must have heard the message. That's why he ran out. He's gone up there to kill him. We have to hurry." She tried to push past him, but Dan caught her arm.

"Shelby, hang on. What in God's name are you talking about? Why would Nick—"

"It's to do with the Morelli case or something. Please, Dan, there's no time. I can explain in the car. Nick's on his way up to the cabin, and unless we get there—"

"Wait a second." He pulled her to a stop again, his voice sounding calm and collected compared to the panic in hers. "Before we go rushing off anywhere, does Nick even know where Aidan's cabin is?"

Of course Nick knew where the cabin was! He'd been there last night. He'd shot Aidan. Shelby was about to confess to Dan what had really happened last night when he interrupted her.

"Aidan's party," he said.

"What?"

"Aidan's retirement party last year. It was at his cabin. I remember John told me he invited Nick." He paused briefly. "All right, Shelby, listen to me, I'll drive out there, check things out. But I want you to stay here. It's not safe for—''

"What? No! I'm going with you, Dan."

"Shelby, this isn't something that—''

"No!" She jerked her arm from his grasp and started for the stairs. "I won't just sit here and... No. I'm going. And that's final.''

JOHNNY HAD WEIGHED the dangers in returning to the cabin. But if Shelby *did* leave for New York, if they truly had no future together, what did it matter if he put himself in danger?

Not that he really was, though. Most likely Nick would have looped back last night and seen there was no one at the cabin; he'd hardly believe that Johnny would've been foolish enough to return to the cabin. And even if Nick *had* followed him up here a second time, it would be the surest way to finally flush Nick out, using himself as bait.

Still, Johnny had been wary—parking the Skylark out of sight around the back and keeping the shutters closed on the cabin windows. And with the light of day, his outlook had changed somewhat. Maybe there *was* still a chance for him and Shelby.

He checked his watch again and paced in front of the cold hearth. He'd been practically counting the minutes since he'd called home, and she hadn't yet rung back.

Unable to tolerate the silence of the cabin any longer, he went outside to the lake. In spite of the drizzle, he walked up and down the shore for a long time. At least it felt like a long time; according to his watch, it was only half an hour.

Back in the cabin he questioned, not for the first time, the wisdom of leaving a message on Shelby's machine this morning. If it had been a weekday, he wouldn't have dared. But Shelby never had Doreen work weekends, and even if the woman *had* come in, she never touched the answering machine.

He needed to talk to Shelby. He was desperate to tell her how wrong he'd been last night, not only in what he'd said, but the way he'd driven off like that, leaving her alone and shivering in the middle of the parking lot.

From the pocket of his jeans he took out the engagement ring and looked at it for what had to be the hundredth time in the past twelve hours. Nothing in this world could make him happier than seeing it on Shelby's finger—and seeing her smile when he put it there. He wondered if that would ever happen.

What if she didn't call? What if his words last night had hurt her so deeply that, coupled with everything he'd put her through already, she'd never find it in her heart to forgive him?

He couldn't bear that thought. He needed her. He'd always needed her. From the day he'd first looked into her eyes he knew he'd found his home. His place in the world. He lived in Shelby's smile, as though he'd never actually existed until he'd gazed into it.

And now a child. How could he *not* be with her? How could he *not* be there to share the life of their child?

All night he'd paced the small cabin, hearing

Shelby's words again and again in his mind, hearing the fears she'd expressed in that snowy parking lot last night. Justifiable fears, too. She had every right to want to shield their child from the risks his job entailed.

He'd thought of his own father, as well, and the things Shelby had said about losing him. Yes, life had no guarantees. There were a lot of cops on the force who had spouses and children. They took risks every day. Accepted them. And forced their families to accept them.

But Shelby was right. It *wasn't* worth it. Johnny didn't want to run those risks. Not anymore. He couldn't do his job with the constant worry that he might not go home that night to Shelby and their child. Life was too important to take those risks. Shelby was too important. And their child—

The low rumble of a car on the graveled drive outside interrupted his thoughts. He moved to the window next to the front door.

For a second he actually expected to see Shelby, that she'd driven to the cabin, instead of calling. But when he peered through the half-louvered shutters, the car he saw was not Shelby's Lexus....

CHAPTER EIGHTEEN

IT TOOK SHELBY the first fifteen minutes of the drive to fill Dan in on what Johnny had told her—the explosion, the Morelli case, the corruption and his suspicions about Nick. She'd admitted her lie about the bullet that Aidan had taken in the shoulder, telling Dan what had really happened last night. Throughout he'd been silent, concentrating on the road and breaking every speed limit.

For the rest of the drive Shelby had sat in the passenger seat in fearful silence. Her mind never stopped thinking about what might be awaiting them when they finally reached the cabin. She clutched her purse in her lap. Even with the captain of the Fairfield Police Department sitting next to her, she took comfort in the Glock semiautomatic nestled in her purse.

When at last they pulled into the driveway, Shelby let out a shaky breath of relief. She'd expected to see Nick's car, but the drive was empty. And no doubt Johnny was playing it safe and had parked the Skylark behind the cabin, out of sight.

The captain reached past her into the glove box. She watched as he withdrew the leather holster containing his gun and clipped it to his belt before opening the car door.

When Shelby started to follow him, Dan stopped her.

"No, Shelby. Until I know what's going on, you stay in the car."

"Dan, I'm not just going to sit here. Not if Johnny's in trouble." She swung her legs out.

She wanted to run up the walkway to the front steps and burst through the door. He would be there. And she would fall into his embrace and this nightmare would be over.

Once again Dan stopped her. He didn't have to say anything; his hold on her arm was firm, and the significance of his nod clear. She moved behind him as he mounted the steps to the front porch.

It took every ounce of restraint she had not to call out Johnny's name, to wait quietly behind Dan as he hammered the cabin door with his fist. Instantly the door swung open, as though it had already been unlatched.

"John?" Dan pushed the door open farther and at the same time reached for the holster he'd clipped to his belt.

But he didn't have a chance to even touch the gun.

He raised his hands in surrender.

"JOHN." DAN BARNES moved farther into the cabin, his hands still up as he looked from Johnny's face to his gun and back again. "Take it easy, John. What's going on?"

"I don't know yet, Captain."

"Well, maybe you could start by pointing that thing somewhere else."

"I don't think so."

"Johnny, no." Shelby barged through the door, her purse falling to the floor as she tried to place herself between Johnny and Dan Barnes. "It's all right, Johnny. It's Nick. Nick's on his way. I was afraid he'd already be here. He was at the boutique when you called and left the message. He overheard it. Doreen said he raced off, so we have to—"

"Shelby, just stay where you are." Johnny sent her a quelling look and saw the fear in her eyes.

Part of him wanted to put his faith in the captain, as Shelby seemed to have done. But he couldn't. He couldn't trust anyone. All Robert Logan had told him moments before the *Orion* exploded was that it was "someone" with the force. That someone had been milking Morelli for payoffs, and it was that same someone who'd killed Morelli. And Feeney. Who'd evidently blown up the *Orion* and later on attacked Shelby.

Yes, he had his suspicions about Nick. But his gut told him to trust no one, and today he was listening to his gut.

Still holding his gun on Dan Barnes, Johnny pushed the door closed.

"Come on, John. Let's talk about this." Dan nodded to the gun. "Like civilized men. Do you want to fill me in? Shelby told me something about your suspecting police corruption in the Morelli case."

"That's right, Dan. It's all connected. Morelli, Feeney, the bomb on my boat, the threats against Shelby. Maybe even Seth Cushing's death."

"Cushing?" The captain shook his head in apparent

confusion. "Look, John, you've obviously got more information on this than I do. You should have come to me sooner. Before it escalated to this. It's not too late. We'll get IAB in on this thing. We'll work it out. A full investigation. But not this way. Put down the gun, John."

Johnny studied his superior's face, searching for anything that might evoke his trust.

"Please, Johnny," Shelby begged. She stood only inches from Barnes and looked exhausted. "You can't do this on your own, Johnny. Not anymore. This has to end. Please."

"I'm sorry," he said at last, directing his gaze from Shelby once again to Dan Barnes. "I need your gun, Captain."

"John—"

"Look, we'll talk about this, Dan, but I want your weapon first."

Dan exhaled harshly. He glanced at Shelby, and when he turned again to Johnny, he reached cautiously under his jacket. Johnny watched him withdraw the gun from his belt holster, then bend down to set it on the floor. He gave it a nudge with his foot and sent it clattering across the wooden floorboards toward Johnny.

"Okay? Can we talk now?" he asked.

"Just the one?"

"It's my off-duty weapon, John. I'm not carrying an issue gun." He lifted back the lapels of his jacket to prove he had no other holster. "For crying out loud, John, I understand that someone tried to kill you, that you're suspicious, but holding me at gunpoint... Come on, John, this is insane. Let's talk.''

"Someone was taking payoffs from Morelli. I don't know for sure it was Nick. But it was someone on the force. Feeney was going to give me the guy's name, but the night before he was going to meet with me, he wound up dead at the waterfront. I was with another informant on my boat the afternoon of the explosion. All I managed to get out of him was the same as I'd gotten from Feeney. That it was someone on the force who'd put pressure on Morelli and it had gone sour."

"And how does Seth Cushing figure into this?"

"I'm not sure yet. But I know about the unmatched slug, Dan. I know it didn't come from the gun used at that armed robbery we were responding to. And I suspect the bullet was meant for me, not Seth."

"Well, if that's true, John, then a lot of people are taking bullets for you. First Seth Cushing, then Aidan. Who's next? It's time to come in, John. We've got to get IAB on this as soon as possible. Before anyone else gets hurt."

"Maybe you're right, Dan." Johnny let his grip on his revolver relax slightly. There was no turning back now, no more hiding. Nick knew he was alive, so what was the point? He'd have to put his faith in Internal Affairs. And in Dan.

It was when he was about to lower his gun that Johnny caught a better look at the revolver on the floor, Dan Barnes's off-duty weapon.

His conversation with Corky McNair the afternoon of the explosion, before life had whirled into this living nightmare, came thundering back. The slugs from the Morelli and Feeney shootings had been the same—.357-caliber rounds, both from what Corky suspected was a Smith & Wesson 586. The same Distinguished Combat magnum that Johnny saw now at his feet.

"Shelby, move over here," he said.

"What?" There was confusion in her voice, but Johnny didn't dare take his eyes off Dan now.

"I said move over here. Step away from him."

"Johnny, I don't understand. What—"

"Shelby, just do it!"

In his peripheral vision he saw her give Dan a quick glance and finally cross the room to stand next to him. Only when he was able to take her arm and guide her safely behind him did his sense of panic change into a dark anger.

"You're making a mistake, John," Dan said.

"Am I?"

"Johnny—" Shelby gripped his free arm convulsively. "—what are you talking about?"

"You think *I'm* somehow involved in all this?" Dan asked. "Come on. How many years have we known each other? How many cases have we worked together?"

"Obviously not enough."

"John, I've got a wife and daughter. I'd never put myself, or my career, on the line like that."

Johnny nudged the Smith & Wesson along the floor with the toe of his shoe, farther away from Dan Barnes. "Then we'll just have to see what Corky comes up with when he checks the slugs from the Morelli and Feeney murders against this gun."

Johnny saw a glimmer of defeat on the captain's face.

"That's why you were so adamant I not work Seth Cushing's case, isn't that right, Dan? You knew I'd discover the slug didn't match the gun from the armed robbery, and you knew I'd figure out the bullet was really meant for me."

"You're making a big mistake, John. You're grasping at straws. Short ones at that. We need to take this to Internal Affairs." Dan's words belonged to a man who still had hope—hope he might yet talk his way out of the hole he'd dug for himself. But his face told a different story. He knew the game was over. Johnny could see it in his tired eyes.

"Why, Dan? For the money? Did you really need it that badly?"

Dan opened his mouth to answer when all three heard a car pull into the gravel driveway. There was the throaty rumble of an engine and then silence. With his revolver still trained on Dan, Johnny took a step toward the window. He tilted one louver with his finger and between the shutter's slats saw Nick climb out of his black Mustang.

At the same time his peripheral vision caught a blur of movement in the room, and he heard Shelby's scream: "Johnny! My gun!"

Johnny whirled from the window. He brought up his revolver even as he saw Dan draw the Glock semi-automatic out of Shelby's purse. And in the same instant he squeezed the trigger.

But there were two explosions of gunfire.

Johnny's shot disarmed Dan Barnes. The Glock

spun away across the floor as Dan sagged against the wall clutching his arm. But Johnny was only vaguely aware of this, for panic had seized his heart.

"Shelby!"

He lunged toward her.

"Shelby!" he cried again as she crumpled to the floor.

Behind him he heard Nick storm through the door. He was sure Nick said something, but he wasn't listening. For him, there was only Shelby—and the end of his world.

He knelt next to her. "Shelby? Can you hear me? Shel?"

She was unconscious, her breathing shallow. Worse than that was the blood. He'd known that head wounds bled profusely, but nothing could have prepared him for seeing Shelby's blood.

"Oh God, oh God, Shel," he heard himself chanting. He couldn't lose her. He *couldn't*. "Please, Shelby, you can't..."

In the background he heard Nick phoning for an ambulance.

Johnny turned Shelby's head and brushed back her hair. "Come on, Shelby, you can't leave me now. Not after all this. You can't."

And then a hot wave of relief licked through him. The bullet had only grazed her scalp. It was the shock of the blast that had caused her to lose consciousness. She was starting to come around.

"Shel?"

She moaned, then, "Johnny?"

"Shel, you're going to be all right," he told her,

unable to control the quaver in his voice. And when she opened her eyes at last and gazed up at him, he couldn't remember ever feeling such overwhelming relief. "You're going to be all right," he repeated.

Nick squatted next to Shelby, as well, and handed Johnny a cloth. Johnny pressed it to the wound and then looked at his partner.

"Sorry I was late, John. Got lost," Nick said. "You should have told me. I was working my own leads. Had a hunch about Dan."

"And how's that?"

"Diane."

"Who?"

"Corky's assistant. Don't tell me you've never noticed her." Johnny barely caught Nick's wink. "I know about the slugs from the Morelli and Feeney cases. Even had her run them against the one that killed Cushing. When she came up with a match, I knew something wasn't right. Then I followed up on the prints from the break-in at your apartment."

"But Aidan told me they'd come up empty on those."

"Sure. Unless you count a partial that was lifted off the back door. When I had it put through the computer and got a match, I couldn't find any reasonable explanation for why Dan would be using your back door."

"I'm sorry I doubted you, Nick," Johnny said.

"Yeah, well, we'll talk." He nodded to where the captain sat, cuffed, on the floor. "I'll take him out to the car. You all right here?"

"Yeah."

Shelby held the cloth herself now, wincing slightly at the pain.

"By the way, John—" Nick looked back at him "—I gotta say, I'm glad you're alive."

"Me, too, Nick." And when he caught Shelby's gaze again, Johnny knew he'd never spoken a greater truth. "Me, too."

Shelby sat up with his help. "I'm sorry, Johnny."

"For what?"

"For bringing Captain Barnes here. I didn't—"

"It's not important, Shelby. What's important is that it's over now. We can...we can get on with our lives."

Or could they? It wouldn't be easy. There were a lot of things they had to resolve, a lot of changes that had to be made—and a few things that still needed forgiveness.

"I thought I'd lost you, Shel," he said softly.

"You think I'm that easy to get rid of?"

"I hope not." He gave her a smile. "I love you, Shelby."

"I know you do, Johnny."

A smile turned up the corners of her mouth. The smile he couldn't imagine living without. The smile that filled his heart with every emotion under the sun and brought him home. When she hooked the collar of his shirt with one hand, pulled him to her and kissed him, nothing had ever tasted so sweet. And if there had been any doubts in Johnny's mind, they were all banished in that instant.

He'd found his place in the world, and nothing could ever take him away again.

EPILOGUE

"IF YOU MESS with that tie one more time, I swear I'm going to strangle you with it."

Johnny dropped both hands to his sides in defeat and let Shelby take over. He watched her reflection in the mirror as she straightened the silk tie and then ran her hands over the lapels of his tuxedo like a sculptor putting the finishing touches to a masterpiece. When she looked up at him at last, she smiled in satisfaction.

"Did you look this good when *we* got married?" she asked.

"Better probably," Johnny said, and lowered his mouth to hers. As he pulled her to him, her swollen belly pressed against his stomach. The feel of it, the thought of their unborn child, filled him with joy.

"You're going to get all creased," Shelby murmured against his mouth and pulled away slightly.

"Does it look like I care?"

She shook her head, accepting his kiss, and moaned softly—a sound that never failed to send a shock of longing coursing through him. And when Shelby pulled away this time, Johnny could see he wasn't the only one disappointed to end the contact.

"I have to get dressed," she said with a tone of frustration.

But still he held her close. Lifting one hand, he smoothed her hair from her forehead, and as he did, his thumb caressed the slight gnarl of her scar. The scar that marked Shelby's brush with death.

With vivid clarity Johnny could remember the deadly intent on Barnes's face when he'd pulled the trigger, and later the utter defeat in the man's expression when he was cuffed and seated in the back of Nick's car.

Barnes had tried to talk to Johnny then as they waited for the paramedics to arrive. He'd tried to apologize, but Johnny had barely been able to look the captain in the eye. Only hours later, after Nick had come into Shelby's hospital room and told Johnny that Barnes was asking for him, did Johnny leave Shelby's side long enough to go down the three floors to Barnes's guarded hospital room. Even then, it took great effort to meet the gaze of the man who'd tried to take Shelby's life.

Johnny had remained silent as he listened to Barnes's remorse. The captain confessed his involvement with Morelli over the past few years, admitted to the bribe money, and then how he'd turned on Morelli when the industrialist threatened his career.

He apologized for the bomb on the *Orion*. And finally he apologized for the shooting. But when Barnes went on to tell him how he'd been in over his head, how he'd found himself on the verge of retirement with no foreseeable end to the mounting medical bills and how he'd had no other choice, Johnny had walked out. That was the last he'd seen of Barnes one-on-one. After that, there was only the trial and the sentencing.

"Johnny? Are you all right?" Shelby touched his cheek again.

"Of course. I'm fine."

"You were miles away."

He pressed another kiss to her lips. "How'd I ever get so lucky?" he asked, but knew he would never find the answer to that question. "I love you, Shelby."

"I know you do." She gave him one of her brilliant smiles. "But I really have to go, Johnny. I have to get dressed."

She gave him one quick kiss before wiping a smudge of lipstick from his lips and heading out the door. And as Johnny watched her go, he wondered how it was that with each day of their life together Shelby only grew more beautiful.

SITTING ON A BENCH under the shade of the gazebo, Shelby looked across the lush expanse of park lawn to where members of the wedding party were grouped for the last set of photos. The July heat seemed to have little effect on their spirits as they joked and hammed it up in front of the camera. Even Johnny's tux looked as fresh as it had when Shelby had helped him dress several hours ago.

He lifted a hand to his forehead, shielding his eyes from the sun, and caught her gaze. She returned his warm smile and gave him a wave before he was whisked away by Aidan and Kate for yet another photo.

It had been a fairy-tale ceremony, Shelby thought, closing her eyes and feeling the breeze whisper across her face—almost as beautiful as hers and Johnny's two summers ago. Every detail of that day was so vividly etched in her memory that it seemed as though they'd exchanged vows only yesterday. And yet everything that had led up to their wedding—the explosion, her belief Johnny was dead, then the threats and Barnes's capture, even the subsequent trial and conviction—those things seemed as though they'd never happened. At the end of all those nightmarish events, there was only their love—and their son.

Instinctively her arms tightened around the two-year-old asleep in her lap. Kyle stirred but didn't awake. He was the spitting image of Johnny, but then, she'd expected that. And every time she gazed into Kyle's small perfect face, she fell in love with Johnny all over again.

Shelby glanced up in time to see Aidan mount the steps of the gazebo. A tired but contented smile settled on his face as he loosened his collar and took a seat on the bench beside her.

"So how's your bride?" Shelby asked.

She followed his gaze across the lawn to where Kate was posing with Johnny for the camera, the sun shimmering off her blond hair and the brilliant white of the gown Shelby had designed for her.

"Beautiful," Aidan answered, and there was undeniable love in his voice. Together they watched Johnny and Kate do a final pose for the photographer, both laughing. "But you'd better keep an eye on that husband of yours," he added. "If those two keep this up, next thing you know they'll be running away together."

Shelby watched Johnny straighten his tux and

loosen his collar as he looked toward the gazebo. The breeze ruffled his black hair and he lifted a hand to straighten it, his eyes never leaving hers. And even at that distance, Shelby could see the love in them.

"Thanks, Aidan," she said, placing her hand over his.

"For what?"

"For everything. Everything you do for me and Johnny. And everything you did to bring us together...and to keep us together. I don't know if we would have had this life, this happiness, without you. And I don't think I've ever really thanked you for that."

"You have, Shelby," he said.

"Well, I can't thank you enough." She gave his hand a squeeze. Yes, she had Aidan to thank for her happiness today and the happiness she knew she would share with Johnny for the rest of her life. It hadn't been entirely easy, patching things up after Dan Barnes's arrest, forgiving one another, starting fresh. But their love for each other had seen them through, and they were stronger for it.

"You're happy, aren't you, Aidan?" she asked.

"You bet I am." There was no mistaking his sincerity.

"I'm glad. And I'm happy for you and Kate."

"I guess you can't say it didn't take us long enough. Between the agency and Kate running all over the state from one case to the next...well, I'm not sure we could have done it if she hadn't accepted that position with the DA's office. And if I didn't have John helping me out. Thank God he finally took me up on my offer to be a partner.''

Johnny had made his way over to them, and as he mounted the steps of the gazebo, he returned Shelby's smile, then touched her cheek briefly before settling his hand on Kyle's head. Shelby felt the familiar tug in her heart whenever she saw Johnny and their son connect.

''So you think you can handle the agency on your own, John?'' Aidan asked him.

''It's just a two-week honeymoon, Aidan. I think I can manage.''

''I don't know. It's a lot of work for one person.''

''And when have I ever minded a bit of work? Besides, that work is paying for the renovations on the house.''

''Oh, and here I thought it was Shelby's success paying for the new nursery.''

''Speaking of which, we should get going,'' Shelby said. ''I've got a meeting and a deadline.'' She shifted on the bench, and Johnny reached down to take Kyle from her.

''Working to the wire again, are you?'' Aidan asked, standing up, and Shelby nodded as she accepted his kiss on the cheek. ''Well, then, I'll let you two get home. Kate and I will stop in tomorrow on our way out of town. Thanks for all your help, partner.'' He slapped Johnny on the back and headed down the stairs.

They watched him cross the lawn to Kate, and when the newlyweds embraced, Johnny turned to Shelby.

''How are you feeling?'' he asked, cradling the

sleeping Kyle against his shoulder and offering Shelby his hand to help her from the bench.

"A little tired."

He drew her to him, wrapping his free arm around her waist. When he kissed her, Shelby wasn't at all surprised at the desire that surged through her. It never ceased to happen.

He removed his hand from her waist and pressed it to her swollen belly. "And how's our girl?" he asked.

"She's fine. Kicking a lot. No doubt anxious to get out and see the world."

"Just like her brother," he said, smiling. "Come on. Let's go home."

DEBBIE MACOMBER

invites you to the

HEART OF TEXAS

Join Debbie Macomber as she brings you the lives
and loves of the folks in the ranching community
of Promise, Texas.

If you loved Midnight Sons—don't miss
Heart of Texas! A brand-new six-book series
from Debbie Macomber.

Available in February 1998
at your favorite retail store.

Heart of Texas by Debbie Macomber

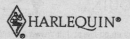
HARLEQUIN®

HPHRT1

Where were you when the storm blew in?

Snowbound

Three stormy stories about what happens to three snowbound couples, from three of your favorite authors:

SHOTGUN WEDDING by Charlotte Lamb

MURDER BY THE BOOK by Margaret St. George

ON A WING AND A PRAYER by Jackie Weger

Find out if cabin fever can melt the snow this December!

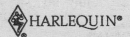 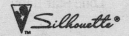